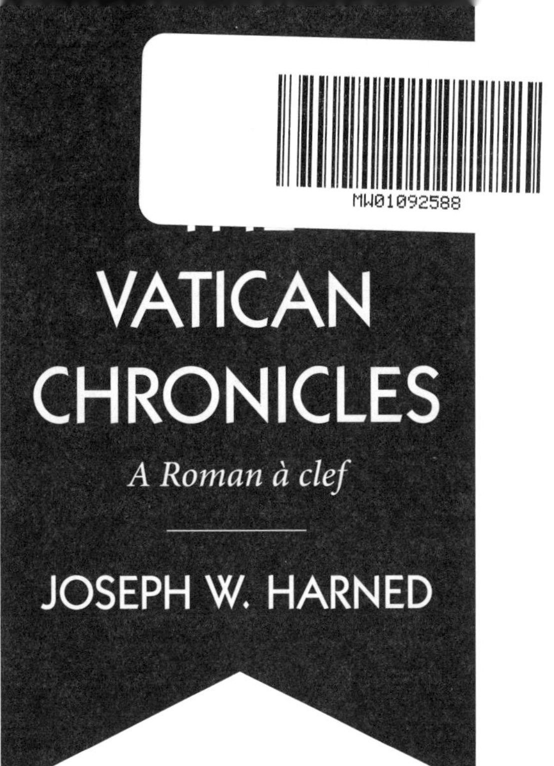
MW01092588
VATICAN
CHRONICLES
A Roman à clef
JOSEPH W. HARNED

TCU
Press
FORT WORTH, TEXAS

Library of Congress Cataloging-in-Publication Data

Names: Harned, Joseph W., 1940- author.
Title: The Vatican chronicles : a roman à clef / Joseph W. Harned.
Description: Fort Worth : TCU Press, [2021] | Summary: "The Vatican Chronicles is a tongue-in-cheek novel about the most dangerous act of nuclear terrorism in the twenty-first century. It is as current as the March 23, 2014 New York Times, in which you will find an article by Michael Shear and David Sanger entitled 'Japan to Let U.S. Assume Control of Nuclear Cache.' The novel is a humorous romp of international intrigue and espionage by a man who spent thirty-three years in the field—a roman à clef that explains how in the real world Messrs. Shear and Sanger allowed the nuclear wool to be pulled over their eyes. The explosive story begins in Washington in the aftermath of a weakened and consequently crippled US intelligence capability, and focuses on the most recent shipment of plutonium by Japan from Cherbourg to Nagasaki. A bizarre attack on His Holiness at the Vatican's summer Palace, Castel Gandolfo, and the murder of a well-known Cardinal in the Vatican hospital lead a much-loved and popular pope and an unloved and unpopular intelligence agency to form an unlikely joint venture to save a key priest at an obscure monastery near Kyoto. As readers, we are treated to a Japan no Westerner is permitted to see, and made privy to a Vatican initiative so daring it may not be revealed. The action escalates with the murder of a monk in a Tokyo Priory, and its attribution by police to the yakuza and right-wing extremists. If seized by criminals, terrorists, or a rogue state, the shipment of plutonium could produce three hundred Nagasaki-size bombs, be used as a powerful instrument of political blackmail, or held for a king's ransom. The most harrowing escapade of nuclear terrorists in our lifetime will succeed unless a handful of Americans and Japanese, aided by the Vatican, can discover who is behind the threat and stop them. The Vatican Chronicles is a short novel written in seventy staccato chronicles. It treats four of the most challenging issues of our time: the future of the Catholic Church, the US intelligence community, nuclear proliferation, and the new Japan—each with a lighthearted, prescient, but insightful touch"—Provided by publisher.
Identifiers: LCCN 2020055713 (print) | LCCN 2020055714 (ebook) | ISBN 9780875657745 (paperback) | ISBN 9780875657813 (ebook)
Subjects: LCSH: Catholic Church--Political activity--Fiction. | Nuclear nonproliferation—Fiction. | Nuclear terrorism—Prevention—Fiction. | Intelligence service—Fiction. | Espionage, American—Vatican City—Fiction. | Radicalism—Japan—Fiction. | LCGFT: Spy fiction. | Humorous fiction.
Classification: LCC PS3608.A74933 V38 2021 (print) | LCC PS3608.A74933 (ebook) | DDC 813/.6--dc23
LC record available at https://lccn.loc.gov/2020055713
LC ebook record available at https://lccn.loc.gov/2020055714

Design by Preston Thomas

TCU Box 298300
Fort Worth, Texas 76129
To order books: 1.800.826.8911

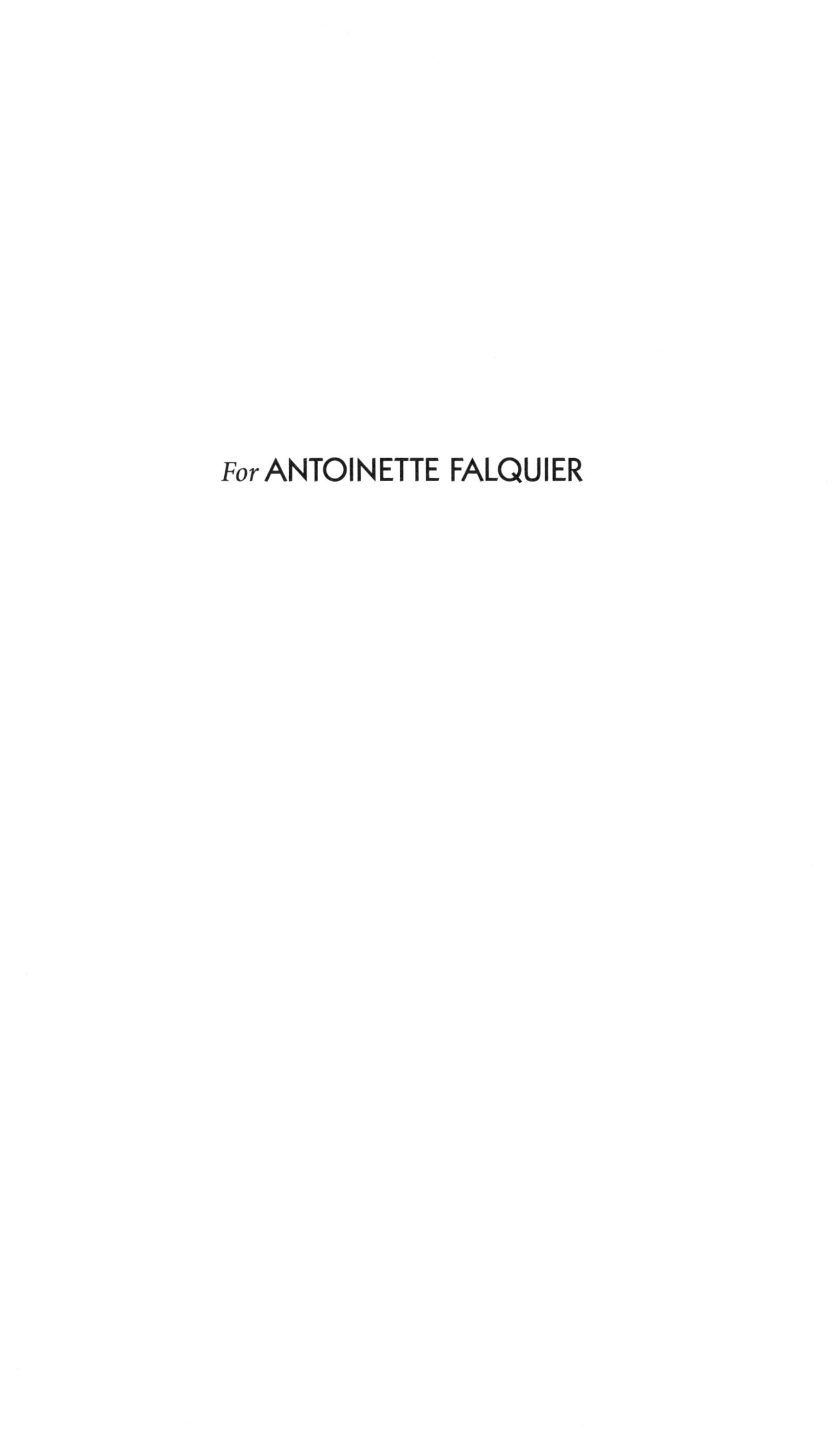

For ANTOINETTE FALQUIER

Undated and unattributed photo of the priests and nuns of Urakami Cathedral in Nagasaki, Japan, prior to the 1945 atomic bombing by US forces.

CONTENTS

— PROLOGUE —

Kyushu Island, Japan, Thursday, August 9th, 1945

"Look! A cricket!" exclaimed the small boy. Standing at the edge of the pond, the five-year-old was pointing to a nearby water lily. The young priest bent over the boy to see and could barely discern the cricket, exactly the same color as the lily pad on which it was perched.

"You're right, Takashi-chan," said the priest. "It's almost 11:00 a.m.," he added. "Your cricket should be home in bed." The cricket chirped.

"Why is he here?" asked Takashi.

Father Junichi Nagano glanced up at the clear blue sky and replied, "I suppose it's such a beautiful day he just couldn't resist. But he'd better watch out, or the dragonflies will have him for lunch."

"No!" said Takashi. The boy took a step into the pond, reached down, and gently captured the cricket in his two small hands.

The priest and the boy had been walking up Mount Kawabira for well over an hour, following the path leading to the wayside shrine of the twenty-six Christian martyrs who had been dramatically and horribly crucified on the ridges of the Mitsuyama mountains embracing the valley and its city below.

Earlier, Takashi and Father Junichi had been to the cathedral downtown, the largest and most beautiful in all of Asia, to pray for the souls of Takashi's parents, killed in an air raid just a week before. The Takanos had been rural farmers who brought their sweet potatoes to town to sell to the university kitchens once a week. This time, they had brought Takashi with them so that the university hospital doctors could tell them the meaning of the red butterfly-shaped mark on the back of Takashi's left hand since birth. They had left Takashi in the waiting room of the clinic while they delivered their potatoes and received their payment at the main kitchen. The air raid alert had sounded as a small group of bombers approached from the sea and, as usual, turned north over their navigators' landmark of the cathedral spire, in the direction of their primary target. But this time, a single bomber, short on fuel, had chosen to drop a bomb on the university. It had killed five people, including Takashi's parents, and wounded a dozen more.

Father Junichi had come to the clinic later that day to give extreme unction to one of the wounded Catholic students and had found Takashi seated on the floor of the waiting room, weeping. When a nurse explained what had transpired, the priest offered to take the child to the mission and orphanage near the cathedral. But once there, Takashi had refused to stay with the Sisters unless Father Junichi promised to return today to visit him and take him for an outing.

Together they had walked the eight kilometers from the cathedral up the Kawabira trail, and while the boy seemed not to tire in the slightest, Father Junichi needed a rest. They decided to stop at the pond to eat the rice balls thoughtfully provided by the mission Sisters. The priest was dressed in the cobalt blue habit, the hooded monk's robe, of his Christopherian Order, and felt uncomfortably warm even in the mountain air after their walk beneath the trees in the August heat. Takashi was dressed in the himino he had been wearing the day his parents were killed, a short coat of thin straw worn by farmers and their families in the summer months to protect them from the sun. The Sisters had given Takashi a child's cotton yukata and a little pair of wooden clogs, or geta, but today he had insisted on wearing his himino, and father Junichi had to carry the geta Takashi had taken off the instant they left the cathedral.

Looking out over the city toward the spire, they heard the plane before they saw it. Today it was quite high.

Father Junichi shaded his eyes and scanned above the terraced fields surrounding the city, but there appeared to be no other planes accompanying this lone bomber. Above the blue tiled roofs of the market district to the southwest, they saw the sun reflect off a great silver egg dropped from the plane some eight thousand meters above Urakami. Then Father Junichi saw that way above and beyond the lone bomber, there were two more planes, two more B-29s. And now the sun glinted clearly off the falling bomb, taking forty-three seconds to fall until it reached five hundred meters above the Urakami cathedral's two towers, when there was a blinding flash of light.

The boy had been looking back at the pond, but the priest had been watching the two additional planes. His right hand had shaded one eye from the flash; but now he could see nothing from his left eye, and felt a sharp pain. He instinctively grabbed the boy and threw them both behind a large tree.

As they lay together on the ground, there was not a sound to be heard. Seconds ticked by. The reflected light around them diminished and was no longer stark white. It had changed to an ominous orange red. Father Junichi carefully peered with his one remaining good eye around the edge of the huge tree toward the valley. A huge column of smoke, flame and debris rose into the air above the Urakami district of Nagasaki. The mushroom-shaped cloud at its top was lit eerily from within by hundreds of orange flashes of lightning.

The shock wave from the blast expanded outward through the city and rolled up the mountain toward them. It pushed inexorably through the terraced fields, destroying anything and everything in its path. The almighty wave's speed and power were terrifying, awesome.

"My God!" exclaimed the priest.

"Did God come to the cathedral?" asked the boy.

First they felt their ears pop forcefully as the pressure wave reached out to them, compressing, twisting, flattening, hurting everything, a silent tidal wave of invisible energy. A moment later the incredible sound and wind followed the shock wave, roiling up the mountainside toward them. Earlier in the day, they had watched a train across the valley. In the first second the sound seemed similar. Then it quickly became unbearable, until, in the next instant, the wind hit like a solid wall, and everything turned black.

When the priest came to and forced himself to open his eyes, he found he was sitting in the pond, clutching the boy to his chest. The giant oak behind which they had taken refuge was now leaning precariously over the water, its branches draped around them. The woods behind were mostly flattened, first by the shock wave and wind blowing out from the blast, and then by being sucked back toward the epicenter with almost equal force. The air had turned cold, and the sun was obscured by a huge black cloud alive with lightning.

The priest gingerly picked himself up and waded through the shallow pond, over the scattered oak branches, to the bank, carrying the boy. The ground was littered with dead birds, squirrels, and insects. As Junichi looked back down the valley, he could see nothing but clouds of dust, smoke, and flames where his city had been just moments before. He tried to speak to Takashi, only to realize they had both lost their hearing. The incredible sound wave had been as brutal to them as the shock wave.

Later, as their hearing began to return, and as the choking air began to clear somewhat, they could make out the rubble of the cathedral where they had worshipped that morning. The heat generated by the explosion was so intense that the stones themselves were actually burning. But almost everything else near the cathedral had simply been vaporized. Other buildings left no trace. People were vaporized in a millisecond, leaving only their deeply etched shadows, cast in the intense flash, permanently engraved into the sidewalks on which they had been standing.

Across the valley, some of the university buildings were still standing. Others were in flames. But of beautiful Urakami, nothing recognizable remained except the burning cathedral stones and the remains of one bell tower. The priest and the boy knelt beside the pond and prayed. The boy opened his palm and looked down. The cricket didn't move.

They were a two-woman band, easy on the eye and addictive to the ear. Peale sang tenor and played a startling guitar. Devine sang counter and played anything handy—usually a harmonica, sometimes an alto sax, often a penny whistle, and once each gig, a ukulele. (She was brought up on the cello but refused to play it in public, too explicit.) They each sang when so moved, and together were the band to go to that summer on the beach. Peale & Devine, with their one-song wonder "Wire Me Two" hitting the charts on the island:

I'm broke and broken hearted over you
Wire a hundred if you still love me
Two hundred if we're through
I'm broke and broken hearted over you.

When the season ran down and the record advance ran out, the agency moved in and recruited them to be our nuns.

President Obama was coming down hard on the National Security Agency (NSA). It was the Central Intelligence Agency (CIA) that had bugged Congress and deserved its wrath. But the NSA hadn't done anything worse than usual. The Supreme Court found that the indiscriminate listening to every chick that peeped was constitutional precisely because it was so indiscriminate. And civilians didn't know the other side of the story: what happens when you succeed.

Knowledgeable folk remembered the great World War II espionage success story of our Brits stealing the Enigma, a German coding device, out from under the Third Reich, cracking the top German codes, and reading the most highly classified messages of our enemies. What the civilians were never told was what happened next. We were overwhelmed with information.

The Germans had twenty-five thousand officers and soldiers cleared to use the information we were intercepting towards the end of the Second World War. The Allies had twenty-five. Why so few? Because we didn't want word to leak out that we had broken the German codes. If they got even a hint of our breakthrough, they would not only change their codes, they would immediately alter the operational orders and secret plans that we had learned about in advance via the codes. So we restricted access to the fewest possible people to limit that risk. But by doing so we also limited our own analytic ability to work on the content, and therefore the real-time utility of the new intelligence.

To address this Achilles heel in the twenty-first century, the NSA extended Top Secret clearances to contract employees to cull the wheat from the ever-growing mountain of electronically evesdropped chaff we were indiscriminately sweeping up. When you do that, no matter how careful your psychological screening—and ours was poor to begin with—you inevitably pick a few individuals who sense the power they could have if they chose to tell all.

And for whatever self-justified rationale, one or more will choose to be the messenger. Hence President Obama's public display of dissatisfaction with the NSA, to distance himself and his administration and Congress from what was in truth the Congress-ordered and administration-approved and now Supreme Court-blessed, legal if repugnant and indiscriminate intelligence gathering that had now generated media-manufactured hue and politically motivated cry. As the late Eric Sevareid poignantly admonished, the greatest industry in America is the manufacture, manipulation, and selling of anxiety.

All of which meant we had to do better. And as has happened before, the pendulum reached its apex and began to swing the other way, from national technical means of gathering intelligence back toward old fashioned HUMINT, from machines back to people, from satellites and drones back to James and Mata. From the NSA to the agency's nuns—two young, free spirits who would soon be enmeshed in the most dangerous act of nuclear terrorism in the twenty-first century…

CHRONICLE II.

How do you rebuild what you've spent decades tearing down, denigrating, and throwing away? How do you re-create a human intelligence network after casting aside the best in the world in order to rely upon "national technical means" instead of old fashioned, feet-on-the-ground, well-trained spies? Either you start over, using the small core of what's left to build upon, or, if you're really pressed, you supplement that core by co-opting an existing network and grafting it onto your own.

At the end of World War II, the US was so unprepared to defend itself in the intelligence war against Russia that it co-opted the Gehlen Organization, postwar Germany's super-secret and super-effective network of spies that survived Germany's surrender and served as America's eyes and ears in Eastern Europe and Russia from 1945 to 1956. The US enlisted its former enemy against the new threat.

And now America needed to quickly rebuild its human intelligence capability. Our own HUMINT network had been sliced and diced by underfunding to divert investment into the new hi-tech space-based boys' toys and drone fleets in the Pentagon and the CIA. When funding got scarce, or the human intelligence side looked like it had a resurgence of interest in Congress, rumors of moles soon undercut faith in human spies. The machines and their masters had remained in ascendency for over three decades.

Then solid proof that US agencies, programs, and contractors were being hacked by the Chinese, Russians, and others became overwhelming, and was leaked first to Congress and then to the public, resulting in a new wave of financing for countermeasures to keep our hi-tech investments from being stolen out from under our mousepads. So while decision-makers were losing faith in hi-tech, they ended up having to double down on their investment in it to try to salvage it from electronic thieves.

That was when the president called in his old point man, and gave him a new job. The president said simply: "I no like; you fix. Whatever you need, let me know. Personally. Starting now." His name, appropriately, was Job.

That evening, as Job had a glass of wine and pondered his next moves, he reflected on and regretted the loss of Arthur Schlesinger, Jr. Wouldn't it have been sweet if Arthur were still around, and here now? In his salad days he had been the resident historian and bard in the Kennedy White House. Over drinks of an evening, he would ever so casually inquire "When the president said this or that, what was the first thing that popped into your head?" And over drinks, fresh from the day, you would answer honestly in the moment, without reflection, without doublethink, just straightforward what you could recall from your reaction to an event a few hours before. It was from these daily personal anecdotes that Arthur was able to produce such vivid accounts of the life and times of the nation's history that he had witnessed. And had he asked Job what went through his mind when the president said "I no like; you fix!" Job would have described to him a two-girl band that the president and he had listened to from the porch of a bungalow on the windward side of Oahu a few months earlier, and how Job thought they could play a key role in the forthcoming effort to recapture America's human intelligence outreach worldwide. Arthur would have loved it!

CHRONICLE III.

The best job in the world is the one that doesn't exist; that way there's no precedent. And if you can manage to arrange to be your own boss, well, that's perfect. Right up there next to perfect is to be working directly for and reporting only to the president of the United States. If it's Ronald Reagan or Bill Clinton or George Bush or Barack Obama, it's all the same if you feel this guy really needs your help to govern.

The problem is the task. Is it doable? If the task is insurmountable, unless you have a Sisyphus complex, stay clear. But if you need to break eggs to make an omelet, and you've got THE man at your back saying go for it, roll up your sleeves and start breaking.

The problem remains, however, that it takes ten years to train up a new, effective espionage network and get it well-placed in the field. When you are dealing with presidential terms of four years, you better have a plan b. That plan b would be to co-opt an existing network. And ideally, that network would already be up and running effectively, most importantly with individual agents in the right places—honest, dedicated, reliable, disciplined agents, relatively invisible, well accepted, educated in the surrounding culture, fluent in the local language, old enough to garner respect but young enough to handle physical adversity, and not vulnerable to blackmail or manipulation by opposition forces. That's asking a hell of a lot. In truth, there probably aren't three people among your family, close friends, and neighbors who meet all of those rigorous requirements, even if you give yourself a free pass!

In 1945–46, the Gehlen Organization was tailor-made to fit US and Allied needs. Former US and Allies spies in Russia and Eastern Europe were scarce, but combined with German, and in particular SS, resources in place at the war's end, a broad and deep network was quickly cobbled together under the newly created CIA to form the beginnings of what would become the Federal Intelligence Service of the Federal Republic of Germany.

Initially highly successful in recruiting new talent, some of Gehlen Org's new talent unfortunately turned out to be Soviet bloc communist moles, thereby compromising the organization, making it vulnerable to attack from detractors, providing a conduit for moles to transit into other Allied intelligence services (e.g., the British), and thus casting a shadow of suspicion over its workings that continues even today. The moral of the story is: If plan b is to adopt an existing network, make sure it's clean, or clean it yourself; conversely, if it is compromised, be careful to use that to your advantage, not your disadvantage.

So Job's marching orders were becoming clearer.

A. Rebuild the human intelligence side of the United States' intelligence community to reach at least its previous levels of commitment and capability circa 1960–70;

B. As plan a will surely be a ten-year effort at best, concurrent plan b will be to find and adopt an existing intelligence network that would ideally have the advantages of the Gehlen example (good agents in the right places at the right time) without the disadvantages of Gehlen (a network that lends itself to being infiltrated, compromised and duped);

C. Have a last-resort "Hail Mary" pass play from the end zone if neither plan a nor plan b works in a timely fashion, and the nation is in critical danger.

"I wonder what I'll be doing with all my free time," said Job to himself.

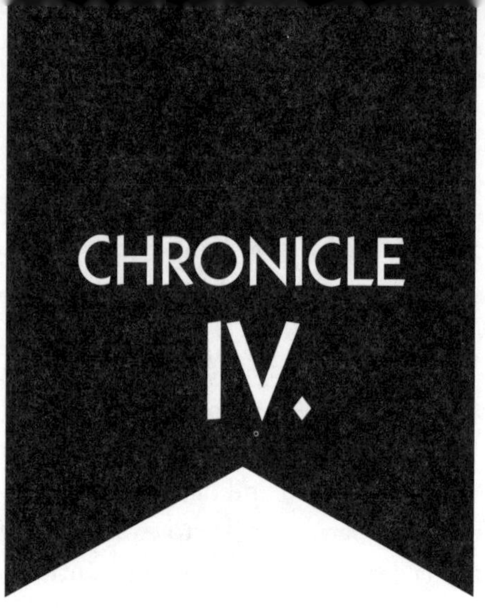

CHRONICLE IV.

The next morning Job phoned Peale and Devine in Hawaii. It was three o'clock in the morning their time, and they were just getting in from a gig on the windward side of Oahu, where he had first met them. The timing was fortuitous. The season was winding down, their one-hit-wonder record advance was pretty well spent, and they were open to suggestions. Job told them he had a serious job offer for them that did not involve music; but given their backgrounds he was sure they would find it challenging. He promised it would pay well. He added they would find tickets to Washington at the airport and would shout them a return trip if they were not accepted by their employer, or if they turned down the offer. They didn't even need to talk it over.

Emery (Em) Peale graduated from Stanford University with a double major: a BA in Japanese studies and a second BA in Asian history. Tall, aquiline, long chestnut hair down to her waist, her most striking and memorable characteristic was a pair of bright, penetrating, celadon blue-green, ever-changing eyes. Job just could not stop looking at them. She mesmerized him.

Surely (Sure) Devine was an auburn-haired hellion from Boston. She had followed the history of arts and letters program at Yale University, which meant she was bright as hell with no marketable trade or skill. Short-cropped hair, emerald-green eyes, and pixie ears, she was born Shirley Devine. In sixth grade, the bullying grade for girls, she was called Surly Devine, Shrilly Devine, Silly Devine, and in a retaliatory strike of self-determination renamed herself Surely Devine. It stuck ever since, or at least the nickname did: Sure. For Sure she was: Sure of herself, Sure of her opinions, her friendships, her causes. Surely Devine was someone you could always count on.

When they arrived in Washington, Job put them up at The Hay-Adams across Farragut Square from the White House, and after they had a good night's sleep and a morning to wander, took them to lunch in the White House senior staff dining room and then a three-minute meet-and-greet with the president.

As agreed, the president recounted how he and Job had both heard them perform during his Hawaii stay, and how he wished them good luck in trying out for their new job. Then he added quietly that he could not think of anything they could do that would be more important to the future of their country.

After that three minutes, if Job had asked them to walk on water, they probably would have tried. What he did ask them to do wasn't that tough, but as it turned out there weren't two women in ten thousand who could have done it with the grace and gumption they managed.

Job asked them to complete the six-month agent training and survival course designed for CIA agents without official cover (NOC's), given at the notorious "farm" near Langley. Moreover, he asked that they complete it in three months rather than six, with agency dispensation, because he needed them to go to Dublin in three months.

Then in Dublin, he asked them to fulfill prearranged special training with the Sisters of Mercy (R.S.M), the toughest bunch of Sisters on any continent, in three months, rather than what usually takes most novices a full year. They were to learn how to be Sisters, and report back to him in six months' time in their novice habits to join in a mission about which they would learn more in due course, but about which they were not to speculate, not even between themselves. "I thought they didn't wear habits anymore," protested Sure.

"They do in Italy," Job replied. "By the time you get back here in six months, you both also need to be fluent in Italian." They settled on payment, surprising to them in its generosity, but available only after satisfactory completion of all three daunting assignments.

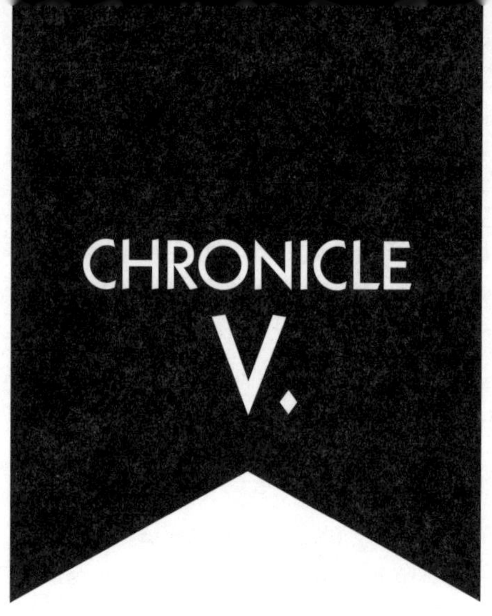

CHRONICLE V.

Everyone seated around the table knew everyone else except for the big guy, the 6'4" gray-haired giant in a black turtleneck, Harris tweed slacks, and Gucci loafers. Then the president came in and everyone stood. He greeted the assembled dozen men and women, and began the briefing without formal introductions:

"Ladies and gentlemen, let me start by thanking you for joining me today. This briefing is classified Cameo Ultra, and goes no further than this room. The tall gentleman on my right is Cardinal Tom Gallagher, who was relieved of his formal duties by the pontiff when he fell gravely ill in Rome at the conclave of cardinals in March of 2013, and has since been undergoing multiple surgeries and rehabilitation at MedStar Georgetown University Hospital. I have asked him to join us today in a personal capacity, as technically he is retired, and does not have an active episcopate.

"Tom, over dinner you will get to meet each of the members of this little group personally. They each head up the human intelligence side of operational intelligence activities at their respective agencies and departments. They are the team I have charged with rebuilding our country's HUMINT capabilities."

Job was seated to the president's left, and watched and listened as he deftly led the group, largely for Tom Gallagher's benefit, through the rationale of the game plan requirements, steps A and B, stressing under B that the network we wished to co-opt had to be up and running, with capable, well-versed agents, respected, steeped in local language and customs, in the world hot spots we needed to monitor.

The president then added a new requirement to our growing list of criteria. We needed motivational leverage on the agents we wished to adopt. The individual agents had to need something that we—and ideally only the US—could, or would, provide. This requirement became a primary focus of the discussion. General brainstorming regarding all the criteria followed and continued over drinks and dinner, with each of the officials taking care to brief Gallagher on his or her purview.

After dinner, the president said goodnight to the team and invited Gallagher and Job upstairs to his study for a nightcap, to review the day.

"Well, Tom, what do you think of them?" the president began, once drinks were in hand.

"Serious, dedicated group," Gallagher said, "and I was surprised that almost every one of them evidenced a genuine sense of humor, which is a 'tell' for me. I was flummoxed from the outset as to why I was here, until one of them told me the team was considering purchasing a family-owned hotel near the Vatican, to use as some sort of hi-tech communications relay station, and asked my advice. She said they would need to put satellite dishes on the roof, generators in the basement, and have living quarters for the agency staff and visitors.

"Apparently, the little place they are looking at is just outside Vatican City, next to the Palace of the Holy Office. That's the office of the Congregation for the Doctrine of Faith, the original home of the Inquisition, and the oldest of the nine congregations of the Curia. It has worldwide reach, as the Church's guardian of faith and morals, and against heresy. It acts as the Church's disciplinarian. And it too is just outside Vatican City, next to the wall and across from their chosen hotel.

"I was asked if I thought it possible to buy the hotel quietly and discreetly. I ventured that instead they needed to think more like Italians, and less like Americans.

"It would cost at least two hundred million dollars to buy, and a good three or four years of legal proceedings to gain clear title from the family and the necessary approvals from the Curia. I told them to stop now before it's too late. Instead, as it's been a family hotel for decades, do it the Italian way—rent the family as well as the hotel, for—say—a million a year. Have the family continue to run the hotel and retain all revenues for themselves. They would also be responsible for paying all taxes, of course. Your folks in return would take over exclusive use of the top three floors, the roof, and the two basements (there are always two basements in Rome), as well as share the upkeep and pay for electricity and water.

"This way, the family is much better off, and so are you. They get to retain ownership of their property, avoid a persecutory windfall tax levy, and make a lot of money in the interim. And times in Rome are tough right now. You, on the other hand, get exactly the location and all the space that you need.

"You should pay for any telltale utilities to hide add-on activity," Tom concluded. "But this way you avoid taxes and legal problems as well as delays; and the whole arrangement costs you much less. Plus, you have the bonus of a built-in cover for your operations: a long-established family business and an ongoing commercial concern."

The president looked at Job, and said, "I think we've found the right man. Let's try to bell the cat."

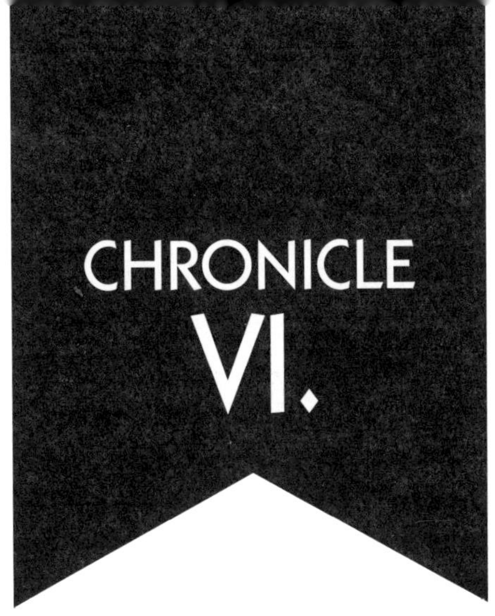

CHRONICLE VI.

The president offered another round. Gallagher declined. "One will have to hold me, thanks," he said. "The doctors at GW still watch me pretty closely. But it's the finest single malt I've ever tasted. Tell me where it comes from."

"It comes from the Edradour, Scotland's smallest distillery, artisanal really, and it's not too peaty. There's only the master brewer and a single assistant. Anything smaller would be considered portable, and outlawed. It's been up in Perthshire in the Highlands since 1825. At some point during Prohibition it was even owned by an American mobster. Today, almost all of their production goes to a single customer, Her Majesty Elizabeth the Second. She introduced me to it, and, with her blessing, I get to purchase a few bottles each month.

"Tom," continued the president, "you look thinner than you did when we were in college together, but you sure look a hell of a lot better than when I came to see you that first day in GW hospital. What's the story? And what's the prognosis?"

"Well, you know I went to the conclave of cardinals to elect a new pope. We had just voted again—as it turned out, for the final time—

when I collapsed. They had to break the conclave to get me to hospital. I'd had a stroke and kidney failure. I was operated on, and after two weeks in the Vatican hospital, flown home.

"Halfway home, I had another stroke. They got me to those great doctors at Georgetown by ambulance from Dulles, and two days later I had a new and different diagnosis. Turns out that for God knows how long, I had a resting heartbeat of thirty. No one understands why, but my heart had simply woken up one day back in Rome and decided I was a hibernating grizzly bear in midwinter. It was beating only once every two seconds, which is so slow clots form spontaneously, and produce all kinds of complications.

"The diagnosis wasn't rocket science, but the doctors at Georgetown clearly saved my life. They operated on me again and installed a special kind of pacemaker directly into my heart. Long story short, after rehab, here I am. Not as smart, but still as tall."

"And the new pope? How did he take all this?" asked the president.

"God, I love him!" exclaimed Tom. "Back in Rome when I collapsed the day he was elected, the next morning he showed up at the Vatican hospital. The first thing he said to me was, 'If I had known that you would take my election so poorly, I would have voted for the other guy.'

"Six months later, he relieved me of all diocesan duties and gave me formal retired status as cardinal, but allowed me to be an active participant in the conclave."

"And that means?" prompted Job.

"Well, back in 1970, Pope Paul enacted reforms to reduce the obvious sclerosis in the Church's archaic institutional system. He limited to one hundred and twenty the number of cardinals with voting power to elect a pope and stipulated that once a cardinal turned eighty he could no longer vote.

"That turned out to be a big deal. For example, when I attended the conclave, sixty-six cardinals no longer made the cut. They could attend the convocation of the College of Cardinals. They could advise. They could admonish. They could eat and drink and schmooze to their hearts' content. But they could no longer vote."

"That's a lot of quality experience and hard-earned wisdom quite suddenly cut off from the decision-making," observed Job. "They must find it frustrating."

"I'm sure they do," said Tom. "In truth, some are even embittered. But just think for a moment of the worldwide television image of the church if Pope Paul had not introduced those reforms. You would have images sent 'round the world of octogenarians and nonagenarians being helped, pulled, and carried up the steps, into the conclave. It would make people wonder: 'Are these sick old men the electors who will choose from *among themselves* a new pope to lead the church in the new century? How relevant are they now? And how relevant will they be in the future?'"

"So how's your own health, Tom?" asked the president, bluntly. "How are you feeling these days?"

"Bored and frustrated, like those old cardinals we're talking about. But hell, I'm only sixty. I just need to find a new direction acceptable to the pope that I can really sink my teeth into. He has asked me to come see him, and I plan to fly to Rome next week."

"Tom, I'm going to put that second drink over here by your chair." said the president. "You may find you'll want it after all. We're about to offer you the best job a retired cardinal could possibly imagine. And frankly it's an offer from your president that you can't refuse."

"Well, I don't know about that, Caesar," said Tom.

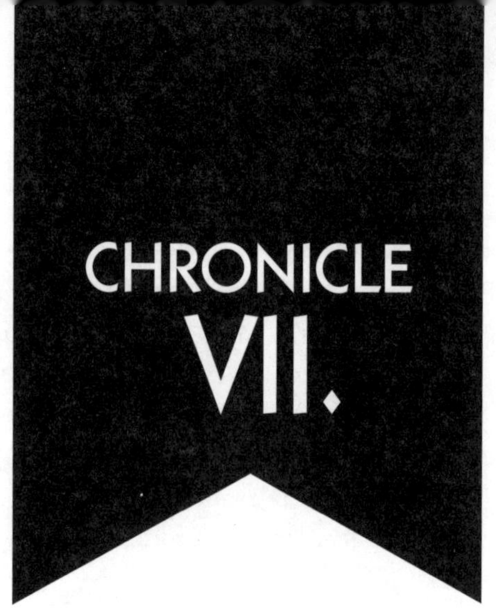

CHRONICLE VII.

"You mean to suborn the entire Catholic Church!" exclaimed Tom in horror, as he reached for the Edradour. The president had briefly just sketched out plan b, our need to co-opt an existing intelligence network.

"No, Tom, you're jumping way ahead of me. But I must admit I do admire the direction you're moving in. Just look at it from a somewhat less ambitious perspective.

"Say for instance, you're a parish priest working sixty miles from Medellin in Columbia. Four nuns are kidnapped from a nearby orphanage and school, and are being threatened with rape, torture, and murder. Tom, you have seen this sort of thing happen around the world repeatedly. What do you do? Pay ransom? With what? You're a parish priest with a subsistence-level income, no savings, and a penurious congregation. Do you call Rome? The Vatican could send you money, if it wishes, but in doing so it knows it is thereby encouraging the same scenario to happen again and again.

"What if, instead, as an admittedly select parish priest in a uniquely tough developing country neighborhood, you could reach into a cabinet and pull out a small satellite phone reserved for absolute emergencies such as this. You don't dial. It's a dedicated phone. It only calls one number. You turn it on and wait ten seconds. A voice says 'Good Evening, Father Xavier, this is Rome. How may we help you?' You describe what has happened, and you are asked to hold the line. You hold. One minute later the voice comes back on and says, 'Please check your watch: we will call you back in seventeen minutes.'

"Seventeen minutes later the phone rings. 'Father Xavier, help is on the way. They will be there before you awake in the morning. Please leave your front door unlocked tonight. Meanwhile, you can sound out your parishioners to learn if anyone has a clue as to where the nuns are being held. No one should go looking for them; but their physical location may already be known to someone locally. Above all, Father Xavier, know this: we are not going to defeat kidnappers, rapists, murderers, suicide bombers, and drug lords around the world by paying ransoms or relying upon suicidal nuns. Help *is* on the way!'

"Within eight hours a stealth jet helicopter with ground-reading infrared capability has dropped off a special force team of men and women who quickly make their way to the priest's quarters while the copter grids the area. By dawn the team is pretty certain where the nuns are *not* being held. By four o'clock the following morning, the team has located the nuns and their captors. Two hours later the nuns are back safe. And when the captors awake and discover that their prisoners have somehow magically vanished, they see on each other's faces permanent tattoos across each brow: 'Jesus says STOP ATTACKING INNOCENT NUNS'."

"Is that actually possible?" asked Tom.

"Yes," Job replied. "When you underwent surgery for your pacemaker, what anesthesia was used?"

"Propofol," Tom replied. "It's great. You wake up feeling refreshed and you don't remember a thing."

"Yes," agreed Job, "that's why they call it 'milk of amnesia'. Our agency techs have weaponized it airborne now, which means they can aerosol it from a plane or helo or drone, release it over a limited area—up to a square kilometer, and anesthetize anyone on the ground, awake or while they sleep. We can then move in undetected, do what we must, and depart. Later they awake refreshed with no recollection of what has transpired. It's like magic. Or a miracle. It's actually pretty dramatic. Our folks also developed a battery-operated tattoo branding iron. It takes four or five seconds to apply a crisp three-by-three-inch image, in color, under reasonably sterile conditions, and it turns out as vivid and permanent as any regular tattoo. It's like signing our work. We shame each perpetrator and leave a permanent message for his or her colleagues and family."

"A righteous version of *The Scarlet Letter*," Tom interjected.

"Let me give you another case," said the president. "A priest in the Central African Republic, or another in South Sudan, careful to steer clear of the tribal, ethnic, and religious conflicts and tensions on the ground that are destroying each of those countries, finds that the water well in his principal village has given out. It's not just a matter of getting a new pump; a new well and new infrastructure are needed, and it's an emergency. These are failed nation states. There's no one to go to. The priest can pray for help. He can ask the UN for help. He can ask USAID for help. But any help has to be timely. In what is effectively a war zone. Meanwhile, his villagers, who can last ten days without food, can only last three or four days without water.

"So he picks up the special little dedicated satellite phone he has been sent from Rome, hears someone on the other end say 'Hi, Father Anthony, this is Rome. What can we do to help?' Twenty-four hours later, again in the middle of the night, two heavy-duty helos in stealth mode land, unload fresh water, setup shop, start up their equipment, and begin digging a new well. In the middle of the night. Twelve hours later the new well is in. The priest has blessed it and the good folks who dug it. Food, medicines and laptops have been distributed. A cursory round of medical once-overs and quick-fixes among the villagers has been completed. And the stealth team has long since departed, having carefully avoided confrontation with indigenous forces, and having been protected during their stay by a small airborne guard force on standby."

"Sounds wonderful," said Tom. "Sounds Christian. But what's in it for you?"

"Well," said the president, "we've had a few trial runs, three of them involving Catholic priests and our black ops teams, to see if the operational side is workable and to get an idea of response times and real-world costs.

"One life was lost. A drug cartel scout fell asleep up in a tree, crashed to the ground and broke his neck. The operations are intended first and foremost to be nonlethal, because we cannot ask the church to get involved otherwise. But I can't help it that the dumb SOB was up a tree when he got sprayed with propofol. I regret his death. On the other hand, Tom, he was part of a band that had kidnapped, tortured, and raped four nuns. So I didn't lose any sleep over it.

"As to gains, when we called the Columbian priest back and asked what the conditions were in real time regarding the cartel in his neck of the woods, we got new, good, reliable intelligence from him on how the drug guys were losing credibility, especially among the youth. They were no longer able to recruit new blood from that area. It turns out that our branding and shaming led to public shunning and ostracizing in a large community that had previously only feared and even respected the drug thugs. We had found a very powerful weapon in our branding iron tattoos, and will continue to use them.

"In the CAR and Sudan, by making friends and winning hearts and minds among the villagers, we were subsequently able to work out information, identification, and location systems with the two priests involved. That's no mean accomplishment. Trying to tell who's who, much less who's where, in covert guerrilla conditions using satellites is chancy at best. Here we had a corrective mechanism in place on the ground to tell us when we were wrong in real time. And in turn we could warn the priests on a daily basis what visitors they could expect and when."

"So you don't always wait for the priests to call you with a problem?" asked Tom.

"We're brand-new at this," Job responded, "and have tried it only three times so far with priests. The idea is to serve as an emergency source of help in return for up-to-date local observations from them. It seems a fair exchange. It helps to build confidence and credibility by coming to their aid first and asking for their observations only after establishing our bona fides."

"And keep in mind," the president added, "we are talking about a very small and select group of priests carefully chosen in the hot spots, the most dangerous and contentious locations around the world. The ones where having someone relatively invisible and reliable on the ground is the best intelligence asset."

"I don't see how I could fit into your plans," observed Tom.

"Oh, that's easy," said the president of the United States. "You get to run the show. From Rome."

CHRONICLE VIII.

The next morning Tom and Job met over breakfast at The Hay-Adams so that Tom could be filled in on the president's proposal. "I didn't get much sleep after that bombshell he dropped," Tom began. Over coffee, eggs, smoked salmon, fresh juice, and warm bread, the president's man endeavored to sketch a more detailed proposal.

"What he has in mind is that you head a small, new organization based in Rome: 'The Foundation for the Propagation of Aid to Parish Priests'—in that hotel we talked about. You would be linked electronically by satellite to our headquarters at Langley, and through them to our station chiefs in every embassy around the world. We would network with the operations of the HUMINT activities of other agencies and departments, like state and AID, as appropriate. Also via Langley we would coordinate directly with our own black operations groups as well as the special forces teams pre-positioned closest to the hot spots.

"Your job would not have anything to do with the operational side of the work. Importantly, you would set the ground rules on our interaction with priests, and monitor all contact. You would also serve as chief public fundraiser. And finally, you would liaise with the Vatican: ideally, get the pope's blessing—or at least avoid denunciation by someone well listened to among the Catholic hierarchy—and keep an eye on the competition next door, the Congregation for the Doctrine of the Faith—with its worldwide reach, high level of sensitivity, low level of tolerance, and disproportionate influence.

"To do this, we would provide you with two staffs. One staff in Rome would be largely Italian American, able to blend in easily, but thoroughly multilingual to field phone calls directly from priests around the world, operating twenty-four-seven. The Langley staff would be a team of experienced black ops pros, integrated with a team of crack analysts. The analysts' job is to research the hot spot, the immediate problem, the priest, the parish. The ops folk then get three chances to plan and be prepared to execute the most imaginative quick fix, with best marks for top speed, low cost, and high drama, keeping in mind that this is a morality play as well as a lifeguard operation.

"If we succeed, within a matter of months you will go from a relative unknown in Vatican circles to a high-value target in intelligence circles. In other words, you will be at risk. Not so much for execution as for rendering—kidnapping—to neutralize you, or at least discover how you do what you do. Because we will do this very well indeed. To help you in general, and protect you in particular, we would like you to meet two 'nuns.'"

Job nodded to the table across from Tom, where Em and Sure were having breakfast. They had been glancing out of the corners of their eyes and turned toward the two when they saw the president's man nod toward them. In their habits and veils, what were previously two young, fit, beautiful women were now sculpted severely in white and black, two perfect, angelic faces with wondrous eyes looking straight through the souls of the two men regarding them. Then they both smiled.

After a moment, Tom turned back and looked daggers at his companion. "You really know how to hurt a guy. I'm a sixty-year-old celibate priest. But I'm not dead!"

CHRONICLE IX.

Tom Gallagher was feeling distinctly queasy, and said so. Sure and Em were trying to be supportive; but they were also trying to ready him for what they knew would be a rough day. It was the morning following their meeting and subsequent briefing together at The Hay-Adams, and the three were now on their own, walking from the visitors' parking area toward the main entrance of the CIA headquarters building across the Potomac, northwest of Georgetown.

They would spend three or four days here being briefed, and then Tom would go through a week of training with Em and Sure at the "farm" to turn them into a team, make certain they could work well together in the field, and read each other's signals and gestures as they moved about as a single, mutually protective unit.

In Rome, Sure and Em would eventually be teamed and mentored with a senior agent assigned by Rome station, who would continue their in-field training for a year or more, liaise with the Rome station chief and embassy, and in general try to help Tom and keep him out of trouble. Of course, that's if he finally made up his mind and took the job; but everyone knew that could not happen until his papal interview in less than two weeks.

This week at the agency, Tom, Em, and Sure would each also have a full day of high-speed defensive and avoidance driving instruction. Tom had bridled at this, saying that he had not yet agreed to accept the job in the first place, and was not all that certain he wanted to play James Bond even if he did accept. He was promptly informed that the course had nothing to do with espionage or derring-do. It simply had to do with survival among Italian drivers in Rome's aggressive twenty-first century traffic.

Em told Tom that the training she and Sure had endured at the hands of the agency taught them to expect a rough morning for him today. The interrogators and briefers he was about to meet would have researched him rigorously—every teacher's negative comment, any honor system offenses, any arrests, a detailed history of sexual preferences and activities, any substance abuses, any behavioral problems, any medications, any peccadillos. "After all," said Em, "you weren't born a priest. They'll ask you every embarrassing question they can think of, back you into every corner they can, drag out every skeleton they can find in your closet, make up ones they can't find, and use any psychological technique short of drugs to strip you bare."

"And that's just for starters. That's how they get down to the bare bones of each and every new colleague. Em and I thought we really knew each other 'til we went through this together and realized we didn't have a clue! When they're done, then and only then do they feel they can build a strong professional bond on a rock-solid base of truth, and establish firm trust. Their words, not mine," concluded Sure.

"Do they understand they are dealing with a sixty-year-old cardinal, a Prince of the Church?" Tom asked with some asperity.

"Of course they do," said Sure, "and they will show you the consequent respect you deserve for at least two—perhaps even three—seconds."

"That includes us," Em chimed in. "They will see Sure and me as part of their team, on their side, not yours, so while we will try to help you, it can only be by preempting them. We will be grilling you, too, Tom. Keep your cool. 'Float like a butterfly; sting like a bee.'"

CHRONICLE X.

There were eight of them, four men and four women, plus Em, Sure, and Tom. Em and Sure took care to sit among the agency types, not next to Tom. Tom looked across the table at a thirty-something hardnosed man who led the meeting and knew instinctively that he was not the senior agency person at the table. The man introduced himself as Derek, and said that before substantive and operational briefings could begin, it was agency policy to "vet" any potential colleague by a process of random, tough questions that fleshed out the detailed and lengthy background checks required by law that had been performed in order to grant Tom the security clearances the president had ordered. He added that everyone, without exception, found this experience unpleasant and embarrassing, and that the agency apologized in advance for the discomfiture. "But we all went through it and found it did weed out those who for one reason or another should not be here. Who would like to ask the first question of Cardinal Gallagher?"

If he had not used the title, at least five of the eight were set with a tough, first hardball question. But that imposing title gave just an instant's pause to all. Sure knew it would, and in her charming, disarming way, she quietly slipped into the instant.

"I have a question, but first I think we should drop the title, as we're questioning the man, not the office, and as I understand it you have no duties and are retired and convalescing."

"Yes," said Tom on cue, thinking, God I like this girl!

"Well then," continued Sure blithely, firmly placing herself on the side of the inquisitors, "I want to know about the sex thing. I mean I just spent six months of enforced celibacy, and I'm here to tell you I don't like it. I know what the church says, but what do you priests actually do? I can tell you I know what I'm going to do!"

Tom knew that Sure was preempting a rougher approach to this subject from someone else and appreciated her parry. After the chuckles had subsided, he replied with a question: "Is anyone else here a priest or a former priest?" He watched carefully. Derek across the table and two others glanced at the tall woman seated at the corner on his right. He knew then that she was the senior officer present. Then Derek said, rather pompously, "That classified information is only available on a need-to-know basis, I'm afraid."

"Well, it's a personal question, so let me give you a highly personal answer. Surely, you won't mind! You told me personally that your father is an alcoholic, and that he joined a twelve-step program when you were nine. You said he stopped drinking, and made amends to you, your brothers, and your Mom, and has stayed sober ever since. Did he ever talk to you about how he handles *not* drinking?"

"Yes, every time I see him!" replied Sure. "Last Thanksgiving he talked to all of us, thanking us for our support. And he admitted that he still thinks about it every day. He said there isn't a night that goes by that he doesn't miss having a few glasses of wine with dinner. But he said it does get easier with time—or at least not quite as hard—to abstain completely as the years go by. And when he's particularly tempted, he said he prays for strength (he's the sole believer in the family) and calls a friend in the program to help him through the moment. He said he takes abstinence one day at a time, and that's the only way it works," Sure concluded.

"Well, Sure," said Tom, "you've just described beautifully and in exquisite detail precisely how I and other priests just like me accept and fulfill our obligation of celibacy, one day at a time."

"And what if you fall off the wagon?!" prodded Derek, with a prurient smile.

"I'm afraid that classified information is only available on a need-to-know basis," replied Tom quietly.

Em and Sure exchanged a quick glance that said, "Float like a butterfly; sting like a bee!"

Tom was doing his very best to maintain a sense of humor, to stay calm and keep a civil tone: but it was after 4:00 p.m., without even a break for lunch, just sandwiches and coffee, and he was tired, cranky, and pissed. This was certainly not the first time he had submitted to one of these probing inquisitions. The first had been at a secret society at Yale, then upon entering the seminary, again before ordination, and finally before he had received the pope's personal call and been given a cardinal's ring. Each had been progressively more intrusive over a longer lifespan, and each had become increasingly less challenging and rather more annoying. He knew he was clean. There was nothing really significant to be found. No showstoppers. But you cannot prove a negative.

He also knew they were not finished with him. Neither Derek nor the woman on his right had asked a question yet. Those two had sent in their six banderilleros to soften him up with sharp pokes here and there, while they hid their long swords under their capes, waiting until the end of the performance to leap between his tired shoulders, over his sagging head, and plant a long sword deep into his heart.

Derek flashed his cape, holding up a sheaf of paper. He would be the first to try. "Tom, I have here copies of tax receipts signed by you and a Father Quinn, cohabiting in Boston with a certain Miss Dagmar in 1977–78. You haven't mentioned her or him earlier, and I wonder why. After all, cohabitation is cohabitation, and according to the record you were in seminary at the time. I thought you were obliged to live there as well. Care to enlighten us?" he asked, with that prurient smile of his.

Tom thought to himself silently, *OK, you SOB, here goes.* Then he said, "Well Derek, I didn't feel it worth mentioning her because she was a real loser. I'm sure you're personally familiar with the kind I mean.

"Father Quinn and I owned a place in Melrose to share costs for her and took care of her. She seemed content enough. We each visited her once or twice a week when either of us could get away, and occasionally rented her out to other seminarians in need of a little fun. They always gave her something extra, too, which helped.

"But she was a real loser. You see, Derek, 'Miss Dagmar' was a horse, a mare, and the 'cohabitation' was her barn. The few times we raced her she came in last or next to last. All in all, a lovely tempered mare, but not a winner, and a poor investment, but a delightful companion to many lonely students."

After the laughter died down, the lady to Tom's right spoke up. *Coup de grace coming?* Tom thought.

"Tom, you can call me Alice D. I'm the deputy director of Clandestine Operations for the agency, and I have but one question for you. Before I ask it, I want you to know that we are finished here. You've passed all the tests, including this last one, and it was indeed a test, with the highest possible marks. I congratulate you. I would welcome you to our family if you had decided to join us, but I understand why that must wait. Tonight you will be feted by the director of the agency, to twist your arm a bit, and I will have the honor of joining you for dinner. Your answer to my question will have no bearing on today's proceedings. But if we are being fully honest here, it is important to me personally, as I too am a practicing Catholic, and I know it must be of critical importance to you."

"Tom," asked Alice, "how does a Catholic priest, a Prince of the Church no less, rationalize working with an agency like ours? I've had to struggle with that question from the perspective of a layperson for over twenty years and would welcome learning your thoughts."

"Thanks, Alice," said Tom, "for making all the rest of this unpleasant day worthwhile. What a great question! And one I'm still battling with myself. But I look at it from a somewhat different perspective. At least the defining terms are different.

"First, you're right, I have not accepted yet, and will not unless and until I am permitted to do so by my own boss, His Holiness.

"Second, the terms of the offer the president made to me were quite clear: I won't be working for you; you will be assisting me—in performing a service for a select number of priests in hot spots around the world. In return, they may be asked to provide me, and through me, your good selves, with information regarding the ongoing status of those hot spots—information which they may choose to provide, or not, as they wish.

"Third, if you put the shoe on the other foot, it is you who had best be prepared to answer the question of why you would expend time, effort, money and risk lives to help some far-off priest in an emergency, solely on the hope—and speculation—that he may prove to be a future asset.

"Every time something terrible happens, the answer should not have to be to commit more of our youth to resolve it, to put in American troops, or even to commit new intelligence assets, when these good priests are already on the ground, for reasons of their own. Trying to help them under the toughest of circumstances in return for their help just has to be better than overcommitting this nation again and again around the world. As an American, and a priest, I fervently believe that.

"So, the short answer for both of us, Alice, you and me, as practicing Catholics, as well as for this agnostic agency, and even our proposed new moral foundation, is that we hope to do well by doing good," he said.

"Of course, there's a more philosophical, and indeed theological answer," he continued. "It's the one I've been struggling with, and I think the one you are searching for, as well—and perhaps some others of you, too," he added, taking care to look directly at each of the other nine individuals in turn around the table.

"I would refer you to the history of a rebel Dominican priest and theologian, Father Jacques Loew, who founded the worker-priest movement after the Second World War. While it started in Marseilles, it represented a powerful and widespread belief among the priesthood that the Catholic Church and especially the church hierarchy were losing touch with the working man. The conflicted reactions of the Roman Curia and

Pope Pius XII, the movement's effect on Pope John XXIII and the Second Vatican Council, and on Pope John Paul II, all show how the church has tried to respond to the challenge that it had gradually become alienated from the modern world.

"That response is incomplete. It needs much more work. But you need to know that the rebel theologian Father Loew spent six years working in the favelas of São Paulo, Brazil, from 1964 to 1969. His concerns began to reverberate throughout South America just as the current Holy Father entered seminary at the Colegio de San Jose in San Miguel, Argentina, working odd jobs in the favelas, and becoming sensitized to the same issues himself. As they say in spaghetti westerns," Tom concluded, "there's a new sheriff in town."

"By which you mean?" pushed Alice.

"I think this pope, even if he doesn't end up approving my project, will understand what I want to do and why I want to do it."

"This is new intelligence," said Alice with a wry smile. "This is the first time, to our knowledge, since the president made his offer to you, that you have told anyone you want to do it."

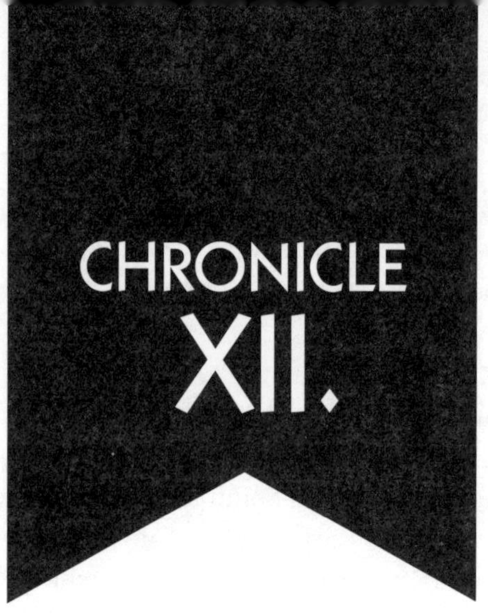

CHRONICLE XII.

Tom led Em and Sure through the labyrinthian maze of the Vatican City. Tom knew his way by now, having visited many times over the past thirty years, but was surprised when he checked in at the front office to be told that His Holiness was not meeting them in the formal appointment rooms, or even in the papal apartments on the top floor of the Apostolic Palace, where popes have lived for centuries, but instead had invited them for an early lunch in the common dining room of the Domus Sanctae Marthae, the modest guest house on the other side of St. Peter's Basilica.

The pope greeted Tom effusively after Tom formally knelt in obeisance and kissed his ring in greeting. Tom introduced Em and Sure—by their baptismal names—as his colleagues. They had both agreed with Tom to wear conservative street dress, rather than their cover-story habits.

"I'm living here, for now, in the Domus," the pope said when he received them. "I can walk to all my appointments in the Papal Palace. As a cardinal in Buenos Aires, I chose to live in my own small apartment rather than the archbishop's mansion allotted to me, and took the bus around town. Here I'm not yet prepared to move into that ten-room papal apartment in the palace. Three hundred people could live there. I even know a circus in Argentina that would love that much space! Instead, here in the Domus guest house, I get to meet all sorts of folks from outside the insular Curia inner circle. Last month, I even threw a party for a visiting group of sixty of my countrymen. Spontaneously. No notice. Everyone loved it.

"Between the four of us," he confided, "I'm actually thinking of not moving into the palace at all. It would symbolize my separateness from the old Curia and its old ways. I was thinking instead of moving into the papal apartment at the Archbasilica of St. John Lateran, which is the pope's personal cathedral as head of the Rome Diocese. Popes lived there for over a thousand years, so there is ample precedent, before they moved into the more sumptuous Vatican apartments. John wanted to live there, too, and had it renovated; but he finally bowed to Curia pressure and remained in the palace. The bottom line for me is that not moving into the palace would make me more accessible to the people.

"But enough about that little controversy. Tell me, Tom. Last time I saw you, you were in the hospital here, close to death. I prayed for you. I see you survived, which means that at least one of us is not in too much trouble with our higher power. And your letter last week said that you wish to ask my blessing for a project that I might find 'repugnant.' You presume to judge me, Tom. Of anyone with this ring, I would think I would be the last fisherman of a mixed lot to be prejudged. At the very least, it's too soon. At best, I may surprise you. So let's have a quick lunch, and then I have another appointment."

Tom felt thoroughly chastised, and rightly so. He was crushed for the president, Sure and Em, and the agency, not to even get to explain their project. He could kick himself for that ill-worded letter he had sent to Rome just ten days ago.

"But enough of my scolding, Tom," continued the pope. "As with everyone who comes to see me these days, I know you want something of me, and I promise to hear you out and give your proposal my full attention. Just not now. Not here. You see, I want something of you, too. And I thank God you are alive and well and here and can hear me out, too. So what I propose is that after lunch, you show these lovely young women a bit of our ostentation, and then join me at 2:00 p.m. to go to Castel Gandolfo for the weekend. Every waking minute of my life here in Rome is programmed, accounted for, budgeted, guided, overseen by the Curia. But at Gandolfo we can spend real time together.

"Unfortunately, you will need to leave these two charming colleagues of yours here in Rome. Before we leave, I will ask our Commandant to see that the Guard keeps a protective eye on them while we're gone, so you need not worry for their safety."

Tom was so relieved he could hardly eat his lunch. He would get his chance at bat after all.

As for Sure and Em, they had not taken their eyes off the handsome, young, fit, colorfully uniformed Swiss guards who stood at attention with their halberds, their huge blades on long pikes, everywhere they looked since they entered Vatican City with Tom. Now the two of them seemed to be the recipients of divine intervention.

CHRONICLE XIII.

After lunch, the pope introduced them to Kurt Uri, who seemed to materialize effortlessly at the pope's side. Uri, they were informed, was the long-standing commandant of the Swiss Guard, "the oldest active military force in existence."

"I thought that was Her Majesty Elizabeth the Second's Yeomen of the Guard," said Tom. But the moment he said it, and saw the commandant's face, he knew he had made a gaff.

"No, my new American friend," said Commandant Uri, meaning just the opposite, "while Britain's Yeomen were founded in 1485, predating the official start of our guard by twenty-one years, they are but a part-time body with a purely ceremonial role. We, on the other hand, have fought in defense of His Holiness for over five hundred years, at times losing up to 147 of the then 189 guards in a single battle in his defense, which is why we carry Pope Julius's imprimatur 'Defenders of the Church's Freedom.' But then I know you Yanks aren't much for history."

The pope intervened, none too soon, to say that Tom's two colleagues were in Rome for the first time, and would not accompany Uri, Tom, and himself to Castel Gandolfo. Perhaps Kurt could ask one or two of the guards to introduce Em and Sure to the Eternal City while he, Tom, and Kurt were away for the weekend.

The commandant seemed to notice the two young woman for the first time, and his entire demeanor changed abruptly. He actually beamed with delight. "Of course," he replied, "and I have two worthy halberdiers for such an honor, Emile Charnet and Jean Michel Arnot, both from Yvorne, above the Lac de Lausanne. They are scheduled for leave this weekend, but I am certain under the circumstances they could be persuaded to sacrifice their trout fishing to accompany the two of you around Rome." He stepped aside and spoke briefly into his hand-held radio in German, the operational language of the guard. Within a matter of minutes, the strikingly handsome answers to Em and Sure's prayers materialized just as effortlessly as Kurt Uri had a quarter hour earlier.

“This is where I’m no longer my own man,” said the pope. “On the ground, I can still walk, or take a bus, carry my own bag, make my own phone calls, live in the guest house. But once we’re off the ground, Kurt takes command,” and he nodded toward Uri. “He won’t let me be driven to the castle because of the traffic, the vulnerability of a car, and the threats we’ve received. But I think what really bothers me is that I feel like such a spoiled kid on these helicopter rides. The view is transcendental.”

“Threats?” I asked, surprised.

“Oh, you can’t shake things up without being threatened. There are always threats against any pope. But I seem to have cornered the market. The ultra-conservatives and literalists are always unhappy. And with Pope Benedict’s reforms being pursued rigorously, we are defrocking priests at the rate of over two hundred a year now. I’m not seen as Mr. Nice Guy.”

The pope, Tom, and Kurt were aloft in one of the papal helicopters over Rome, each wearing earphones and lip-mikes so they could talk to and hear each other comfortably over the sound of the helo’s engine. Kurt, who as commandant of the Swiss Guard was in effect the pope’s secretary of defense, chief of security, and principal bodyguard, undertook a short orientation and history lesson, clearly for Tom's edification. He pointed out that they were headed southeast up into the Alban Hills at an altitude of some 1,400 feet to Lake Albano and the cooler temperatures of the Apostolic Palace of Castel Gondolfo, the summer residence where popes had enjoyed the cool climate, fresh air, long walks in the vast gardens, the silence (especially), and the blessed absence of petitioners, for more than four hundred years. It was a place of prayer, contemplation, consultation, and even decision-making.

During the Second World War, Kurt recounted, it was also a place for hiding Jews and birthing babies. Literally thousands of Jews and other Italians needing refuge, many of them pregnant women, passed through and were hidden away inside the walls, the Roman catacombs and the medieval grottos of the castle, over the course of the war. With Pope Pius XII's approval, the papal chambers were used as a maternity ward, and his papal bedroom a birthing chamber. One result was a surfeit of babies named Pio, Italian for Pius, and Eugenio, Pius XII's given name. But the belief that the pope's castle was inviolate was shattered the morning of February 10, 1944, when the Allies bombed this territory of the "neutral" Vatican. Over the next few days, some five hundred corpses were dug out of the wreckage.

While Tom knew that Pope Pius had less than a spotless record overall in regard to helping the Jews, supporting the Allies, and eschewing the Third Reich and Benito Mussolini during the war, the role of his summer palace and the Allied bombing were facts new to him. It was becoming clearer to Tom why Kurt, a "neutral" Swiss, might not be overly fond of Americans. But then again, come to think of it, the Swiss enjoyed the same mixed World War II reputation that Pope Pius XII had. While this was probably a subject to be avoided with Kurt, Tom knew he needed to ask about those threats the pope had mentioned.

As the white and blue helicopter gracefully circled into the wind to land, Tom got a 360-degree view of the castle's grounds. He was prepared for the beauty, but not the size. Castel Gandolfo was larger than all of the Vatican City. While the Castel and the town named for the Genovese family of Gandolfi were built around 1200, the Papal Palace itself dated from the time of Pope Urban VIII in the seventeenth century, and as Kurt emphasized in his continuing travelogue with obvious pride, had been designed by Swiss architect Carlo Maderno. But in addition to the palace and the surrounding formal landscaped and sculpted gardens, there were also fish ponds, an arboretum, natural conservatories, the Vatican Observatory with its world-class collection of meteorites, the Villa Cybo—which served as a school for the Maestre Pie Filippini religious educational community, the Villa Barberini—where Roman Emperor Domitian ordered the bloody persecution of Christians during the first century after Christ's crucifixion, the Pontifical Church of St. Thomas of Villanova dating from 1658, apartments for the live-in staff of twenty-one, plus greenhouses, cattle barns, and even a fine herd of twenty-five prize dairy cows.

"Pope Benedict told me right after my election, when I came to see him, 'Here at Gandolfo I find everything: a mountain, a lake; I even see the sea.' It's not your average summer camp," remarked the pope with a wry smile.

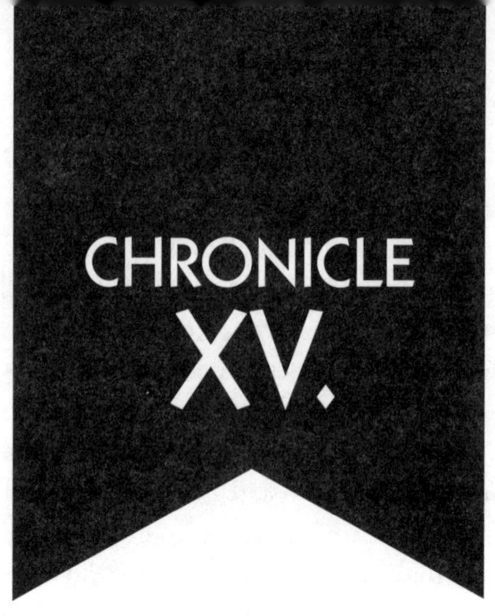

CHRONICLE XV.

That evening, at the pope's invitation, Tom and Kurt joined His Holiness in the Papal Refectory—effectively the pope's summer palace kitchen, for what was to be an informal "light dinner." Kurt just kept showing up, and Tom was getting the impression that he was more than chief of security and bodyguard; he increasingly seemed to be the pope's personal confidant—with the distinct advantage of not being a member of the Curia, not even a priest, but a man of the world—yet one who clearly knew where all the Vatican bodies were buried, so to speak, and who for whatever reasons was clearly loyal to this pope. Tom was re-evaluating Kurt.

The pope introduced Tom to Sister Lucia of the Maestre Pie Filippini Order, whose convent shared the Castel grounds. Sister Lucia was almost as tall as Tom and looked like she could take him on in a fair fight. She ran the Castel, and the papal apartments in particular. "Il Papa is infallible in all things," pronounced Sister Felicia, "except the care and welfare of his good self. That's my job!"

"Sometimes," said the pope with a wink, "she even lets me cook. Last month I made a carbonada criolla for Pope Benedict."

"It was actually pretty good," observed Kurt.

"Kurt knows if he doesn't like my cooking, he goes straight to hell," remarked the pope.

For dinner, after the pope's lengthy grace, they dined on Sister Lucia's tortellini verde in a spiced vegetable broth, fresh trout from Lake Albano at their doorstep, a salad from the extensive kitchen garden, a wedge of *Paglietta*, which Kurt dubbed Italy's answer to Camembert, and some just-baked crusty bread, followed by a tiramisu, all served with a light, white *Verdicchio del Castelli di Jesi* that Tom found he didn't know and wanted to meet again.

But it wasn't the food that received Tom's undivided attention. It was the pope's tutorial, his "Vatican chronicles."

"No one yet understands the extent of the sacrifice that Pope Benedict made for the Church. Yes, clearly, he had become part of the problem, because for years bishops had been lying to the Curia and the succession of popes. The succeeding Curia, and particularly the Holy Office, chose to compound the lies or at least ignore the truth, and by the time Benedict discovered the full reality of the situation, the enormity of it was simply appalling and unconscionable.

"And I'm not talking only about the sexually deviant priests preying on their congregants for decades, and the abhorrent practice of their bishops playing whack-a-mole with those priests rather than following Church law by revealing them and turning them over to civil authorities. I'm also including in this horrific mess the less-publicized, subversive activities associated with organized crime, and the questionable transactions and crimes, even murder, connected to the Vatican Bank.

"Pope Benedict was personally responsible for instituting rigorous reforms, making sure the college of cardinals were made aware, to a man, of the reasons for all of his actions, and then resigning to pay for the egregious errors of the Church's ways in the eyes of the world. So, yes, he inherited and was made part of the problem. But he realized it, crafted the stringent reforms, and took upon himself the public guilt and personal penance as pope. As his successor, the guy with a new broom coming in to make a clean sweep of things, I am profoundly in his debt, and unlikely as it may seem, we have become good friends.

"I've been sorting out the Curia, particularly with this last round of elevating cardinals, and will continue to do so with the next round, but I must leave further implementation of the reforms to them for the time being, if their credibility is to be restored. Meanwhile, I have an even bigger challenge facing the Church that I must deal with.

"I first heard of it as a seminarian, in the favelas of Argentina and Brazil. It was a kind of radicalization that I took seriously at the time, but then it was limited to a few priests who worked with the very poor. It has grown steadily since and played a significant role in the thinking of John XXIII, John Paul II, and mainstream thinking among the more liberal laity.

"It started out with a whisper. 'Capitalism is not the answer.' That issue was the starting point for the communist party's recruitment during and after World War II. And it worked because of the seed of truth: 'Unbridled capitalism breeds a caste society of economic classes.'

"Then we saw in the Cold War and the collapse of the Soviet Union that Communism is not the answer, either. In fact, no ideology—no '-ism' or economic system—has been able to resolve the growing problem of income inequality, the growing gap between the haves and the have nots within and among nations. In other words, the promise of upward mobility is not being fulfilled.

"The Church must address this challenge if it is to be deemed relevant in the twenty-first century. If the wealth of eighty-five or eighty-six richest individuals today exceeds the total wealth of over half the world's population of 3.5 billion people, we are no longer talking about 'income disparities' or income inequality. It's obscene!" exclaimed His Holiness with fervor.

"What is meant by this can be seen all over the world. In South Africa, for example, one political party continues to make the traditional argument that all you need is more jobs: give people enough jobs and they will become self-enfranchised and pull themselves up by their own bootstraps. But radicalized priests are arguing today that this is not enough, that subsistence urban jobs are no better than subsistence agriculture or subsistence mining. They just create a permanent underclass with zero upward mobility.

"Instead, these politicized priests and their followers argue, what is needed are good jobs with fair wages that permit education, and more importantly re-education, training and re-training, savings and investment, on the part of workers. That is how they define upward mobility; and that is how they redefine a successful capitalist society and a real growth economy. So, for them the answer is not just jobs, but good jobs with fair pay, education and re-education, training and re-training, and importantly a piece of the action, a share in the ownership of the means of production.

"If this is what 'radicalization' means these days, then I stand with the radicals. But the conservatives inside my church and yours are accusing them of being socialists and communists, with their capitalism-at-any-price rhetoric. We are losing priests around the world because of this schism. It's tragic. And it is as much of a problem in America and Britain and France as it is in South Africa and Columbia and India. We must address it if the Church is to remain relevant."

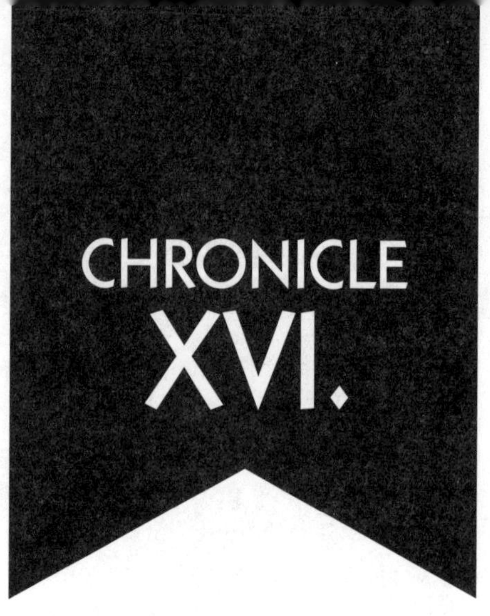

"But aren't we supposed to be politically neutral?" Tom asked over the tiramisu and coffee.

"Oh, bullshit!" exploded Kurt. The pope winced, but saw what was coming, and let Kurt take aim at Tom's query.

"How you Americans can be so incredibly arrogant and at the same so misinformed and naïve is beyond my comprehension, until I realize once again that you know nothing of history," Kurt continued. "Your man Webster decided that 'neutral' should mean 'not taking sides,' and you have believed him ever since, when every European politician, every pope, and certainly every Swiss knows that neutral means taking both sides!

"At the end of the Middle Ages, Switzerland was a poor country. Young men often sought their fortunes abroad. The use of Swiss soldiers as royal bodyguards and the pontifical army stemmed from the reputation of Swiss mercenaries beginning in the late fifteenth century. We fought in almost every important battle of the day in Europe, often on both sides.

"We are seen as collaborators in World War II by you Yanks, but even though we had Germany as our next-door neighbor, we—like Sweden—

did not succumb to the Nazi war machine. Like Sweden, and for precisely the same reasons, we sometimes made concessions and breached our neutrality in favor of both sides, the Axis powers of Germany and Italy, and the Western Allies. But for the most part we tried to remain independent and 'neutral.' And throughout the Cold War, while we were 'neutral' and therefore never joined NATO, in fact we were consistently a better ally of the United States than some of your so-called allies! So, for a poor little country in the middle of everything, we've not done badly for ourselves, and have avoided being bombed and invaded."

"Well," said the pope, "now that we've gotten to know each other so much better, I suggest a good night's sleep is in order, as Tom and I have a tough morning ahead of us." With that, he bid the two men goodnight and retired. Kurt, as a peace offering of sorts, offered Tom a nightcap, and Tom accepted.

Over a Strega, Kurt zeroed in. "Tom, it isn't often we see a cardinal accompanied by two young ladies. Tell me about them."

"Oh, those aren't ladies," said Tom, smiling to himself at the hackneyed old saw, "those are my spies. They're CIA agents-in-training. They each know sixteen ways to disable you without mussing their hair. You haven't seen them in their habits yet, but their cover is that they are nuns, Sisters of Charity to be exact. I must say they look angelic."

Kurt was totally nonplussed. When he began to recover his composure, he carefully said, "Does His Holiness know this?"

"Not yet," replied Tom, "I was saving it for breakfast."

A few moments later, the hi-tech phones of two Swiss guards, Emile Charnet and Jean Michel Arnot, automatically decrypted an urgent text message warning each of them that agents of the CIA were attempting to get into bed with the guard. "You're a little late, commandant," they each concluded separately, smiling.

CHRONICLE XVII.

Over breakfast the next morning with the pope and the ubiquitous Kurt, Tom took meticulous care to present the president's proposal in as objective a way as he could manage. He outlined plan a, and the urgent requirement to rebuild the human intelligence side of America's and the West's intelligence capability. He then made the case for plan b, the concurrent need for assistance from an existing network of trustworthy observers who were already well-established in the right hot spots at the right time. Finally, he added an undefined plan c, a wish-list, last resort "Hail Mary" pass-play from the end zone if neither plan a nor plan b was working effectively in a timely fashion, and danger was imminent.

He then recounted for His Holiness and Kurt the three examples the president had provided, in all the detail he had been given, trying hard to stick with the facts and not let his enthusiasm show—setting out the aid that would be provided to a select group of priests, and exactly what would be asked of them on a voluntary basis in return. He concluded with the offer that the president had made to him personally, to head up the communications network from Rome, and added that his colleagues, Em and Sure, were CIA agents in the guise of nuns, serving as facilitators and bodyguards. Finally, he said he would do nothing, and would go no further with the president's proposal, without the pope's blessing.

"You mean to tell me we took two CIA agents to lunch at the Duomo?" exclaimed the pope. "The Curia would dine out on that tidbit for a month if they knew!

"Tom, you've given me a lot to think about," the pope said after a moment, "and I'll not reject it out of hand. But I will need time to ponder and pray about it. Right off the top, there are two things I don't like. First is telling priests 'This is Rome calling.' You're not a tourist board. Either it's the Vatican or it's not. And second, saying 'Jesus said stop attacking innocent nuns.' Laudable sentiment; but Jesus didn't say it.

"As to the Church getting into the intelligence game, it's always been there. In the fourteenth century, there were two competing Holy Sees, and two popes, one in Avignon in France, the other here in Rome. The growth industry of the day was spying on each other!

"In the fifteenth century, the Catholic Monarchs Ferdinand and Isabella used the Spanish Inquisition's spies to learn everything there was to know about their enemies, and then the Church persecuted them mercilessly. You Americans think that the most important event of 1492 was the discovery of America; but it wasn't. I'm pretty sure somebody would have found it eventually. The most important event of that year was the expulsion of all non-Christians from Portugal and Spain by those Catholic Inquisitors.

"In seventeenth-century France, Cardinal Richelieu personally established the most extensive intelligence network of his time. He ended up more powerful than his king, was renowned for his deviousness, and called the *Eminence grise*, Europe's Cardinal of the shadows."

"While there's ample precedent for the Church's involvement in international intelligence activities," remarked Kurt, "I wouldn't call those particular examples morally supportive of your case, Tom."

"Now it's my turn to ask something of you," the pope continued. "Let's walk in the gardens, and I'll take my turn as petitioner."

CHRONICLE XVIII.

While the formal, sculpted gardens of Castel Gandolfo were truly magnificent, and the whole complex of the summer palace significantly larger than the Vatican, to Tom's surprise the pope was headed out back for their walk. Kurt diplomatically had begged off and left the two of them alone.

"I prefer to walk in Sister Lucia's kitchen garden when I want to think and pray, rather than out front with all the formality," said His Holiness. "It seems more friendly, and earthy—and all these vegetables and spices and herbs always make me hungry!

"The reason I wrote asking you to come to Rome," he continued, "apart from the fact that I wanted to see you and check on your recovery, is that I recalled that you attended university with the president, and were friends with him after his election. Of course, that was before I found out he was sending you to see me. I wanted you to take a message to him—one that I cannot entrust to the usual channels—the Curia, or our ambassador, the Papal Nuncio in Washington. It's something of a riddle.

"Shortly after my investiture as pope, I received a visit from a Muslim head of state. I thought at the time that it was simply a polite diplomatic gesture. It turned out to be more than that. How much more I can't tell. I need your president's help. And I cannot tell you exactly who my visitor was. But I can say he brought me a beautifully decorated antique box, sixteenth century Iznik I would guess. He remarked that while it was empty, he would fill it with a riddle.

"He told me if I identified the fifteen key generals among all the contesting forces in the Middle East today," the pope recounted, "I would be surprised to find that eleven of the fifteen share a common trait that could help lead to Middle East peace. He would not be pressed on the issue but stressed that a time was soon coming when this information would prove to be valuable, when that common trait would override all other loyalties and interests: Shi'a, Sunni, Wahhabi, Palestinian, Pharaonic Egyptian, all.

"Tom, I have worked on this riddle, but quite frankly it's beyond me. I can't share it with the Curia and keep the promise I made; but I can't act on it either if I cannot figure it out. So I thought of reaching out to you, and through you, informally, to your president. Perhaps he and his advisers can make sense of it. I should add that I would not make so much of it were it not for my trust in and respect for the source."

"On first hearing," said Tom, "I'm just as flummoxed by it as you. But I'll be happy to talk with the president personally and keep it confidential and low key."

"I thank you," said the pope. "Now I think I'd like to be left alone for a while to think about all that you have told me." As the pope turned slightly and smiled, Tom automatically moved toward him, leaned forward and started to kneel to kiss the papal ring, when out of nowhere he was kicked by a horse—or at least that's what it felt like. He heard a slight pffftt, and felt like a horse had just kicked his left shoulder.

He ended up down on the ground, dazed, full of adrenalin, staring at a small, dark man with a pencil mustache and wide eyes some forty yards away. Tom quickly struggled up, hurting and dizzy, and charged the man from a halfback stance, using the adrenalin and all his six-foor four-inch frame to be as intimidating as possible. The man's eyes widened even further. He dropped the silenced pistol and fled, with Tom pounding after him, around toward the front of the palace.

It should have been no contest, and it wasn't, but not with the outcome Tom expected. One moment he was fifty feet behind the would-be assassin, and the next instant the short man just disappeared—right in the middle of the palace's formal gardens. Tom looked right and left, and then began to carefully grid the area around the point where he lost sight of the little guy.

Kurt came rushing up with two of the Swiss guards exclaiming, "You took a bullet for His Holiness!"

It was then that Tom's feet went out from under him. He crashed in a heap on the ground beside Kurt. The pope rushed up; his cassock covered in blood.

"Oh my God," croaked Tom when he saw the pope.

The last thing he remembered was Kurt saying gently

"Don't worry Tom, it's not his blood; it's yours."

CHRONICLE XIX.

"You've been shot, Tom," said Em. "You're in the summer palace infirmary. We flew out with one of the Vatican surgeons, who's scrubbing now to operate on you to try to find the bullet."

"Why here, rather than back in the Vatican hospital?" asked Tom.

"Kurt's orders," replied Sure. "He doesn't want word to get out that there's been an attempt on the pope's life. He's told the staff that some foreigner fired at you over a personal quarrel. And he has changed the pope's schedule, and is flying him back to the Vatican this evening so he can give a Sunday morning blessing over St. Peter's Square tomorrow from his balcony, and be seen alive and well to quell any rumor that may have been started here this morning."

"Does he know who did this?" asked Tom.

"No," said Em, "and apparently only you saw him."

"Let me give you a description before I go into surgery," Tom offered. He described the dark little mustached man in blue coveralls, and Sure tried to sketch him. When she had finished a draft, she showed it to Tom.

"That's him, but his eyes are wrong. They are more weasel-like, very frightened, and mad as a hatter."

Sure was adjusting her drawing when the surgeon came in, followed by the His Holiness and Kurt. Without further ado, the surgeon gave Tom an injection that immediately made him even woozier.

As Tom was being wheeled into surgery by the infirmary nurse, the pope leaned over and said loud and clear, as if talking to someone inebriated, "Thanks for this morning, Tom! And stop attacking innocent nuns—you can quote me on that!"

Tom had enough consciousness remaining to realize that the pope had just given him the green light for his project. He closed his eyes and smiled.

The surgeon, on the other hand, frowned darkly at his patient.

CHRONICLE XX.

When Tom next awoke, he felt refreshed, no pain to speak of; but he clearly remembered His Holiness somewhat obscurely blessing his project by coded reference to the tattoo. *Must be propofol*, he thought.

The nurse by his bedside rose and exited quickly as Kurt came into the room. Kurt's demeanor toward Tom had clearly changed. He acted more like a brother and fellow conspirator. "We have the pope's blessing to proceed," were the first words out of his mouth. Tom noted the "We." Not "How do you feel?" Not "The operation went well, and they found the bullet!" Rather a sort of "Why are you still lying there when 'our' project has a 'go' and 'we' have work to do!"

Tom was a bit slow to catch on. Then Kurt reached in his pocket. "Here's our top medal, highest honors and all that, for courage and valor under fire. You took a bullet for His Holiness. You are now officially an honorary member of the Swiss Guard, with the rank of major. I would kiss you on both cheeks, but you Yanks don't go in for that. So consider yourself officially kissed.

"When they first brought you in here, you weren't seriously wounded, but had lost a lot of blood. We're the same type, so they hooked us up for a direct transfusion, which was the quickest and most efficient way to handle the emergency. Incidentally, as a consequence, you're now half Swiss, and will get cravings for Emmentaler and Yvorne. But while all this transpired, His Holiness would not leave our sides. So I took the opportunity of rounding out his education on modern Vatican involvement in the intelligence business.

"I told you that the examples he recounted to you earlier were not morally supportive of your case. So I gave him a few of my own that clearly were. I've been around here a long time. During the Cold War we ran an extensive clandestine network in Eastern Europe and the USSR, most aggressively under John XXIII and John Paul II, directly aiding Western efforts against anti-Catholic Communist regimes. And we had begun even earlier to combat leftist Third World guerilla movements that were trying to co-opt our priests to advance their revolutionary agendas, though on a more modest scale.

"In fact, your former National Security Adviser Zbig Brzezinski once told me personally he thought America would have been better served if Jean Paul had been president and Jimmy Carter had been pope, given Jean Paul's geopolitical savvy versus Carter's naiveté. And Ronald Reagan extended full diplomatic recognition to the Vatican only after being briefed on how our priests could operate in Poland and Latin America with unrivaled grassroots presence, solidifying an exchange of information which has continued under Pope Benedict and to this day. So in my role as the Vatican's 'Secretary of Defense,' I chose to weigh in on your side. After all, you took a bullet for His Holiness. As far as I'm concerned, you're on the side of the angels."

"Not intentionally!" exclaimed Tom. "It just happened."

"Your project is the right thing to do, in keeping with all that we have been doing," concluded Kurt. "So get out of that bed, because we've got to catch an assassin, and we've only a couple of hours in which to do it!"

"You think he's going to try again?"

"Of course! That's what assassins do! As long as that blue and white helicopter hasn't departed, he knows His Holiness is still here, and he has another chance before the pope returns to the relative safety of the Vatican. You're the only one to have seen him. I need you out and about to try to recognize him. Surely and Emery are down in the village with my men and copies of your sketch; but I need you to come with me to help in the search. You have a flesh wound that will hurt like hell tomorrow. Let's move now while you're still numbed-up and I can get you looking."

"What if he recognizes me?" asked Tom. "Won't he flee? Or shoot?"

"I've asked Sister Lucia to help us with that." Kurt opened the door of Tom's room and Sister Lucia, who had been seated patiently outside, came in carrying a large, black bundle. She spoke rapidly in Italian to Kurt, and while Tom had learned a modicum of the language from his earlier visits to Rome, this exchange was so fast and so lengthy that he couldn't track it.

"What did she say?" Tom asked. "She said 'Yes'," Kurt replied.

Em and Sure were resting their feet after traipsing the entire village with Emile and Jean Michel, and were enjoying an espresso at the corner café in the little lakeside village of Gandolfo below the summer palace, when they saw Kurt and Sister Lucia approaching them, accompanied by a second sister, also of the Filippini Order given the habit she was wearing, but with her left arm in a sling. Em was the first to realize that the second sister was their boss draped in one of Sister Lucia's habits; then Sure caught on and burst out laughing as well. "It was the shoes that gave you away," said Sure, which just started everyone roaring.

"You two make terrible spies," remarked Tom crossly, "if you can't keep a straight face!" "Very unprofessional," added Kurt, with a wink—by which time Em was now doubled over, hiccupping, and Sure was covering her mouth to keep from spraying everyone with espresso. It was Sister Lucia, of the teaching order, who brought discipline to the gathering by drawing a ruler from her vast sleeve and threatening the lot of them sternly with a burst of Italian invective. Kurt translated meekly: "As our lives may depend on this charade, get serious!"

They moved to a larger table at Kurt's behest for a council of war. "I think we must now change our tactics," said Kurt. "This is a relatively small town even with the castle, but we've had no luck. On the other hand, all my professional instincts tell me the would-be assassin is still here because the pope is still here. The shooter will want to try again if he possibly can. While we have the sketch, I now believe we should ignore it. He will have changed appearance: no mustache, different hair, change of clothes. Plus, he has lost his pistol.

"One reason Tom is still with us is that this assassin is not a pro and was using a World War II weapon with old ammunition that no longer packed its original punch. My guess is that he will now attempt to use a rifle, having lost his pistol, and while a rifle may be easier for us to spot, unfortunately chances are that it will be more modern and thus more accurate and dangerous.

"All we really have now is his height and age. Tom guesses about 5 feet 5 inches, or 1.6 to 1.7 meters, and late middle age. I've informed the rest of the summer palace guard to watch for anyone of this height and age, especially if they are carrying anything that might conceal a rifle. Here is a grid map of the area with assignments and radio frequencies. Emile and Emery will work as a team, Jean Michel and Sure as a team, Tom is with me. Sister Lucia I would ask you to remain here at the café to keep your eye on that wall over there. Sister Lucia knows, but the rest of you don't, that that wall hides the little entrance to the tunnel we used during the war to get children in and out of the palace grounds unnoticed.

"Everyone please keep radio silence unless you see something suspicious; but if you do, don't hesitate to let us all know. We have just under two hours before the pope departs and then our assassin will go to ground. We need to find him before then. Let's go!"

Anyone older than forty and shorter than two meters in height was stopped, queried, stopped again, re-queried, all to no avail. An hour and a half went by without a word. Then Emile and Em called in. "Kurt, what does the palace cowherd look like?" asked Em. "I don't recall, why?" replied Kurt.

"Because it's getting late, and no one has brought the cows in for milking. They're unhappy. Something's wrong," responded Em.

"This is Sister Lucia. I heard you. The cowherd is from the town. His name is Luigi Stoppa. He's short, about 1.6, and about fifty years old.

Normally he would never let those cows suffer. I can't imagine him trying to kill the pope. But I know he protested the Priebke affair."

"That's our man!" broke in Kurt. "Everyone on this channel: we are now specifically looking for Luigi Stoppa, age fifty, height 1.6 meters, probably armed and intending to make a last chance attempt on the pope."

Hardly were these words out of his mouth when three rifle shots rang out from the direction of the corner café.

"Hold your positions," ordered Kurt, "this may be a diversion. Tom and I will investigate immediately, and keep you informed."

When Kurt turned the corner, he was brought up short, with Tom almost knocking him down as a consequence.

In front of them, sprawled on the ground, was a short, bald man whom they could only assume to be Sr. Luigi Stoppa. Seated on top of him was the muscular and large Sister Lucia, smiling happily, holding the rifle she had just fired.

"What happened?" exclaimed Kurt.

"It's our cowherd, Luigi Stoppa," replied Sister Lucia, "he was headed for the children's tunnel with the rifle when I told him to stop. He pointed the rifle at me, so I took it from him and hit him on the head with it."

All Kurt could manage to ask was "Did you fire the rifle, or did he?"

"Oh, I did," replied the good Sister, smiling happily.

"Why?!" managed Kurt. "Always wanted to," she replied. "Papa used to have one but would never let me try it. Besides, I thought it would bring you running. Seems it has."

CHRONICLE XXII.

An hour later, His Holiness had safely departed for the Vatican by a well-guarded helicopter—Kurt would catch up later in the evening; Sr. Stoppa was safely ensconced in the Gandolfo village jail, charged with shooting Tom—with no mention of any attempt on the pope; Sister Lucia was busily overseeing the preparation of a well-deserved dinner in her own honor—for what was now called the Café clutch of bravados—at which she was invited to recount her capture of Stoppa in colorful detail, and for which His Holiness had ordered at least six bottles of chilled Asti Spumanti Papal Reserve to be consumed in her honor and his absence; and in the meantime the team of four young CIA and Swiss Guard operatives were using their extensive training and secret skills to milk two dozen really unhappy cows.

As Kurt poured Tom three fingers of Poire Williams to ease his pain and brighten his outlook before their dinner, Tom asked "What is the 'Priebke affair' that Sister Lucia referred to as motivating Stoppa?"

"It's a long, messy story," replied Kurt. "Very Catholic!"

"Back in the fall of 2013, the semi-secret traditionalist Priestly Fraternity of Saint Pius X, which opposes the liberalizations of the Second Vatican Council—especially the opening of relations with Jews and Judaism—wanted to have an ex-Nazi, Erich Priebke, a war criminal, receive the sacrament of a public Catholic burial right here near Gandolfo on Lake Albano. Local church authorities refused, saying the deceased had not repented. The fraternity argued that he had been baptized, confessed, and received absolution, so was technically forgiven even if he did not repent or demonstrate remorse. Hence an impasse.

"Long story short, he was refused a public Catholic funeral. There were protests. Old fans of Il Duce, neo-Nazis and anti-Semites, tainted a group of Catholics who believed the fraternity had a reasonable theological argument that Christ paid for all sin, no matter how abhorrent, so that once baptized, confessed and absolved, you should receive a Christian burial even if you are so blind as to not recognize your own sins. Stoppa blamed the decision of the local Catholic authorities on the old pope, and he retaliated against the new pope. Who's to explain the logic of a madman?

"I talked earlier by phone with the leader of the fraternity in question and am absolutely satisfied that this was the aberrational act of a lone crazy, not the fraternity. He was appalled, and profoundly disturbed at what transpired, and has every reason to keep it secret along with the rest of us.

"So I owe a great debt to you, Tom, and to the forceful Sister Lucia, whom we will fete tonight. You will both be in my prayers, and His Holiness could not be more grateful. Which is why he approved your project with such alacrity. After my history lesson on Vatican intelligence gathering, of course!

"Before he took off this evening, he left a list of 'suggestions' for you, a copy of which he gave to me. He asked that you peruse these and give him your reactions once you're up to returning to Rome. I've already read them, and conclude that we've got work to do, and I thank God this man is on our side, for I would hate to be up against him! These are his 'suggestions'":

1. Think bigger. Not just Catholic priests. Monks, Bishops, Cardinals—if they are in the right place at the right time, they should have a phone;
2. Think bigger still. Orthodox priests, Muslim Imams, Protestant missionaries, Jewish Rabbis: if they are in jeopardy, where we can, let's help;

3. Don't answer the phone from "Rome"; you're the Vatican—not the Pope, but close enough; and quote me not Him on the tattoo brand to be accurate;
4. You have detailed plans a and b but not c, the so-called Hail Mary pass from the end zone if all else fails. Even if all else doesn't fail, I have a plan c. More about that later.
5. I have given Kurt a short list that I would ask be given top priority for receiving phones ASAP.
6. Tomorrow morning, when you return to the Vatican and see the surgeon at the hospital to check on your arm, please take the time to visit at length with Cardinal Mamoru Matsumoto, who is there with terminal cancer. I will have prepared him for your visit, and Kurt can fill you in;
7. Don't drink too much Asti—I need you and Kurt back in Rome tomorrow; but do please make sure Sister Lucia knows how much we all owe her and love her for her diligence and strength. She is a rock in the foundation of our church. Please read that part to her tonight, and you and Kurt both hug her for me; if I hug her she'll crush me like a walnut.

"Have you looked at this list, Kurt?" asked Tom. "There's something odd about it."

"No," replied Kurt. "I read the note but just glanced at the list of priests. What strikes you as odd?"

"Well, they're not all Catholic priests; there are a few sisters, one Church of England priest, a Lutheran pastor of all things, two Rabbis, three Imams—in all a total of twenty-three individuals in the field in hot spots you would expect in sub-Saharan Africa, North Africa, the Middle East, Southeast Asia, and South America. But the first name on the list stands out as being in the least likely place I could imagine as a 'hot spot,' in fact probably the most tranquil location I know: it's the name of a Catholic priest in a small monastery just outside Kyoto!"

CHRONICLE XXIII.

Called the Gemelli University Hospital after its founder, Franciscan Friar Agostino Gemelli, the private teaching hospital of the Catholic University of the Sacred Heart, two miles north of the Vatican's emergency side gate at the Porta Sant'Anna, serves as the Vatican's hospital as needed. It was here that seriously wounded Pope John Paul II was rushed for emergency surgery following the assassination attempt instigated by then KGB head Yuri "the pope is our enemy" Andropov, and thankfully bungled by a young, incompetent Turkish agent under Bulgarian control. (Andropov feared that the appeal of the Church in general and this pope in particular would grow arithmetically in Poland and expand geometrically in Eastern Europe. And, of course, Andropov proved to be prescient.)

There is a suite on the third floor of this hospital reserved for the pope, but this evening it was occupied by Japan's Cardinal Matsumoto, at the pope's insistence. Under extraordinary circumstances, His Holiness had agreed to hear the dying cardinal's final confession and wished now he hadn't.

While the cardinal was close to death from terminal cancer, and would certainly succumb to the disease—according to his doctors—within the next few days, the pope had asked Kurt to place the cardinal's suite under guard—but could not tell him why without abrogating the seal of that confession. So His Holiness simply told Kurt that apart from imminent death from cancer, there was additional reason to fear for the cardinal's life.

And because he could not break the seal of confession, he had asked Tom to see the cardinal tomorrow morning, and in turn asked the cardinal to share with Tom what he had confessed to the pope. In this way, and only in this way, could His Holiness then ask Tom to act directly on the information the cardinal had shared in his confession, information that clearly required urgent action on the part of the Vatican and the West.

That would all take place in the morning. It was just after ten o'clock in the evening on the third floor of the hospital. Nurses were cracking windows for the night and making sure their charges were comfortable or asleep. The bored uniformed halberdier of the guard was surveying his hallway.

Because this was the floor housing the pope's suite, there were additional security precautions in place: a private, coded elevator, the only one to reach that top floor; security cameras covering that elevator and every stairway and hallway; security cameras in the pope's medical suite itself; infrared cameras and heat sensors monitoring the suite and all doorways; regular hospital guards on the floor and the additional Swiss Guard, all twenty-four-seven.

While not an impregnable fortress, Kurt was satisfied that no one could get in or out without being noticed. The cardinal had received a significant number of visitors—Japanese diplomats from the embassy, senior churchmen from the Curia, Japanese businessmen and their ever-present minions visiting Rome, all paying their last respects to His Eminence while he was still alive to receive them. But they had all been identified and screened in advance.

Then about 1:00 a.m., after the third-floor shift changes in personnel were completed, something odd began to happen in the soiled linen cart at the end of the hallway. The soiled linen slowly began to grow. A white form appeared, what seemed like a small white head, then a torso—ever so slowly—and finally the all-white form of a diminutive woman in some sort of body stocking, but with no holes for eyes, mouth, or ears. Then, quite suddenly, she simply vanished.

One instant there was a white shape, and the next instant there was a blank tiled wall. With grout lines. Reflecting light. Just like someone flipped a switch—there one second, gone the next.

And that's exactly what the operator of the Q-suit did. She pressed a switch. The six layers of her form-fitting white machine—for it was indeed a machine, though she was the only moving part, worked flawlessly on its first real-world field trial. Layer one, closest to her skin, absorbed and dissipated her perspiration, keeping her comfortable. Layer two heated and cooled her as necessary, while dissipating her body heat entirely to make her invisible to infrared cameras and heat sensors. It managed to do this while stabilizing her core body temperature in wind up to sixty miles per hour and weather between negative ten and ninety-five degrees Fahrenheit, allowing her to operate anywhere at any time, with her built-in night vision lenses.

Layer three was the battery breakthrough which powered the suit's personal comfort zone and total body heat dissipater, and more importantly its primary function, the cloaking system generated by layers five and six. The battery was integral to the suit itself, as pliable as denim cloth. It scavenged its energy directly from the electronic environment it found itself in—from the energy in the Wi-Fi, radio, television, and other electronic signal transmissions all around it.

This marvel of science was developed by Shuman Cray Lee at Stanford University, stolen from his computer by the Chinese, purloined from theirs by the North Koreans, intercepted from theirs by the Russians, and purchased surreptitiously by some Japanese.

But it didn't work. At least until a frustrated Wharton-trained Japanese CEO picked up the phone one day and called Shuman Cray Lee direct:

"Hi, Shum, it's your old buddy from Wharton, Tadeo Miki."

"I'm not at Wharton. I'm at Stanford."

"Okay, so I want to be your new buddy from Tokyo. I'm sitting here with our prototype of your battery. It doesn't seem to work."

"Are you the guys who stole the drawings off my computer?!"

"No. That was the Chinese."

"So how'd you get them?"

"Long story. Bottom line, the Chinese haven't made them work. Nor has anyone else. I'm betting you can. Answer the knock on your door."

"Nobody's knocking. Oh, now they are." There was a pause. "Some Japanese suit just gave me a briefcase full of money. Then he just bowed out."

"You'll also find first class roundtrip tickets to Tokyo and reservations for a Japanese garden room at the Okura, the best hotel in the world. Incidentally, the briefcase is a million in cash, just so you don't have to spend time counting it. I'm betting you didn't put how to make the battery work on your computer intentionally, but that you do know how to do it. And I would be pleased to give you the equivalent of nine more of those briefcases just to come and talk to me about doing a bit of work with us. And that's just for starters."

"Wow. You sure know how to warm an indebted college kid's heart! Yes. Okay. I accept. At least to listen. See you in Tokyo. Give me a day to rest up in the hotel and think before we get serious."

That's the conversation that produced layer three. Layer four was an equally supple storage system for the energy layer three harvested undetected from its ambient electronic environment. Invented in Japan.

Layer five was a computerized picture-taking and transmission system that used some two hundred tiny cameras on the surface of the Q-suit—layer six, effectively a wearable TV screen—to capture the surrounding area in nine hundred pixels per square inch, in order to reproduce a computer-corrected version as if on a flat surface, visually eliminating the curves and bulges of the suit wearer—essentially making the suit invisible.

What you would see, if the Q-suit and its wearer—the agent—weren't blocking your view, is pictured on the suit. So you see the tiled wall, or the hallway, or the linen cart, not the Q-suit; and the computer keeps the lines straight as you perceive them even though they are projected on the curving surface of a human form. It's as if the suit and the agent were transparent, and you are looking right through them.

As long as the agent doesn't make any sudden moves, the Q-suit allows the agent to be a chameleon, changing appearance to blend precisely with the surroundings, and doing it so accurately that you can be just two or three feet away, and as long as the agent doesn't make any noise, he or she remains imperceptible to you.

When Kurt later examined the tapes of that night on the third floor, the infrared cameras and heat sensors were blind to the intruder because of the suit's heat dissipater. The visual tapes showed only a white form briefly rising from the soiled linen cart, then nothing for fifteen minutes until a pillow levitated over the cardinal's head and he was quietly smothered in his sleep.

After the murder was discovered, when Kurt's team found a listening device in the suite, Kurt realized they had failed to take the threat seriously enough from the very start. He sent his team back in and had them look again. Chagrined, they found a second listening device, of different manufacture.

Tom arrived from Gandolfo later that morning. Kurt had to give him the bad news, adding that His Holiness was furious to lose one of his own to whom he had offered sanctuary. Kurt noted that one of the devices found was of Japanese manufacture, and the other Chinese. "But that doesn't tell us anything, except that at least two unrelated agents had His Eminence under surveillance. These two devices were commercial products, off-the-shelf stuff anyone could buy, not government issue. It could be anyone. I believe the cardinal was killed because someone overheard the pope ask him to talk with you this morning and wanted him silenced before he could reveal whatever secret he was keeping."

CHRONICLE XXIV.

Trastevere. Tras-té-vere. Just the word alone makes any Roman smile. It means "across the Tiber," across the river, not here—over there. Of the fourteen neighborhoods created by first Emperor Augustus after the collapse of the Roman Empire, thirteen of them were on the right bank, the east bank of the Tiber River. Only one was on the "wrong" bank, the left or west bank, and he named it Trans Tiberim, which became Trastevere. Actually, all one needs to know to understand Trastevere is that its fourteenth century coat of arms, which continues as its symbol today, is the golden head of a lion on a red background flagrantly sticking out its tongue at the thirteen other Rioni or "neighborhoods across the river."

To say that Trastevere has a "mixed" reputation understates the issue. In the Middle Ages its maze of narrow, winding streets left no room for carriages; and even later when streets were widened and cobbled, and sidewalks added, navigating them required expert knowledge and total sobriety, neither of which was often to be found.

Isolated as they were, alone "beyond the Tiber," the inhabitants of Trastevere developed a culture of their own, with the only connection to the rest of Rome a small wooden bridge built on pilings, the Pons Sublicius. By six hundred BC the neighborhood was full of sailors and fishermen, with immigrants from the east joining them over the next few centuries, mainly Jews and Syrians.

In the Imperial Age, it became somewhat gentrified. Clodia, Catullus's friend, moved in, as did Julius Caesar, who built a garden villa, Horti Caesaris. Today, Trastevere maintains its multicultural character, its narrow, cobbled streets, and its medieval houses. As a consequence, it has attracted tourists and teaching institutions catering to foreigners. But it is still the first love of all native Romans, and those who live there still call themselves Trasteverini. There is only one neighborhood that surpasses it in popularity: its next-door neighbor, also on the "wrong" side of the Tiber, the Vatican.

When you want to eat well, you go to Rome; and when you want to eat well in Rome, you go to Trastevere, which has more good cafes, pubs, and restaurants per inhabitant than anywhere else on the continent.

After two weeks of all work and no play, Tom invited Kurt, Em, Emile, Sure, and Jean Michel to an evening in Trastevere—his treat.

He led them through a warren of Trastevere's wonderfully crooked cobblestoned alleys and walkways, all within an easy stroll from the Vatican, to a little family-owned and -operated restaurant that boasted the oldest cellar in Rome. Tom had known the family for over twenty years and was received like the prodigal son.

After all the *abbracci* and *baci*, Tom introduced his friends to the three owners, Romeo Catalani, who managed that marvelous cellar; his wife and magical chef, Elena; and their knowledgeable son, Francesco, who served their guests while Romeo pushed them politely and ever so gently up the learning curve of Italian history and cuisine.

First Romeo whisked them all down the worn stone steps into the cellar, remarking that "You are going back in time seventy-five years with each step down. And when you get to the bottom, you will be in a space over a century older than the Coliseum."

"Tell them what that space was originally used for," prodded Tom with a smile.

"It was one of the earliest synagogues in Trastevere," replied Romeo. As he spoke, he opened a cellar-cooled bottle of what he called a "white" Lambrusco wine, which was in fact rosé in color, and poured everyone a glass.

"The synagogue was founded by Nathan ben Jechiel," he continued, "who lived from 1035 to 1106, in the basement of his beautiful medieval home, with its loggia and arches. On the base of this column over here you can still make out Hebrew characters carved into the marble. The address was thirteen and fourteen Vicolo delle Palme, the alley of palm trees, as palms were planted around the house in memory of Judea.

"Incidentally," he added, "the wine you are drinking is made from a grape that dates from before the time of Christ, when it was grown right here on the bank of the Tiber by the Etruscans. It was popular during the Roman Empire and is still produced today in the Emilia-Romagna region to our north. It makes both a white and a red, depending on how long you leave the skins in contact with the juice, and both are always pleasantly frizzante or slightly sparkling, what the French call *petillant*. We enjoy it because it goes with almost anything and has an unusually low alcohol content. It's our 'no fault' recommendation for Americans because, like almost all ancient wines, it's slightly sweet. The French, and the nouveau-Californians, don't like that—which makes us appreciate it even more."

Romeo refilled their glasses and guided them back up the worn stone staircase to their table, where Elena was ready to reveal her art of the evening. Tom explained that her menu changed with the season, and as she used only fresh, local produce, what may be available on the menu changed from day to day.

And then there were Elena's special discoveries. For example, this morning at the market she had found beautiful, fresh, tiny artichokes that were irresistible.

Kurt spoke up, saying "Tom, why don't you and Elena choose for all of us. Between you two, we can't go wrong!" And that's exactly what transpired. Tom retired to the kitchen with Elena to pick, choose, and taste, and when he returned, he was all smiles. "I think we're in for a treat," was all he would say.

What followed was not what any of them would have ordered on their own, but a meal that not only treated their senses but intrigued their intellects, as each recipe dated from the time of Julius Caesar. They began with a small portion of artichoke clafoutis, an ethereal baked essence of artichoke. This was followed by a single calamari stuffed with eggplant and poached in white wine, perfect against the last of the white Lambrusco. After a pause and more conversation, they were each treated to a small portion of fresh linguine in a minced truffle sauce, with Romeo pouring a red Lambrusco to accompany it. The main course, again served sparingly in small portions, was roast pork that had been cooked for days in red wine and a myriad of spices, served with braised lettuce. And for those who wished, a dessert of lemon *givré* ended the meal on a light, tart note.

Over coffee, Kurt observed, "I've lived in Rome for most of my life, but I can't remember a meal I enjoyed more. And I don't even know the name of your restaurant! I didn't see it when we came in, and as we didn't use the menus, I still don't know it."

"Well," replied Tom, "the name depends on who you are. Let me show you. If you're Trasteverini, the name of the restaurant is **Spirito di Vino**, the 'Spirit of Wine.' But if you're an *habitué* from the Vatican, the name is **Spirito Divino**, the 'Divine Spirit' restaurant!"

"Before we end this evening," continued Tom, "I want to thank all of you for these last two weeks of unstinting work. We were all depressed by the loss of Cardinal Matsumoto, and frustrated by our inability to track the agent, much less look behind the crime at the cause and the identity of those who hired the agent. But all of you persevered, and we are ahead of schedule in getting up and running.

"And tomorrow we go fully operational. Our first fifty satellite phones are being delivered around the world, initially to the twenty-three priority cases chosen by His Holiness plus the first twenty-seven high potential cases identified by Washington. Our communications equipment is installed and tested, and our staff is up to speed and in place at our third-floor hotel-headquarters, the offices of the new Foundation for the Propagation of Aid to Parish Priests.

"His Holiness has added an imprimatur to his blessing, his personal design for our papal insignia. It is a simple cross beneath a white rose. 'I thought "sub-rosa" appropriate,' he told me with a big grin!

"I have been asked to fly to Washington tomorrow for a meeting with cabinet and congressional officials on new developments of direct interest to us. I'll be back by the end of the week. While I'm gone, Kurt will continue to oversee us on behalf of His Holiness. I'm putting Sure in charge in my absence. And Em, in light of what happened to Cardinal Matsumoto, and given your background in Japanese studies and your language ability, I want to ask you to deliver the phone in person to the pope's highest priority priest, the Japanese monk in Kyoto. What's his name?"

"Father Takashi Takano," replied Em.

CHRONICLE XXV.

The president's point man welcomed Tom back to the White House, saying, "As I'm the guy that got you into all this, I hope you don't hold it against me. The meeting's about to start. We're simply calling you a consultant at this point, and not referring to your church title. We have not briefed this group on your project, and don't plan to unless and until we develop a track record of success."

"And if we fail?" asked Tom.

"If the project fails, then they have no need to know!"

Senator Daniel P. Laughton, co-chair of the US Senate Select Committee on Intelligence, struck the table with his open palm, and the cross talk ceased. "This special group is now in session. What are we called this time?" "Omega Nine, Sir," someone replied. "Okay, Omega Nine is now in session. I apologize for getting you all out here on a Saturday, but the president has commissioned us on short notice to provide him, informally, with our views on the risks of this forthcoming Japanese plutonium shipment, and I'm due to deliver our concerted opinion to him personally at Camp David this evening. I've asked Admiral Hackett to join us; Admiral, welcome to Washington's most elite coffee klautch. Also joining us is Tom Gallagher, a White House consultant here at the president's request. Welcome, Tom.

"I also want to welcome back our committee's own guru, Dr. Bob Travis, home from Moscow, where he has been working on the follow-up with the Russians to the Krapotkin affair[1]. The late general's partner, Admiral Alexey Rostov, continues to serve as a consultant to our president, and is a member of this working group and with us today. Alex, our congratulations on your recent marriage to Connie, and all good wishes to you both!

"Now, to today's agenda. I need to brief the president this evening on what the Japanese are doing, why they are doing it, and what the risks are as we perceive them here today. Frankly this would have been a hell of a lot easier if we had maintained the high quality of our good old-fashioned human intelligence capabilities, and if we could still use our hi-tech intelligence capabilities to continue to spy on our allies. But we allowed our HUMINT shop to deteriorate while we invested in hi-tech. And now we've sworn off listening in on our allies with the hi-tech gear we invested in at the cost of HUMINT. We've cut off our ears to spite our face!"

---

[1] The theft of former Soviet strategic nuclear weapons from Ukraine by KGB General Georgiy Krapotkin and Admiral Alexey Rostov, and their subsequent disposition, are set out in *GAMBIT* by Antoinette Falquier & Joseph Harned.

CHRONICLE XXVI.

“Do they know about Cardinal Matsumoto’s murder?” whispered Tom to the president’s point man. “What murder?” he whispered back. “The Vatican announced he died of terminal cancer.”

Senator Laughton continued: “Kathleen Conover is with us this morning from the agency. As NIO for Japan, you are in a good position to start us off with a background summary.”

“Happy to, Senator. We all remember the Japanese ‘economic miracle,’ and the rapid rise in oil prices that followed it. The Japanese have no domestic energy to speak of, apart from some coal, and when OPEC began to apply the screws, the Japanese realized how dependent on oil they had become. In a little over five years, they therefore produced a second miracle, an efficiency miracle, whereby they could produce two and a half times the product with the same amount of energy.

“Concurrently, they followed France’s example and invested heavily in nuclearizing their electricity supply, switching from oil-fired plants to the first nuclear-fired generation. Problem was they realized they were just switching dependencies, from oil to uranium. So they bought into the argument of building a second generation of nuclear reactors, called breeder reactors, which produce more plutonium fuel than they consume. It was an elegant solution with the seductive attraction of a perpetual motion machine—almost. Breeders are in principle very efficient, and with just a modest supply of fresh uranium, they could keep the country growing for centuries.

"Theoretically. On paper. The physics and chemistry and engineering are all hellishly complex, but the logic is straightforward. While Japan worked on designing and building a new generation of breeder reactors, it would ship its used or spent uranium fuel from the first-generation reactors to France and the UK, where reprocessing plants could extract the plutonium Japan needed to start its second-generation breeders.

"Once Japan's breeders were up and running using this starter kit of plutonium, they could then produce the additional plutonium fuel necessary to keep the breeder reactors going. And the modest amount of new uranium needed for the process would be coming from stable and safe suppliers like Australia and the US, thereby assuring Japan of secure supplies of electricity at reasonable cost for the foreseeable future.

"When you reflect on it, this was a pretty compelling strategic plan. What went wrong was totally unforeseen. First, commercial breeder technology turned out to be much more difficult and costly to develop than anyone had imagined initially. Second, the price of uranium fell by eighty percent, making plutonium fuel a prohibitively expensive alternative. Third, the price of oil has gone down rather than up as everyone had predicted. Fourth, non-Arab oil producers have dramatically diluted the ability of the Middle East producers to drive world prices higher at will, much less to single out individual nations like Japan for oil blackmail. And fifth, the combination of fracking and intense gas exploration has changed the import-export picture worldwide, turning once dependent nations like the US into much more self-reliant producers, further weakening the Middle East suppliers' leverage.

"As a consequence of all these developments, the countries that have been scrambling to design, build, and commercialize breeder technology have now halted their breeder programs. The US and UK breeder programs are essentially dead. The breeder programs in France and Russia have been shelved indefinitely. Everyone's decision-making regarding further development is on hold until the technology may actually be needed.

"Everyone, that is, except Japan. Japan is still determined to forge ahead. Japan has had a rash of serious nuclear accidents, most triggered by tsunamis generated by typhoons. The accidents have revealed systemic problems and safety concerns in their first-generation reactor plant designs. And rather than undermining Japan's faith in nuclear energy, their answer seems to be to push for a new generation of safer plants. But the private sector can't afford it. Since 1973, the electric utility industry has put over six billion dollars into Japan's breeder program and the associated technology. Now they've had it. They've told the government that if it wants the breeder, it can damn well pay for it.

"And here's the uniquely Japanese aspect to the conundrum: the Japanese government is simply not strong enough to say no! The Japanese public is angry with the public utilities for not making nuclear safe, as they had promised. And they are furious and frustrated with the government, which they view—quite accurately—as undermined by corruption, graft, and scandal. With revelations of payoffs and yakuza criminal influence decimating government leadership, including a series of prime ministers, it appears that Japan's highly centralized system and revolving-door politics have fallen victim to rogue politicians and bureaucrats willing to rig Japan's economic life for personal gain and power. The only time the ruling party, the Liberal-Democratic Party, lost control—back in 1993—a coalition of eight parties attempted to govern for ten months, and it was as if there was no government at all.

"There is no viable alternative to the LDP, no political opposition ready to challenge them effectively, take over, and actually govern. Consequently, the weakened Japanese government is faced with a unique kind of gridlock, not unlike that which we face in America: unable to make major decisions that reverse existing policy or change the status quo.

"Eventually, of course, there will be political reform. The Japanese people are too committed to democratic institutions to permit this political decay to continue unchecked. At some point, Japanese business, banking, and industry will withhold funding from the LDP until reform occurs. But until that happens, the government is not about to change policy on the plutonium issue.

"And while the breeder may eventually enhance Japan's energy supply security, the import of its reprocessed plutonium from the UK and France will actually decrease its national security! This is because if it imports plutonium, even though it's for use in breeder reactors, Japan's neighbors will see Japan as moving toward nuclear weapons capability.

"Moreover, the physical transport of four thousand pounds of weapon-capable plutonium some seventeen thousand nautical miles from Europe to Japan, by a nation with no navy to protect it, and a constitution that prohibits the projection of force to defend it, is sheer folly in today's world of international terrorism.

"That's enough plutonium for three hundred Nagasaki-size bombs! And that, Senator Laughlin, brings us full circle as to why we are here. While their breeder program has been on hold, so have Japan's shipments of plutonium. But now that their program is being taken up and refinanced by the government, the shipments are to resume, beginning this weekend, from Cherbourg. And we have so little intelligence on what is happening, what route is planned, or how the shipment is being protected, that the agency is in the dark and deeply worried."

CHRONICLE XXVII.

"Thank you, Dr. Conover," said the senator. "Once again you have managed to turn a complex situation into something I can actually understand. It is an art which endears you to this ersatz think tank of ours. And it brings us to our own Dr. Bob, our in-house master of confusion. Bob, I know that as a student of Herman Kahn you always try to construct surprise-free projections. I've spent too much time in Washington to believe in them. But I do think the effort is useful. It stretches our imaginations if not our credulity, exercises our intellects, and puts our arms around the issue at hand. So have at it, my friend, and just ignore my carping skepticism."

"Thank you, Senator, for that fulsome vote of confidence," began Dr. Robert Travis of the Senate Select Committee on Intelligence staff. "I want to use Nassim Taleb's paradigm, as amended by Slavoj Žižek, to lend some discipline to our thinking."

"Bob," interrupted the senator somewhat testily, "while I do understand the need for all this, it makes me fidgety as hell. Let's skip the academic footnotes."

"There are four categories of questions we need to ask," Bob began again:

"First, what are the *known knowns*, the things we know that we know;

"Second, what are the *known unknowns*, the things we know that we do *not* know;

"Third, what are the *unknown unknowns*, the things we do not know we do not know—the infamous black swans;

"And fourth, last and most troublesome, what are the *unknown knowns*, the things we do not want to admit we know.

"Dear God," exclaimed the senator, "I was doing fine with Dr. Conover. Now you're ruining my morning."

"A few examples will help clarify why this is a useful discipline, Senator," continued Dr. Bob, unfazed by his boss's heckling.

"The *known knowns* are simple enough. We know the Japanese are about to resume plutonium shipments because they told us as much. We offered to help protect the shipments with our navy, stipulating that Congress required that Japan reimburse the US for the costs of doing so. Japan declined, saying allies are allies, not rent-a-cops; if they wished to hire mercenaries, they'd get back to us.

"So much for Congress making foreign policy. While I understand the congressional intent, it was not the way to get the Japanese to agree to accept our protection. And as a result, they're going it alone. First, they thought they might be able to transport the four thousand pounds of plutonium by air, via Alaska. But the Alaskan members of our Congress raised such hell for fear that a plane crash could disperse plutonium oxide powder across the ecologically fragile tundra, poisoning the area for thousands of years with the most toxic substance known to man, that they reverted to planning a sea route, using the same ship they used for their first shipment twenty years ago.

"Since that first shipment, and after learning that Japan now has over thirty-five tons of plutonium stored in France and the UK awaiting shipment, dozens of nations have declared that they would not permit any plutonium-carrying vessel to enter their territorial waters. South Africa and many of the Pacific Island nations went even further, declaring such shipments prohibited within their 'exclusive economic zones' which, under the United Nations' Law of the Sea Treaty, extends two hundred miles from their coasts. Bottom line is the Japanese won't be able to stop along the way to refuel. So their little transport ship has to carry enough fuel for the seventeen thousand-mile journey."

"Four thousand pounds of plutonium doesn't take up much space on a ship," interjected former Soviet Admiral Alex Rostov. "But seventeen thousand-miles' worth of fuel would turn it into a mini-tanker. My guess would be that they'll try to develop some way to refuel at sea."

"Good point, Alex," responded the senator. "Perhaps you could elaborate on how they might go about that over lunch today. It would seem an obvious area of vulnerability."

"We've already talked about some of the *known unknowns*, which range from the timing, the route, the course and speed of the vessel, and importantly the Japanese plans to protect it, to the overwhelmingly critical question of identifying any adversaries—rogue states, pirates, or terrorists—planning to interdict the shipment and hijack it for the purposes of either nuclear proliferation or blackmail. These are the primary risks the president wants to hear about from us tonight.

"Then there are the *unknown unknowns*, the black swans. These are the things we haven't imagined, factors we haven't even thought of, the unexpected events for which we are unprepared. If I were prescient and could identify and list those for you, I'd have unlimited job security!

"And last, the troubling *unknown knowns*, the things we refuse to acknowledge. First and foremost is that our human intelligence capability in Japan is abysmal. Dr. Conover, would you like to reveal the bad news?"

"To be an effective spy in Japan," observed Kathleen Conover, "you not only have to look Japanese, you have to be native-born Japanese. And we have had very little success in recruiting well-placed native-born Japanese to spy on Japan.

"American-born Japanese, even if fluent in the language, lack the cultural tells and innate prejudices to pass as native-born for long. And Japanese born overseas are treated as second class persons, having somehow betrayed the homeland.

"The Japanese are in practice the most racist people I know. Japan's centuries of cultural isolation produced an ingrained racial arrogance and intolerance. That's why the Japanese show little remorse for the war or shame for the occupation of other countries, and the enslavement of other peoples, particularly their women. Moreover, even today they remain fundamentally misogynistic. Women exist to entertain, comfort, and serve. While they may no longer always walk four steps behind their man physically, they still do so psychologically. Just ask any Japanese woman who has tried to start her own business—unless it's to entertain, comfort, or serve.

"To complicate matters, there is a little-known caste system in Japan: The Burakumin, Japanese who treat the dead, both humans and animals, are unseen and unacknowledged by their fellow Japanese—like India's untouchables, or those figures in black that move the furniture and change the sets in Noh theater, they simply don't register in Japanese perception. It has been that way since the eleventh century Heian period for butchers, leather workers, undertakers, executioners, and their descendants. And Japan-born ethnic Koreans are severely discriminated against as well, seen as a race apart. Consequently, about sixty percent of the yakuza, the Japanese mafia, are recruited from the Burakumin, and about thirty percent from the ethnic Koreans, because they identify with the 'outcast' nature of the organization.

"Long story short, while Japanese aesthetics are acknowledged and admired worldwide, they remain impregnable as a people for our intelligence agencies. We have a miserable track record when trying to understand, much less penetrate, Japanese society at any level, and no success to speak of at the decision-making level. All our useful intelligence on the Japanese has been garnered by 'national technical means.' And now that electronic spying on allies has been drastically curtailed, we're largely in the dark."

Tom thought to himself: *I guess my idea of sending Em to Kyoto on her own was not my brightest.*

CHRONICLE XXVIII.

Em had been issued a $2,600 business class ticket on All Nippon Airlines (ANA) from Rome to Osaka, with a five-hour layover in Frankfurt. She promptly took it to an Italian ticket scalper, sold it for $2,200, and bought a Turkish Airlines $870 Rome-Osaka round-trip economy class ticket with a six-hour layover in Istanbul. That gave her just enough transit time and extra cash to shop the wondrous Istanbul medina for an Ottoman carpet perfect for the apartment she shared with Sure, and have it shipped back to Rome while she continued her journey.

Terribly pleased with herself, she settled back in her economy nonstop Turkish Airlines seat from Istanbul to Osaka, enjoyed their commendable seasoned lamb on little wood skewers with a glass of wine, and slept like an angel. Once in Osaka, she took the train directly to Kyoto and made her way to the Christopherian Monastery on the eastern edge of the old town, halfway up a wooded hill, where she inquired at the gate for Father Takashi Takano. She was surprised to hear that he had received word from His Holiness that she was en route and looked forward to meeting her. He was away at the moment, would be back shortly, and had instructed that she be shown to his private quarters to make herself at home until his return. Tom had advised her before she left Rome to wear her habit, and she was happy now that she had. Curious as to how a monk lived in a Catholic monastery, or at least in this one, Em welcomed the opportunity to do a little snooping in this bastion of celibate males.

The monk who welcomed her said that as this was a weekend, she was free to wander about after he showed her to Brother Takashi's quarters. She would find other outsiders, visiting family, friends, and neighbors, within the monastery until compline, the last service of the working day. All he asked was that she restrict herself to using the visitors' bathroom facilities by the front entrance.

Father Takashi should return by compline. Each Saturday he climbed to the martyrs' shrine farther up their little hill. Was she aware that he was sixty-six and walks with a stick? No, Em had replied—they had not met before. Should she address him as father or as brother? "He is a priest," replied the monk, "so he is Father to you and Brother to me," the monk concluded with a smile.

Father Takano's quarters were revealing. Many of his books concerned the history of Nagasaki, the war, the bombing of the city, the stories of survivors, the rebuilding. There was a lot of published and unpublished material from Greenpeace regarding the Japanese breeder technology program. And then she found the poetry. Em made a quick decision. She had two hours before Father Takashi was due back. Instead of exploring the monastery grounds, she decided to explore Father Takano's mind.

CHRONICLE XXIX.

One poem Em found was a formal, rather stilted haiku signed Yamamoto, an admiral in the Japanese Navy, but not the infamous admiral of World War II. It was dated 1929. This was a much earlier Admiral Yamamoto, a devout and prominent Catholic, Shinjiro Yamamoto, who took the name of Stephen at baptism, and as a senior admiral accompanied Japan's emperor to visit the pope in the Vatican in the 1930s. It was this Yamamoto who at about the same time helped raise the funds to purchase this monastery for the Christopherian Brotherhood, according to a note accompanying the poem.

Em saw another poem, again a haiku with its classic thirty-one Japanese syllables, carefully framed beside Brother Takashi's shaving mirror. It was amateur calligraphy, ink on rice paper, and looked to be the original, dated "New Year's Day, 1940." And it was signed Yamamoto Nagasha. Em suddenly realized that this was the other Admiral Yamamoto, the admiral who had planned what would be called *kishu-seiko*, the successful surprise attack on Pearl Harbor the following year. She pulled her notebook from her saddlebag, the ones nuns wore on their hips beneath their habits, and began to translate the poem:

Being my own,
It seems large,
This tiny cabin;
I yawn, I sprawl,
I do as I please.

A perfect haiku by an admiral in his sea cabin; and a perfect sentiment for an existentialist priest in his monastic cell. Em reflected on her studies at Yale about this Admiral Yamamoto, recalling that he had been born Isoroku Takano, the son of Sadayoshi Takano, and had taken the name Yamamoto when he was adopted into the Yamamoto family after the death of his parents.

Here was the one Japanese naval officer who went to Harvard, kept up with his alumni dues, served as an attaché in Washington, and became thoroughly familiar with America and Americans. He had strongly opposed an alliance of Japan with Germany and argued against any war with the United States—to the point of becoming a target of the Japanese right wing, which threatened his death. He argued with his superiors before Pearl Harbor that a preemptory attack on the American navy was the only way to wound it, but that such an attack would only awaken the resolve of a nation whose superior industry and productive capacity he had witnessed firsthand. America, he argued, would inevitably prevail in the long run. Japan's defeat, he both wrote and said, would just be a matter of time, if Japan chose war.

But if he was not well listened to, he did obey orders, orders that came from His Imperial Majesty the Emperor—not just his sovereign and liege, but his divine god. When asked to plan a sneak attack on the most vulnerable American asset, he used his strategic skills to do just that.

Could Father Takashi Takano believe that he was a descendent of this World War II admiral because they shared a last name? It was a common name. But otherwise, why the interest?

Then Em recalled that Admiral Yamamoto's blood father, Sadayoshi Takano, an old samurai, had himself been adopted into the Takano family when he married into it. Em could not recall Sadayoshi's samurai name, or his birth name. Perhaps Takashi just liked the idea of orphans making good. Or perhaps Em should just wait and ask the good father and stop trying to read his tea leaves!

Em sat down at the father's tiny desk and opened his laptop computer. The door to his room was closed, and she still had a good hour to wait until compline. The computer was password protected, but the trusting father had stored the password in his laptop's own memory.

She was in quickly and rooting about. And the first tab she found was so unexpected it nearly caused her to faint: there was the usual pause as the little computer, like some ten billion other devices connected to the internet that day, used a series of digital addresses to get where it was going, and then a second pause for mutual authentication, so the addressee knew it was talking to someone it would want to talk to, but in this case there was a third pause while an automatic online encoded algorithmic decryption on each side cued a synchronous secure dialogue. And finally, just a second or two later, the screen opened and Em saw she was welcomed to *XINSI BAOZHANG JIDI*, the national cyber security agency of the People's Liberation Army of the People's Republic of China. *Oops!* thought Em, just as Father Takano opened his door.

The old man stopped and took in the scene, the nun at his desk, his opened laptop, the Chinese classified cyber security website on the screen. Raising his walking stick, he exclaimed: "*Anata wa supaidesu*! You're a spy!"

"Hai! Yes!" replied Em.

"Oh, thank God," said Father Takashi in fluent English, "Heaven knows I have no use for a nun! And here I thought His Holiness must have lost his marbles when he sent word he'd sent a nun to see me. I've clearly done him a great injustice. In fact, this is brilliant! Now I'm delighted he sent you, and happy you've made it safely. Good cover, too! But I must say you didn't hold out long under my tough interrogation," he added with a chuckle.

"I wasn't supposed to," said Em. "And I have a lot more to tell you. I was told to reveal my identity to you from the start, including the fact that I'm not officially a Sister."

"Sister, you're more of a sister than you know. But I'll make all of that clear to you as we go. We first need to attend compline. After compline, we begin the grand silence here, during which the whole community, including our guests, observes silence through the night until the morning service, Matins. Silence is not what you and I need. So after compline, what we'll do, you and I, we'll take the night bus to Nagasaki.

It's more comfortable than flying. There's a change to a local early in the morning in Fukuoka; otherwise it's essentially door to door. We'll arrive in Nagasaki in time for breakfast. Then I can take you to the place you need to experience personally to understand what is happening here, and to report it all back to His Holiness."

Seated comfortably next to Father Takano in his cobalt blue monk's robe and cowl on the "Moonlight" bus to Nagasaki, Em sipped rice wine with her fresh sushi dinner and mused about a novel of her youth, the 1936 spy thriller *Night Train to Lisbon* by Emily Grayson. "Night bus to Nagasaki" just doesn't seem to cut it, she concluded. "Why aren't we on one of the famous Japanese bullet trains?" she asked, somewhat petulantly.

"Look," said Father Takano, "we're going from Kyoto, for a thousand years our Imperial capital, to Nagasaki, a port on the coast, from one small inland town on our main island of Honshu to another small town on the coast of a different island, Kyushu, about an hour from the city of Fukuoka. This is the cheapest, quickest, most efficient and comfortable way of getting from here to there. So don't kvetch. Besides, it keeps my watcher handy and in sight."

"You have a watcher?" asked Em. "We're being followed?"

"Six rows back, opposite side of the bus, dark-haired man in gray cap, gray jacket with a bulge under left armpit, ear buds, tinted glasses. Don't look now," added the father, "but take a good look when you get up to use the bathroom."

"How long have you been followed?" asked Em.

"Oh, about twenty-five years," replied the father.

"Who trained you?"

"Self-trained. Mostly by reading de Villiers' SAS books."

"So who do you work for?"

"God," said Takashi Takano, "or at least I like to think so. After all these years, I figure I'm on the side of the angels."

"Who pays you?" continued Em.

"No one. I'm an impoverished Christopherian monk."

"Well then, who do you give your information to?" pressed Em, undeterred.

"Always my cardinal, and sometimes Greenpeace. I've been feeding intel to Greenpeace on occasion for twenty-five years. Intel about the Japanese nuclear-electric utility industry, nuclear reprocessing, Japan's Self Defense Forces, and its import of reprocessed plutonium from France and the UK. Before my cardinal died of cancer in Rome, he was going to tell His Holiness of my work, and of my recent discoveries. I'm the anti-nuke Christian underground guru in Japan. Have been for a quarter century."

"Your watchers know all this?" asked Em incredulously.

"No! No!" replied Father Takano. "I'm being watched for totally different reasons, thanks be to God. I'm watched because I serve as confessor to several crypto-Christians in the government. I'm watched to protect them. That's why they come all the way to Kyoto to see me. They are good people, relatively speaking, relative to other bureaucrats and politicians at least, and are taking great risk professionally in secretly maintaining and practicing their faith. Christianity has always been seen here as a repudiation of heritage; and nowhere is heritage more important politically than in Japan. That, in a nutshell, is why there are so few Japanese Christians. The system is protecting me in order to protect their secret."

"Well, I have bad news for you," said Em. "Your cardinal, the archbishop of Nagasaki, did not die of cancer in Rome; he was murdered. And we believe he was murdered in order to silence him before he could share with my boss, Cardinal Tom Gallagher, what he had told the pope in his final confession. You see, by confessing it he tied the pope's hands. And he was killed before he could act on the pope's request to share his secret with my boss. So I'm here at the pope's behest to bring you a phone, an encrypted direct line to the Vatican, for your emergency use. And also with a request from my boss, Cardinal Gallagher, to tell me what you can about what got Cardinal Matsumoto killed."

"Jesus!" said Father Takashi. "And that's a prayer, not an expletive," he added quickly.

Father Takano and Em had breakfast across the square from the new little cathedral of Nagasaki, built in 1959 to replace the grand Urakami cathedral destroyed by the nuclear bomb dropped on August 9, 1945. Afterwards, he took her to see the remains of the original fifty-ton bell tower, which had been blown into a small stream about thirty-five yards downhill from the remains of the first cathedral. Too heavy to be moved, the Japanese congregants diverted the stream around it in the years that followed so that the tower's remains would not be undermined. It was all that was left of Asia's largest cathedral, and it lies "in state" at the foot of a little rise, *in memoriam*.

"Two-thirds of Nagasaki's Christians died that day," recounted the father. "Almost all the teaching Sisters and orphans in my orphanage and school. The man who saved me, Father Junichi, and I led the few survivors back to the pond up the mountain where we had been when the bomb went off, and we camped there. Eventually, we received food from the outlying farms, tents, and some schoolbooks, and we harvested the new crop of boys and girls who had survived but been made orphans by the blast. At the end of summer, we moved into temporary shelters near the university.

"Seventy-three thousand, eight hundred and eighty-four men, women, and children died in a millisecond that morning. Vaporized. In the next few minutes, an additional 195,727 people were irradiated, poisoned, burned, or injured by the blast and radiation. I want to show you where I viewed it all from, with Father Junichi, and tell you what transpired afterward. It will be a bit of a walk and a climb, but if I can do it at my age, you shouldn't mind."

"I think I'll be following in your footsteps in more ways than one," remarked Em. "Tell me, Father, how did Christianity come to Nagasaki in the first place?"

"With great difficulty, many murdered martyrs, centuries of repression, campaigns of persecution, political intrigues, and infighting among missionaries—between Jesuits and Franciscans, Protestants and Catholics, Spanish and Dutch, Buddhists, Confucians, and especially the Shinto religion. And those were the good times! We've been hung, quartered, crucified, outlawed, and thrown in a boiling spring not far from here.

"But don't get me started! Because I think we're our own worst enemy. Every time our missionaries become even somewhat successful, they get involved in politics and trade and attempt the repression of competing faiths, and once that happens, the wheels come off. As the French say, 'on a perdu les pédales'—you've lost control of the outcome, and you know it's going to get ugly. I'm considered something of a heretic in my monastery because, on balance around the world, I believe missionaries have done more harm than good."

Em realized she'd struck a nerve. This was the first real emotion the good father had shown. She pressed on: "What's the Shinto religion you mentioned?"

"Well, dear Sister, that is the one thing that is pure Japan. Shinto—which means the way of the gods—is the original Japanese belief in nature, and lasting respect for those who have gone before. Nature worship and ancestor veneration are fundamental to the Japanese character. No dogmas, no moral codes, no sacred text, no canon, just a natural pantheism and mythology whose primary ethic is respect, and whose worst sin is desecration. In fact, that belief system is close to your own Native American beliefs. And it's not surprising. The Japanese and American Indians probably both derive from the same northeast Asian origin thirty thousand years ago.

"However, on top of that is a layered feudal system with an emperor who is considered not only the high priest but is himself divine. It is his duty to celebrate the worship of his ancestors, who are the gods, and intercede with them on behalf of his subjects. So think of the Native American belief system, but add an overlay of imperial Mayan sun god.

"While Confucius, or Master Kong, formed his social ethics in China some five centuries before Christ, his teachings didn't reach Japan until AD 285. The Confucian value system was welcomed here and seen as complementary to Shinto belief, emphasizing ethical concepts and practices of virtue through personal endeavor, family values, humaneness, and altruism—without the rewards of an afterlife or belief in intervening gods.

"Then Buddhism was introduced into Japan in AD 552, when the king of Korea sent Buddhist statues and books as a present to the Japanese Emperor. Two years later the first two bonzes or Buddhist priests that Japan had ever seen came from Korea. Some Japanese nobles argued that a new religion would not be seen favorably by the Shinto gods, who after all had protected the country and allowed it to prosper, but after thirty-five years of struggle, the growing group of nobles who became partisans of the growing group of bonzes prevailed, and Buddhism was accepted as the first among two coexisting religions.

"I'm not going to go through the whole megillah of the twenty-eight different flavors of Buddhism for you, but the one that stuck in Japan is Māyāna, which encourages everyone to complete vows of giving, discipline, forbearance, effort, meditation, and transcendent wisdom. Today's top physicists and mathematicians have noted that Buddhism is the only world religion to have foreseen and made room for the current string theory projection of multiple universes. The Dalai Lama often cites as his favorite Māyāna verse: *For as long as space endures, and for as long as living beings remain, until then may I too abide to dispel the misery of the world.* I like that one, too.

"It was from three influences, Shinto, Confucian, and Buddhist that the warrior class—the samurai—hammered out their strict code of conduct, *Bushido:* the path of the Samurai. It is founded first and foremost on loyalty and honor, not unlike the code of knighthood in King Arthur's court. It borrows courage and endurance in the face of death from Buddhism; the honoring of your ancestors and loyalty to your sovereign from Shintoism; and the appreciation of beauty and culture from Confucianism.

From this intellectual amalgam the samurai produced the code of the perfect knight: *the samurai has not two words; he serves not two masters; he gives his blood for duty.*"

"Whoa, whoa," said Em. "I'm not letting you get away with this. I accept that you're supposed to be a priest, but how do you know all this, and how do you get away with using words like 'kvetch,' or 'megillah' — which I haven't heard since I left Yale—much less know about Howard Johnson's twenty-eight flavors!"

The priest laughed with obvious pleasure. "When Father Junichi was posted as the Chritopherians' representative to the Vatican, he took me with him," he replied. "I attended the American School in Rome—now the International School—until I was eighteen, and then returned to Japan to graduate from Kyoto University before I entered Catholic seminary and became a priest. I began English and Chinese in Rome, with all those embassy kids, both American and Chinese, and continued both languages in Kyoto. As to religions, I teach a graduate seminar in comparative religions and comparative cuisines at the university."

"Comparative religion and cooking?!"

"Well, yes. I learned to cook in Rome, where I had to work to pay for my school tuition. I started out by washing dishes in Trastevere. I graduated to marmiton, and was diligent, and learned how to cook. It was six years of the best training in the world, and they paid me!

"Years later, when I was invited to become an adjunct professor and teach a graduate seminar on comparative religions at Kyoto, the second most prestigious university in Japan, I was chagrined because no one signed up. The graduate students knew it wouldn't be a gut course; and they knew it wouldn't get them hired by big corporations, either.

"So I rewrote the prospectus: comparative religions and comparative cuisines. Here was intellectual challenge, and a fallback skill set! I was overwhelmed with applicants and limited the seminar to just a dozen 4.0 graduate students each semester, half women and half men. Lots of students ask to audit the course, but I limit it to just my twelve disciples each semester. It's a three-hour session each week, and next week is Berber beliefs and North African cuisine. I'm quite a chef, if I do say so myself, and the course is always oversubscribed."

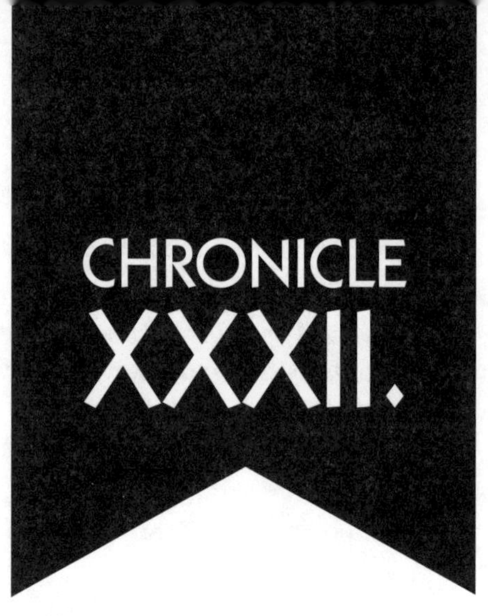

"But I haven't yet addressed your question directly," continued Father Takano. "Christianity arrived in Japan in 1549, and in Nagasaki in 1569, in the form of the Society of Jesus, evangelizing Jesuit missionaries. And that's what put the cat among the pigeons. No more of this coexisting religions and amalgams of beliefs: the Jesuits played a different game—winner take all.

"They were soon followed by Franciscans, Dominicans, Augustinians, plus Presbyterians and other Protestants, who were all treated to the same Jesuitical disdain as was directed at Buddhists, Confucians, the many Shinto, and the odd Taoist. The Jesuits found themselves in ascendency when they could arrange to be protected and encouraged by the regional Shogun or warlord. And they were promptly persecuted when they fell out of favor. Consequently, they had a labile existence. Initially they had extraordinary success, eventually recruiting over eight hundred thousand souls and converting powerful shoguns to the Church.

"But old shoguns, in fear of their mortality, die. And new shoguns are often influenced by different voices. One new shogun in particular, Hideyoshi, who came to power in 1596, listened to the bonzes, the

Buddhist monks, who were losing converts, wealth, and power to the Jesuits. Hideyoshi declared the Jesuits to be spies, an advance guard of Spanish and Portuguese colonizers wanting to control Japan's commerce. It is said that Dutch and English ship captains were heard to agree. As a warning, Hideyoshi promptly crucified three Jesuits, six Franciscans, and seventeen Japanese Christians—including two young altar boys—on crosses on the hilltops and ridges surrounding the three sides of Nagasaki. In case they didn't get the point, he burned one hundred and thirty-seven Jesuit churches, their college, and their seminary. This led the locals to observe that it's going to be dangerous to be a Christian, and that apparently one Jesuit is worth two Franciscans or five Japanese.

"Other martyrdoms followed, and by 1640 the expulsion of Christian missionaries and the destruction of their churches and schools was mostly complete. Some three hundred thousand Japanese Christians had been put to death. And for over two centuries after 1640, Japan remained incommunicado, isolated as a culture and a people.

"This led to all kinds of strange developments. For example, by 1853, when Japan was reopened by US Commodore Matthew C. Perry's expedition with the black fleet, silver in Japan was deemed twice as valuable as gold—which, when discovered, immediately created the original 'carry trade.' But the two-hundred-year isolation also produced an exquisite inward-looking refinement of the Japanese arts of porcelain and pottery making, woodcraft, painting, silk screening, textile design, poetry, theater, and music. On the other hand, the isolation reinforced xenophobia, cultural arrogance, racial intolerance, and a hidden caste system.

"To my mind the most extraordinary development occurred here in Nagasaki. When missionaries were allowed to return, one of the very first, Father Petitjean, was met in Nagasaki by fifteen Japanese who wished to ask him three questions. Remember, Em, there had not been a priest here for more than two centuries. On March 17, 1865, the fifteen asked Father Petitjean if he acknowledged the pope in Rome, if he venerated the Blessed Virgin Mary, and if he and his brethren lived lives of celibacy. When the priest affirmed all three questions, the fifteen Nagasaki Japanese made known to him that there were over forty-four thousand crypto-Christians who for ten generations had kept the faith clandestinely, awaiting the day when priests would return and they could openly practice their religion without fear. When the news reached Rome that Petitjean had found forty-four thousand congregants for Christ, the pope immediately elevated him to Vicar Apostolic of Japan. And to this day, Japan's archbishop is always established here, in Nagasaki."

They had reached the pond where Father Takashi was headed. The old oak was still leaning across the water. The priest smiled to see the tree that had protected Father Junichi and himself all those years ago. He sat down beside it to rest. Em turned back and gazed at the city across the valley. "It's beautiful," she said quietly.

"I miss the wonderful blue of the tiled market roofs," Takashi remarked. "There has never been a blue like that before or since. It was as if a slice of heaven was used to cover our old market. After the blast, all Father Junichi and I could see was roiling black ash, flames, and lightning. When we eventually went back down to the valley, even the stones of the cathedral were burning."

"Why have you brought me here?" asked Em.

"Because I fear it's all going to happen again," said the priest.

CHRONICLE XXXIII.

"Do you know who is responsible?"

"I can take a guess," replied Father Takashi. "It could be a secret society called the Society of Izanagi."

"Never heard of it," said Em.

"I would hope not," retorted the priest. "If you had before, it might have cost you your life. It could have done just that for Cardinal Matsumoto."

"So why are you telling me?"

"I need help to stop it from happening. I feel guilty because I think by informing the cardinal I caused his death. Or, I'm a lonely old man and tired of carrying this burden alone. I don't know. Take your pick."

"Okay," said Em, "all of the above! First, in the field I get to call the shots. And I want you to know I'm here for the duration. As we like to say—help will shortly be on the way. Second, if it weren't for the late cardinal, His Holiness would not have sent me. So the cardinal managed to accomplish exactly what he set out to do. And finally, you're no longer alone. You've not only got me, you've got a team in Rome and Washington.

We can get the wheels turning right now if you'll just use that phone I gave you, and then pass it over to me."

The priest did as he was asked: called the Vatican, identified himself, and asked for help. Then he passed the phone to Em, who was quickly transferred to Sure.

After a long talk with Sure, Em wished she hadn't been quite so forthcoming. Sure reminded her that the last thing the agency could get involved in was direct action on the ground in an allied nation. That was anathema to a highly sensitized president and Congress after the allies' reactions to the NSA. Sure would talk with Tom to see what options might remain open, if any. In the meantime, Em needed to find out exactly what was happening in Japan; who were the principal actors, what was their intent, their capability, and their timing?

Em repeated all of this to Father Takashi in detail after the call, reiterating her own commitment to remain in Japan for the duration, whatever that might mean, but making it clear that she had overstated her team's ability to respond under the circumstances. Clearly chagrined, but no less determined, she attempted to start again.

"Knowing now what you went through here as a child, I can begin to understand why you've worked as an intelligence source on all things nuclear for your cardinal, the Church, and Greenpeace for twenty-five years—and why you are so opposed to the misuse of nuclear power," observed Em.

"I thank you for getting that right!" replied Father Takashi. "I'm *not* opposed to nuclear power; only to its misuse. In fact, nuclear power is the only solution I see to the environmental crises we are refusing to face. By using our atmosphere as a sewer, we are altering our environment so rapidly that the present extinction rate in nature is ten thousand times greater than normal, reducing biological diversity short term, and curtailing our own future long term. We are our own cataclysmic asteroid. The only way to alter that course is to adopt safe and clean nuclear power. And to do that, we can no longer be sold a bill of goods by electric utilities taking shortcuts, as was clearly the case here in Japan.

"So when I oppose misuse, I'm not only talking about nuclear proliferation by rogue nations and terrorists, I'm talking about nuclear-electric industries that lie to their governments and their nations by designing plants that are not well planned, but calling them safe; locating those plants on geological faults or seaside below tsunami level, and then declaring them secure; undertraining, underpreparing, and underequipping their employees but boasting that they are the world's best emergency responders. It's unconscionable! And it's *post hoc ergo propter hoc* thinking. 'We haven't had an accident yet, so we must be safe.' By doing this, these utilities have undermined public confidence in, and government reliance on, the one policy response that—if used correctly—could get us out of our environmental morass."

"And the Society of Izanagi?" asked Em.

"Oh, they would want to steal the plutonium to build bombs," replied Father Takashi, "if they're the ones after it."

CHRONICLE XXXIV.

"Who are they?" asked Em.

"To understand the answer to that question, you need to understand something about the history of Japan. We have the oldest continuous hereditary monarchy in the world. We have had one hundred and twenty-five emperors, dating back to six hundred and sixty years *before* Christ, and continuing to our current emperor, Akihito.

"Legislative authority and the choice of a prime minister are the right of our bicameral legislature, called the Diet, convened first under the Meiji Constitution of 1889. For a long time after the war a single party, the Liberal-Democratic Party, held power. Then in 1993, for the first time in over forty years, they lost. A coalition of eight minor parties attempted to govern for the next ten months, but the result was chaos at home and lack of credibility abroad. In effect, there was no government.

"While politicians come and go, the continuity of our government is in the hands of a few apolitical bureaucrats at the heads of the ministries and agencies. These men, and in Japan they are of course all men, are like the permanent undersecretaries of the British government, the rock-solid, dedicated professionals who keep the nation safe at night no matter what political vicissitudes may trouble their elected political 'superiors,' the ministers.

"During those ten months when Japan appeared to have no effective government, and was in fact more vulnerable than it ever had been before, the most powerful fifteen of these Japanese bureaucrats met in secret and formed the Society of Izanagi, the Shinto god who created Japan, believing themselves to be the direct inheritors of the burden of the royal samurai, the emperor's own personal guard, to protect the nation.

"In short, they believed that the political future of the country was too important to be left to the politicians. They had spent entire careers witnessing the profligacy, graft, greed, corruption, and criminality of Japan's elected leaders, even including a few of its prime ministers, and felt to a man that the politicians could no longer be trusted with decisions of the utmost importance to the future of the country. In the absence of a coherent government, during those vulnerable months, they would take the initiative. And then simply inform any succeeding government that it had inherited a *fait accompli*.

"Seeing how easily Japan could be made vulnerable by the whims of a democratic electorate, their first decision was to prepare the country for nuclear weapons capability. Their goal was not that Japan should acquire nuclear weapons, but instead that it should have a clear, direct, and relatively transparent path of escalating to that capability. Then, over a series of years, or even months, it could overtly walk that path if it chose to do so, using each step incrementally to counter moves or respond to rising tensions on the part of potential adversaries. As the only country in northeast Asia without recourse to nuclear weaponry, this seemed a sound, sane, and safe way to resolve an issue that was politically toxic to elected politicians. This was the way of the Izanagi, the secret royal samurai.

"There are no plans currently for Japan to produce nuclear weapons. If there were, I would know. I've spent twenty-five years building my network of *tuyeaux*, my friends, contacts, and informants. But the experts, the technology, the materials, and the money are all in place if needed. That's the work of the Izanagi.

"We also have a three-stage rocket, the Epsilon, and the ballistic missile capability, to make delivery anywhere around us credible. So without building a single nuclear weapon, or assembling a single nuclear warhead-carrying missile, we've become a *de facto* nuclear power, thanks to the Izanagi. Why they would now change their minds and try to divert this shipment of plutonium to build bombs rather than breeder reactor fuel is beyond my comprehension. But they are the only people in government with the knowledge and power to do it."

CHRONICLE XXXV.

To their mutual surprise, the satellite phone Em had given to Father Takashi, and which he had then used to call Rome, started to ring. Father Takashi put it to his ear and said "*Moshi, Moshi*?" He handed the phone to Em, saying "It's for you."

It was Sure. She had reached Tom, and relayed Father Takashi's request, Em's concerns, and Sure's cautionary response. Tom was with the president at Camp David, together with Senator Laughton and Alex Rostov. They had discussed the matter together, and Tom had just called Sure back. First, he wanted to tell Sure her initial reaction was spot on. He concurred. More importantly, so did the president. But they all felt Father Takashi was on to something, and they needed to respond quickly, learn more, and support Em and the father in the field. Could Father Takashi meet with an adviser to the president, Admiral Rostov, in Tokyo or Kyoto in four days' time? Father Takashi responded that he knew of Rostov's work as cofounder of Russia's RADACT 2000.[2]

He would like nothing better than to have the opportunity to meet Rostov, but he was obliged to be in Beijing in three days, to reopen the

---

2 See GAMBIT by Antoinette Falquier & Joseph Harned.

Christopherians' little monastery that was being returned to them by the Chinese government after seventy years, when the Christopherians were evicted and expelled from China in 1948. Could they possibly meet in Beijing instead? It turned out that Rostov thought Beijing a much better—and more secure—meeting place than Tokyo under the circumstances, and they made a date for four days hence.

"I'm really looking forward to meeting that man. He's a legend in Greenpeace because of what he did on behalf of thousands of irradiated Russian seamen with his RADACT foundation,"[3] Father Takashi declared. "And I must admit I'm encouraged that an American president is smart enough to have a Russian adviser."

"What do you mean by that?" asked Em.

"Russians understand history," replied Father Takashi. "We Japanese are the only people who can understand Americans. It's because we shut ourselves off from the rest of the world for over two hundred years. And essentially that is what America has inflicted on itself. American youth know nothing of history and geography. They are ignorant of the two world wars their grandfathers and great grandfathers fought to defeat fascism in Japan, Germany, and Italy. They can't even tell you what fascism is, much less what it was. The headlines of American newspapers today don't report the world; they report what has happened at the local zoo!

"I was taught by my roommates at school in Rome that Americans can't be bothered to learn other people's languages and cultures. Just like us Japanese! For both Americans and Japanese, our sons and daughters have died half a world away for reasons average citizens cannot fathom, in places they've never heard of, and cannot even find on a map, yet they acquiesced because failure to do so would have meant failure to support the troops and the nation.

"Both Japanese and Americans believe they are superior rather than privileged, entitled rather than fortunate, chosen rather than just plain lucky. As a consequence, both America and Japan are about to learn what it is like when countries that are nine time zones deep, not three, or 1.1 billion strong, not a few hundred million, pass us by without even a 'by your leave.'"

---

3 See GAMBIT.

CHRONICLE XXXVI.

Father Takashi was barefoot, stripped to the waist, wearing only a pair of shorts emblazoned with a Chinese counterfeit logo for the Harlem Globetrotters. He was whitewashing a wall of one of the fourteen monks' cells in the old Beijing Monastery of Saint Thomas the Apostle, which had served as a police station since 1948 when the Communists had taken Beijing from the Nationalists, closed the monastery, and forced the Christopherians and other missionaries to leave the country. The Nationalists had taken refuge on the island of Taiwan.

Father Takashi had so far managed to get whitewash in his hair, on his shorts, and on the wall in roughly equal amounts. It was the ceilings that defeated any attempt at neatness. Back to back in the same cell, dipping whitewash from the same bucket in the center of the floor, was Lieutenant Xiao of the Chinese People's Armed Police Force, the nation's enforcers, wearing nothing but his People's Liberation Army khaki underwear, now nicely mottled in whitewash.

The monastery had been a police station and "soft-holding" or re-educational prison as long as Xiao could remember. Until the previous week he had been in charge, when out of the blue he had received orders to transfer his detainees, have his men clean the place out, and turn it over to Brothers Takashi and Liu, arriving this week from the Christopherian Priory in Tokyo. Xiao and his sergeant had done as ordered and had then been further directed to help facilitate the return of the premises to their original purpose. They had set out to remove all trace of the monastery's interim use as a prison by the police, and to return it to its stark monastic simplicity, which to them meant a clean, whitewashed prison without the graffiti.

The two brothers, Takashi and Liu, were surprised by and appreciative of the help, unaware that Xiao and his sergeant had been ordered to make certain that no potentially embarrassing traces remained from the use of the police station to hold certain prisoners taken at the time of the Tiananmen Square incident on June 4, 1989. Indeed, Xiao had found miniature graffiti scratched into the plaster in two of the cells, anti-government messages which he managed to cover over with the vigorous use of a wire brush and the liberal application of whitewash.

Xiao certainly did not appear to Takashi to be in any way embarrassed by the use of a sacred monastery as a police station and prison. Over breakfast together that morning, Xiao had responded to a question from Brother Liu by recounting his role in the June 1989 "episode." He had not yet become a policeman, he said, and was still serving in the army, the PLA, when he and his men were ordered to move from their barracks outside Beijing to surround Tiananmen Square in the heart of the city. Protestors had taken over and occupied the square ten days earlier, and now that the world's media were picking up on the story, the government had determined that the square must be "pacified," and the inner city of the nation's capital returned to normal.

But the appearance of armed troops, armed personnel carriers, and tanks had only served to incite the protestors to riot. No one he knew in the PLA, attested Xiao, approved of the ensuing violence. And his sergeant concurred. Certainly no one was proud of having fired on their fellow countrymen. But when the protestors began throwing cobblestones and torching vehicles, the green troops felt threatened and had overreacted. And Xiao swore that he had heard the order to fire from his commanding officer.

When subsequent arrests filled the city's jails, this little police station with its fourteen monastic cells had been turned into a soft-holding prison for twenty-eight "connected" student protestors, students who had been involved in violent activity but whose parents were sufficiently well-placed or well-connected in the government hierarchy to preclude "hard-holding" under more normal, distinctly unpleasant prison conditions.

For reasons of national security and reliability, the troops involved in the Tiananmen "incident" were split up, reassigned, and moved around the country. In order to stay in Beijing with his wife and newborn son, Xiao had used connections to wrangle a transfer from the PLA to the Armed Police under the Security Ministry. His wife had proudly sewn the yellow piping of the Armed Police onto his PLA uniform, and eventually, after two promotions, he had been put in charge of this little soft-holding prison and police station—until last week.

Xiao said he had enjoyed running his police station and soft prison. Soft-holding prisons in China were supposed to be run not for punishment but for the reform of detainees. The day-to-day work and discipline were designed to reduce prisoners to the point of admitting their crimes against the state and against society, and then to educate them to the view that anti-state and anti-social behavior were one and the same, and that protests and violence were self-defeating and harmed innocent fellow citizens.

The object of this re-education was to instill respect for the order and governance required to allow 1.1 billion people to live and work together in relative harmony and peace. Drug dealers, molesters, murderers, kidnappers, armed robbers, and other violent criminals were dealt with differently: they were shot. Once. Each. In the head. It was swift, effective, and worked wonders for the prison system budget. "As Deng Xiaoping taught us," said the sergeant, "kill a chicken to frighten the monkeys."

But Xiao found that with the well-connected and over-privileged students who still remained in his charge, the system of re-education hadn't worked well. They lacked the basic fear of authority and the malleability of the masses that resulted from systemic repression of individualism. These were the nails that stuck up and should be hammered down. They had become "westernized." Rather than model prisoners, these privileged ones had turned into recalcitrant martyrs. Then three weeks ago came the order to release his remaining prisoners. And two weeks later he had been informed of another liberalizing gesture: the government decided to return the police station to the Christopherians and to permit them to reopen it as their monastery.

Father Takashi and Brother Liu had listened intently to Xiao's story, and welcomed his offer to pitch in with his sergeant and help refurbish the old building. As the two teams—Brother Liu with the sergeant and Father Takashi with Lieutenant Xiao—moved from cell to cell carrying their buckets of whitewash and brushes, the brothers took the opportunity to ask practical questions about Beijing and the monastery's neighborhood. The lieutenant, armed with the ultimate priority of a direct order in the names of Chinese President Xi Jinping and Prime Minister Li Keqiang, asked that a phone be installed. When it was installed the following morning, Xiao spoke with his sergeant: "I don't know what they can do for our country or for the Party. But if these guys can get a phone installed in Beijing overnight, they've got real connections!"

The sergeant assumed Lieutenant Xiao was referring to the brothers, and not to Comrades Xi and Li.

CHRONICLE XXXVIII.

Father Takashi had brought Brother Liu along with him to Beijing from the Priory in Tokyo as a test. Brother Liu had been with the Christopherians now for almost three years. He was Chinese. He had come from China to Tokyo to enlist in their order. He was not the first; as well as Japanese and Americans, the monastery had trained many Chinese and Koreans, and now included all four nationalities, plus the odd Canadian. But Brother Liu was different. He was a spy—recruited, trained, and sent to the monastery in Tokyo by the Guóānbú, the People's Republic of China's Ministry of State Security, the civilian spy agency.

Liu's problem was that his heart wasn't in it. He confessed as much to Father Takashi. All he really wanted was to get out of the PRC. Father Takashi sat him down and told him he could go to hell in a handbasket, or to heaven in a habit, but he couldn't do both. Like the samurai, he couldn't serve two masters.

So Liu turned his computer and his codes over to Father Takashi, and his heart over to God. And quietly Father Takashi took over Brother Liu's communications with the *Guóānbú,* pretending to be Brother Liu, and providing them with far better intelligence on nuclear matters in Japan than Liu could ever have obtained access to, and bided his time for the day when these new *guanxi*, these secret special connections, might prove useful.

Meanwhile, Brother Liu had been promoted *in absentia* by his employers in Beijing for doing such an unexpectedly good job on his first assignment abroad and was not about to be reassigned. Father Takashi was secretly quite proud of this. When he explained it all to Em, after she discovered the computer in question, at first she thought it was "a hoot." Then she was seriously intrigued and passed the word to Tom that they had a small but fascinating window into the famed *Guóānbú*.

Earlier today Father Takashi had assigned Brother Liu to find out from Lieutenant Xiao's sergeant where they could buy a bottled-gas stove, beds, bedside tables, lamps, maybe even a refectory table and benches, and used but serviceable bicycles, all needed to make the monastery operable again. Tentatively at first, and then more directly as his curiosity overcame his natural reserve, the sergeant began asking questions of his own. What would the little monastery do? What was it like to be a monk? How did Brothers Takashi and Liu become Christians?

It was nearing dinnertime, and Liu and the sergeant were almost finished with their whitewashing, when Lieutenant Xiao returned, laden with steaming pots and bamboo baskets of food, a large bottle of Chinese beer, and the chef-owner of a little neighborhood restaurant nearby who had insisted on accompanying him. He introduced himself to Father Takashi, Brother Liu, and the sergeant, saying that he had known Lieutenant Xiao and had served the police station for years. He presented Father Takashi with a copy of his new menu, which included the telephone number of his restaurant, suggesting that in future, the monastery simply "call out for Chinese" and his son would deliver! He hoped they would enjoy their dinner this evening, and he would stop by tomorrow to pick up the pots and baskets.

Father Takashi was delighted by this welcoming gesture and told the man so. The dinner turned out to be excellent, except for the ducks' feet soup, a gelatinous porridge with rubbery orange webbed feet floating on the surface. They gave Father Takashi the impression the ducks must be upside down, collectively holding their breath, in some kind of mass suicide drowning. Lieutenant Xiao and his sergeant seemed to relish this country delicacy. Brother Liu gave it a pass. And Father Takashi couldn't even look at it.

During dinner, more questions were asked, as the four began to bond over beer. The sergeant wondered what life as a monk was like. Brother Liu replied, "We each own a change of clothes, live rent free, and have steady work—what more could you want?"

"Well," said the sergeant, "I was wondering what you do about women?"

"We pray for them," said Brother Liu with a smile.

"What he means," added Father Takashi, "is that we lead lives of celibacy. The Christopherians follow the Rule of Saint Benedict, which sets out the purpose and obligations of a monk's life. And then there's the requirement of celibacy, of course."

"Don't you find that difficult?" asked the sergeant.

"It gets harder every day!" quipped Brother Liu.

"But the life we've chosen has its unique rewards," added Father Takashi hurriedly.

"Just be careful how you spell unique," muttered Brother Liu.

"What are those rewards?" pressed Lieutenant Xiao.

"Our lives cover a broad range," replied Father Takashi. "Some monks withdraw into solitude and silence, while others are teachers, or run schools, parishes, missions, clinics. Since the Middle Ages, thousands of abbeys have had different approaches to living out the rule. Monasteries have never been centralized or standardized. But each is a community of love and care in which we work, study, pray, and seek God.

"Saint Benedict counselled poverty and work to the glory of God. The problem is if you work really well, you don't remain poor. Through the centuries, tensions built up between these two admonitions. How can an individual monk remain poor if his community has become rich? Saint Benedict himself realized his rule had its own internal contradictions. He added at the end of his writings that any community could choose to ignore his advice if the monks collegially found that it didn't work for them.

"Some orders, like ours, put more emphasis on work and study; others emphasize poverty and worship. And then there are those who ignore work to the point that poverty is assured. The Christopherians have tended to work hard and teach well. Consequently, we're no poorer in fact than we are in spirit."

"Except for women," added the sergeant.

"Amen," intoned Brother Liu somberly.

Father Takashi thought to himself, *If this trip has been a test for Brother Liu, he's passed it.*

Then he directed a comment toward Lieutenant Xiao: "You asked about rewards. I can tell you from my own experience that in every monastery each monk supports and cheers the other members of his little community. It's the one place where a man can dedicate and give himself to God without distraction, and where God can quietly communicate with, and even illuminate him in return. It's where each individual is seeking spiritual enlightenment, and at the same time is fully aware of his essential role in the community as a whole. That's the closest thing to heaven on earth that I can imagine."

This was the first time Brother Liu had heard his mentor speak so eloquently about the life they had now both chosen. Any doubts he still harbored about his own choice were quickly disappearing.

"That does not sound like the PLA!" said the sergeant, with a laugh.

After reflecting a moment, Lieutenant Xiao said, "No, but I'm beginning to see the attraction, the appeal of such a life."

"If you do see," observed Father Takashi, "then you've just answered the unasked question: 'What are we doing here in China?'"

Xiao looked at the two brothers in turn, nodded, and said "Yes. But we are all children of the revolution. While we are now infusing our nation with a healthy mix of market economics and consumerism, we are still taught that Christianity is a competing system of belief. It's foreign and new to us."

"Not really," countered Father Takashi. "Christian missionaries served here from 1583 to 1948. And the Chaldee Breviary of the Church of Malabar in India confirms that Saint Thomas the Apostle came to China following his journey through India in the year AD 64, just thirty-one years after the Crucifixion. That was during the Eastern Han Dynasty of your Ming Di, in the seventh year of the reign of Yong Ping. The Chinese Emperor had sent two court officers to India to learn about the rumored 'new religion,' and they returned in the company of Saint Thomas. That's why this monastery is named in his honor."

"There's more evidence of Christianity in your city of Xian Fu," added Brother Liu. "In 1625, when workmen were digging a house foundation, they discovered a monumental stone, a monolith of black marble, three meters high by two meters wide. The inscription carved into the stone told of a man of eminent virtue named Olopen, who in the year AD 635 came from Da Qin, the Roman Empire, to Xian Fu, bringing 'sacred books.' The then Chinese Emperor had the books translated, found the doctrine they contained to be good, and decreed their publication. That's how the Bible first reached the Chinese people. So in fact," concluded Brother Liu, "we Chinese were among the very first to learn of Christ's teachings, and among the earliest to receive the written Word."

"And if we're going to continue the work of Saint Thomas," admonished Father Takashi, "I hope all three of you will accompany me tomorrow morning on my quest for a stove and furniture! Christopherians are noted for their hospitality, and tomorrow afternoon Admiral Rostov arrives. We have a monastery to furnish, and at the very least will need a place for him to sleep comfortably. Moreover, I admit to being tired of the camp cots and sleeping bags Brother Liu and I have been using. I was hoping the three of you would join me in making the rounds of the secondhand shops and stalls tomorrow, and then help carry it all back here."

The sergeant declared, "Lieutenant Xiao is known as a master of logistics. I suggest we put ourselves in his hands."

Xiao smiled and said "I'm not a master of anything, but I have done some homework and have a little surprise for you. Please by ready to leave at 0800."

CHRONICLE XL.

The following morning, Father Takashi and Brother Liu heard a truck pull into the courtyard shortly before 8:00 a.m. They found Lieutenant Xiao, his sergeant, and the driver sharing a pack of cigarettes. "Ready to go?" asked Xiao.

"Yes, but we want to know the secret you referred to last night," said Father Takashi.

"My secret is Mr. Chen of Huaxia—the Huaxia arts and crafts shop on Dongsi Road. Actually, the official name is the Beijing International Trade Company, and it's been in Mr. Chen's family for three generations, since even before the revolution."

A half-hour later, the PLA truck and its five occupants pulled up in front of a small, nondescript, dark, and dusty shop set back from Dongsi Road. Mr. Chen had obviously been awaiting their arrival and stepped out of the door to greet them. Inside, he scrabbled about to find chairs and stools to seat his five guests and offered them tea. Once this Chinese protocol was complete, he showed the brothers through his shop, which while small and narrow, appeared to extend a full block. Even though the shop was dimly lit, Father Takashi could see that it contained everything from used furniture to extraordinary antiques, Chinese antique furnishings and rugs, porcelains and pottery, opera costumes, puppets, Chinese and Japanese scrolls, glazed roof tiles, antique jade, great old wooden chests, Korean and Japanese *tonsu*, and—to Father Takashi's surprise—several pieces of *ko-Imari nishiki-de*, eighteenth-century Japanese multi-colored Arita porcelain, called brocade-ware because of the colorful designs were taken from Edo period court textiles. He made a note to himself to return to study these.

It was all a feast for the eyes, but neither brother saw the kinds of things they needed for the monastery. Brother Liu began to explain their needs to Mr. Chen, but he interrupted to say that Lieutenant Xiao had made him fully aware of what was needed. Xiao had also made him aware of the personal interest Comrades Xi Jinping and Li Keqiang shared in the reopening of the little monastery. What he had to offer the brothers was not in this shop but in his warehouse on Chongwenmennei Street, just a few minutes' drive.

Everyone piled back in the truck, ceding the place of honor to Mr. Chen, and drove to the warehouse, following his careful directions. It looked completely boarded up. Mr. Chen, Lieutenant Xiao, and the sergeant used a tire iron to pry the boards loose from a large doorway. Then Mr. Chen used three keys to unlock three locks and opened the door. The inside of the warehouse was pitch black. As their eyes slowly became accustomed to the darkness, the brothers began to perceive what appeared to be mountains of furniture stretching into the distance. Mr. Chen lit a small lantern and led everyone single file, snaking through the aisles in the valleys between the mounds of furnishings until they reached another large, old, locked door. Here Mr. Chen brought out yet another key, ushered them into an inner room, and turned on overhead lighting.

What the brothers saw before them took their breath away. Piled along one wall were more than a dozen narrow beds, simple in design, obviously sturdy, made of quite beautiful wood visible beneath the dust. Then there was a long and handsome refectory table, complete with benches, that could easily seat twenty people, made from the same lovely wood. And in a corner of the room was a pile of matching chairs, stools, and small tables.

Smiling happily, Mr. Chen motioned them over to the far side of the room, and pulled a sheet off a wonderful cook stove, large enough for a small restaurant, that immediately made Father Takashi want to start cooking. Then Mr. Chen dramatically opened the doors of several clothes closets, and pointed to piles of linens, blankets and towels, all carefully wrapped in plastic.

"Good Lord!" exclaimed Brother Liu, "This is exactly what we need. Everything!"

Father Takashi turned to Lieutenant Xiao and asked quietly how much he thought Mr. Chen would want for the lot. Before Xiao could reply, Mr. Chen declared, "Of course this is what you need! But you haven't caught on, have you? These are the furnishings of your old monastery. My late father bought them from Lin Piao in 1948, for an antique jade ring, and stored them here. He knew some day you would return. I must admit, I did not believe it, but out of respect for his wishes, I never sold them. So here you are."

Brother Liu looked at Father Takashi and said, "We're overwhelmed, Mr. Chen. We are deeply honored that your father had faith in us, and most grateful to you for keeping these things all these years, in such beautiful condition. We can never repay your kindness, but please allow us to at least to reimburse you for your expenses, the storage costs, and of course the antique jade ring."

"Oh, these things are not for sale," said Mr. Chen. "They are yours to take. In fact, I have my men standing by to help. My father and I were only guardians until you returned." He paused, and then added. "But there are two favors I might ask you to consider."

"Of course," said Father Takashi quickly.

"First, I would ask you to say a mass for my father and mother, when you get up and running again."

"Nothing would please us more!" said Father Takashi.

"Second, and this is important, I would ask you not to tell anyone that I have given these things to you. I am called 'the tiger' locally, because I'm the toughest bargainer in the business. I always get the best prices. Always. And I don't want you to ruin a reputation that has taken three generations to build!"

"Agreed!" said Brother Liu, and extended his hand to seal the bargain, as did Father Takashi with a smile.

When everyone got back outside in the sunlight, they found that four of Mr. Chen's assistants with two of his delivery vans had joined the PLA truck and driver to help haul everything. The stove alone would fill a truck. With this much help, the task would be done in a single morning.

Takashi took a few minutes more to draw out Mr. Chen, saying he would be invited to the first dinner inaugurating the stove, as well as to the mass for his parents. It turned out that Mr. Chen was not Catholic or even Christian. He just liked to "hedge his bets,"' as he put it. And he relished the thought that the reopened monastery would be the product of three respected Chinese: Xi Jinping, Li Keqiang, and Mr. Chen.

CHRONICLE XLI.

When the embassy car and the US ambassador's aide de camp delivered Alex and Connie Rostov from the Beijing airport to the courtyard of the little police station, the ambassador's aide was certain there was an error, and he sure as hell was not going to be the one caught making it. "You can't possibly want to stay here!" he exclaimed. "My map shows this is a soft-holding prison and police station! Let me take you both back to the ambassador's quarters, or at least to a four-star hotel. We can't have a presidential adviser bunking in with the PRC Security Ministry!"

"Calm down, my friend," replied Admiral Rostov. "First, I'm here on a personal visit, unofficially, and want to keep the lowest of profiles, which is why I objected to your using the embassy car to begin with. Second, the Security Ministry turned this former monastery back to its original owners, the Christopherians, last week. They occupy it now. Third, we're here to see them, not Chinese officials, and will be leaving in a couple of days, so a short stay here will be no hardship, will it, Connie?"

The ageless beauty of Connie Zimmerman Rostov, lately of San Juan, Vieques, Zermatt, and Washington, had already captivated the ambassador's aide. She glanced at the little nineteenth-century courtyard and cloister, looked directly at the aide, smiled, and said "No," thereby putting a definitive end to the discussion.

They were greeted at the garth by Father Takashi and Brother Liu in their cobalt-blue cassocks. A bear of a man, Alex Rostov embraced the father rather than shaking hands, almost lifting him off the ground, and said in his ear, "I bring you greetings and thanks from my president. Your information has proven invaluable."

"And which president would that be?" inquired Father Takashi, in all innocence. Father Takashi recovered quickly from the surprise that Rostov was accompanied by his wife. Here was a woman of easy grace and unaffected elegance, who appeared to have realized her fantasies as well as her ambitions. She and Alex had the air of two happy newlyweds, clearly in love with each other in that quiet way of savoring life that comes with age and experience. We're going to have to do something about the communal bathroom, Father Takashi reflected.

He had had barely enough time to install the furniture and the wonderful stove and make the beds. He was not up to trying to cook tonight, so had reserved at the neighborhood restaurant whose owner had greeted them earlier. He explained to Connie and Alex that they would be attending a banquet this evening in honor of Mr. Chen and the extraordinary remembrance of his father. Knowing that the Rostovs wanted to keep their visit as discreet as possible, he would simply treat them as two of the monastery's guests, without further fanfare or introduction.

Everyone who had participated in today's proceedings was invited, in the egalitarian approach to celebrating good fortune. So not only would they be joined by Mr. Chen, the honored guest, and Lieutenant Xiao and his sergeant, who managed the *guanxi* and masterminded the morning, but Mr. Chen's four assistants and Lieutenant Xiao's driver would join the festivities. Together with the Rostovs, Brother Liu, and himself, Father Takashi counted twelve at the table.

It always amazed Father Takashi to see what happened when such a diverse group of people with such different levels of education, variety of beliefs, disparity of backgrounds, and conflicting loyalties broke bread together over a few glasses of wine. It turned out that the common denominator in this case was produced by the chef, when he served a whole, steaming red snapper in black bean and green onion sauce. Fishing. Everyone at table had done it in their youth, and most at some time since, with more or less success, and several truly amusing disasters that the victims were willing to recount to the delight of the table. Fishing turned out to be the leveler to which each of them could relate.

The restaurant owner-chef was astonished that his courtesy call on the monastery and Father Takashi was paying off so quickly. He had explained that with such a small neighborhood establishment, it was something of a problem to produce a full Chinese banquet for twelve people on such short notice. But it was the kind of problem he wished he had more often! Judging from the way everyone tucked in, Father Takashi felt that the chef had outdone himself—particularly with the tender pork chow mein. While the other guests enjoyed fresh lychee in plum brandy sauce for dessert, Father Takashi stepped into the kitchen to explain to the chef that from time to time he had to cook for a monastery of fourteen monks in Tokyo. Would the chef part with his family recipe for the wonderful pork chow mein? The chef said that he would be honored. He would dictate it to his daughter and give it to the good father before the evening was ended.

CHRONICLE XLII.

Back at the monastery after dinner, Alex Rostov quizzed Father Takashi about what he knew of the Japanese nuclear energy program in general, the breeder reactor program in particular, the plutonium shipments from Europe, and most particularly, what arrangements for their protection the Japanese had in place. Rostov was amazed at the breadth of knowledge exhibited by Father Takashi, until it was explained to him that this had been Father Takashi's area of specialization for more than twenty-five years.

"So they are currently en route from Cherbourg," summarized Father Takashi, "with the plutonium on a refurbished British nuclear fuel carrier, a double-hulled freighter called the *Akatsuki Maru*, protected by a lightly armed escort vessel, the *Shiki-shima*, manned by the Japanese Maritime Safety Agency—the equivalent of the US Coast Guard. They had to refit the freighter to be able to travel up to twenty thousand nautical miles because with that much toxic plutonium, no one wants them any closer than two hundred miles to the coast of any country. So they can't refuel anywhere, or even shortcut through the Panama or Suez Canals. As a consequence, they had to add fuel tanks for propulsion and electric power, turning the little freighter into a mini tanker. And to make matters more difficult, they can't shorten the route by getting anywhere near the Strait of Malacca, or the Red Sea, or from Mindanao in the Southern Philippines south along the Sulu Archipelago to Sabah, for fear of terrorists. And they are carrying 1,700 kilograms of plutonium, about four thousand pounds, enough plutonium to produce three hundred Nagasaki-sized bombs, which makes a tempting target for rogue nations as well as terrorists."

"Sounds like a piece of cake!" cracked Connie. "What could possibly go wrong?!"

It was then that the monastery's telephone rang. At first, Father Takashi didn't recognize the sound, not having received any calls on the new phone. And then he couldn't remember where they'd put it. But when Brother Liu finally tracked it down, Father Takashi answered in Chinese, switched quickly to English, and then just listened. Several minutes passed, and then father Takashi said, "Thank you, Em. I will call you back as soon as I know our plans."

When he turned back to the Rostovs and Brother Liu, Father Takashi looked ashen and profoundly grieved. He took a deep breath to steady himself: "Brother Tomoyo of our monastery in Tokyo has been working with Emery Peale to try to find out more about who might be trying to interdict the plutonium. He has just been found dead in his cell. Apparently he was murdered."

CHRONICLE XLIII.

Alex and Connie Rostov had agreed to accompany Father Takashi to Tokyo in the morning in light of the unfortunate news. Brother Liu would remain in Beijing an extra day to welcome the new monks and candidates arriving from the Christopherians' monastery on Taiwan to take over the newly reopened Saint Thomas the Apostle Monastery in Beijing.

Cardinal Tom Gallagher's role had been explained to Alex at Camp David when they met with the president. Tom had phoned Alex from Washington shortly after hearing of the murder from Em and Sure, with news of further disquieting developments. During the night the trackers at the agency and at the Pentagon had lost track of the *Akatsuki Maru* and the *Shiki-shima*.

They had been tracking them visually and electronically, using both ships' unique electromagnetic transmission signatures, via satellite. The two small ships still had almost three weeks to go at sea before they could be expected to reach Nagasaki. The US Navy had recorded their engine sounds departing Cherbourg and could listen for those unique signatures from submarines and buoys along any presumed route. But both ships had vanished overnight. The Japanese government had not said a word.

And the president was most reluctant to intervene officially or overtly. Tom said that under the circumstances, he had spoken with his people in Rome, and was flying directly to Tokyo from Washington with something Alex might find useful.

According to Father Takashi, the first flight from Beijing to Tokyo the next morning with three available seats was the Japan Airlines nonstop departing at noon. A five-hour flight, a one-hour time change, and the unavoidable ninety-minute struggle through traffic from the airport into town, would get them to the Chrisopherian Priory about 7:30 p.m. Alex phoned Tokyo's Okura Hotel to tell them he and Connie would be arriving two days ahead of their planned schedule, and was told that the Okura was as usual fully booked but could accommodate them if they would accept to stay in a Japanese-inn-style ryokan room on the garden rather than a Western-style hotel room. Connie was delighted with the prospect, and Alex quickly accepted the extra cost.

He then made a second call, to the US Embassy in Tokyo, and left word with the night duty officer of his change in plans, asking that the ambassador and the White House be informed, and that the agency station chief arrange access to secure communications in "the bubble" the evening of his arrival.

After a quick nightcap, Father Takashi showed Alex and Connie to their separate, newly whitewashed cells, with their old fruitwood beds newly made up, blessed each of them, and bid them both goodnight. Connie came into Alex's small cell, looked at the narrow bed, and remarked that from her point of view monasticism had its drawbacks. Alex gave her a kiss. "You'll like the Okura," he said. "It's the most civilized place in the world."

"I'm just a simple priest," began Tom, "but with all your whiz-bang technology and eye-in-the-sky satellites, as a taxpayer I'm a bit disappointed you managed to lose the *Akatsuki Maru* and the *Shiki-shima* so easily!"

He was having dinner in the White House executive mess with the president's man before catching the 11:00 p.m. flight to Tokyo, and was wondering how to explain to Admiral Rostov and Father Takashi that the most powerful nation on earth had misplaced the little plutonium-carrying Japanese two-ship convoy.

"First, you're not a simple priest. You're a complicated cardinal. Second, it wasn't easy: it took millions of dollars' worth of hi-tech equipment and hundreds of man hours of experts. But you've got to understand that nothing in this business is full time in real time. Satellites come and go, pass by every three or six hours. And geostationary satellites are never, ever where you want them to be when you really need them. We're talking about Cherbourg here, and the French and Spanish coasts. It's not what you would call a high priority area of inquiry for us under normal conditions!"

"So what happened?"

"As best we can tell, they disappeared by prearrangement, because they wanted to disappear. In my humble opinion, I think everyone has underestimated the Japanese running this goat rodeo from the get-go! While their Coast Guard has the duty, their ship captain is a Lieutenant Mamoru Ito from the Self-Defense Forces, a real hotshot our agency has touted as a long-distance runner with a good chance of eventually making admiral and running the whole show. Even at his young age, he has developed a following and loyalties within the JSDF. He's not going to risk a promising career by taking a chance on losing the plutonium shipment."

"So how did he manage evading detection?"

"I figure first he turned off all electronic emissions, ceased all radio communications, and covered his ships' sonar signatures by adding the recorded sound of other engines. And then during the night, he used plywood, paint, and coated mylar sheeting to subtly alter the visual configuration of the two ships, changing their outlines, and hiding the *Shiki-shima*'s light armaments, just enough so that their profiles on the horizon no longer matched the originals.

"And, of course, he will have painted over the ships' names on the sterns and given them new, innocuous names. Anyway, that's my best guess as to what's happened.

"Then," continued the president's man, "I believe Lieutenant Ito did exactly what he was sworn not to do. Rather than staying the proscribed two hundred nautical miles from everyone's coast, I believe he set out to mix himself innocuously in with all the coastal clutter of small ships closer to the coast all along the route to Japan. I think he's been sneaking up along the way ever since, just blending in, doing what the Japanese do best—not standing out waiting to be hammered down but disappearing in the crowd.

"And I think he has co-opted Greenpeace to go along with this strategy. Originally Greenpeace was to follow the *Akatsuki Maru* all the way to Japan, with protests planned in each country along the way. But even Greenpeace has gone dark. I think Lieutenant Ito has explained the danger if Greenpeace tells everyone where to find the plutonium, and cut a deal whereby they can protest the arrival in Nagasaki all they like, but will refrain from targeting the vulnerable route, for fear of contributing to the nuclear proliferation they so strongly oppose. They're reasonable folk and have consistently had better Intel on the Japanese than us."

"Do you have any confirmation that your view is correct?"

"We haven't picked up anything from Japan, because we're constrained these days in eavesdropping on allies. But we did overhear one brief phone call into China yesterday that would seem to confirm my view."

"The Chinese are involved?"

"No. The call was to your Father Takashi Takano, in Beijing. From the Greenpeace vessel."

CHRONICLE XLV.

Alex and Connie accompanied Father Takashi directly from the airport to the monastery to meet with the Japanese homicide police. "This is a most unfortunate way to introduce you to our Priory," said Father Takashi. Em was there to ease the situation, welcome Father Takashi home, and introduce the two senior municipal police officers. "These officers have awaited your arrival," began Em, "in order to run through for all of us what they have found out since Brother Tomoyo's body was discovered last evening." The more senior of the two homicide officers took that as his cue and, in deference to Father Takashi's official guests, recounted in fluent English the recent developments.

"We are here tonight in the hope that one or more of you can shed some light on what has happened. We've questioned the monks and candidates who were in the monastery at the time of the murder, and I don't mind telling you that frankly we are baffled. Let me detail what we have discovered so far."

Referring to a notebook he took from his pocket, the officer began: "After work yesterday, all the members of this little community, except for Father Takashi and Brothers Liu and Tomoyo, attended Vespers in the chapel. Everyone was aware that Father Takashi and Brother Liu were in Beijing. It turns out that no one had seen Brother Tomoyo all day.

"Emery Peale, who we gather is Father Takashi's protégé, has testified separately that Father Takashi had suggested she discuss her current research project with Brother Tomoyo in Father Takashi's absence, indicating that Brother Tomoyo's past life experience might shed some light on her thinking. This she had done; and Brother Tomoyo had told her he might have news for her on his return to the monastery last evening. She waited for him but did not see him return. Nor did anyone else.

"As time for Compline approached, Father Ryan went to Brother Tomoyo's cell and found the door locked. He knocked, but there was no answer. He called out several times, to no effect. He tried all the keys available on the monastery master key ring, but none would fit the lock, which appeared to be jammed from the inside. Please follow me to the cell in question, but please do not enter it.

"Father Ryan put his shoulder to the door, as you can see—I gather he played football for his seminary." The officer gestured through what remained of the door. "You can also see that Brother Tomoyo's cell has no other exit. Nor does it have a window. The only fresh air it receives apart from this doorway is through the iron grate high on the opposite wall, facing east into the Priory's garden. That opening is covered on the outside by a second wrought-iron grill. The walls of this cell are a half meter thick. The floor is made of eighteenth-century one-hundred-kilo stones that fit together so closely water does not penetrate between them. We've had a master stone mason look at them. There is no other way into this cell than the doorway in front of us.

"What Father Ryan, his colleagues, and we discovered last evening was Brother Tomoyo, face down, spread eagled on the floor, an antique sword plunged through his back with such force that it nicked the stone beneath his chest. The door was closed, locked, and the old key broken off in the lock from the inside.

"Moreover, in examining that grate on the back wall, the wrought iron has not been touched in centuries, and the pattern doesn't allow anything near the size of the sword's hilt to pass through, even if the sword were to be disassembled and then reassembled. And our top forensic team swears on Fuji that Brother Tomoyo could not possibly have done this to himself; in fact, they say the placement of the blow was done by an expert in martial arts, one with great strength and considerable training, causing instant paralysis and death within a matter of seconds. Finally, the sword itself is worth a small fortune."

Admiral Rostov cleared his throat and commented: "It would seem from what you have said that this was some sort of a ritual slaying, and that the victim submitted rather than struggled."

If a Japanese can look impressed, the senior homicide officer looked sincerely impressed. "Yes," he responded, "I agree. As I'm sure you are aware, the traditional Japanese ritual is for the victim to cut across his own abdomen with a razor-sharp knife, and then within an instant have his pain and life ended by a single, expert stroke of a long sword by a trusted friend standing behind him, severing head from body. That *hara kiri* tradition is considered an honorable death. Brother Tomoyo's death may have been a ritual slaying, but it was not an honorable death. It was an execution."

The municipal police officer then asked for and was handed a photograph, which he passed among the small group. It was a picture of Brother Tomoyo's right hand, beneath which, and partly hidden by the sleeve of his cassock, appeared to be a message of some sort. When Father Takashi saw the photo he looked startled, and slowly moved his left hand into the sleeve of his cassock. Connie saw this reaction but said nothing.

"Was Brother Tomoyo right-handed?" asked the officer.

"Yes, as I recall," replied Father Takashi.

"Beneath the right sleeve of his habit," said the officer, pointing to the photo, "we found that as he died Brother Tomoyo used his remaining strength to scrawl a Japanese character in his own blood on the stone floor. It seems to be the character *cho* as in butterfly, although it's hard to tell as it's a complicated character and a bit smudged, and Brother Tomoyo was clearly weakening as he drew it. He wrote nothing more but used the last ounce of his strength to move his arm and cover what he had done with the sleeve of his robe—I would guess to hide it from his assassin."

CHRONICLE XLVI.

"*Pssst.* Alex?"

"Yes, Connie."

"*Shhh.* They'll hear you."

"Who?"

"The police."

"Okay. I'm shushing. What do you want?"

"I want to go to the Okura."

"Why? What's up? It's just a few blocks away."

"I married you for better or worse, in sickness and in health, for murder or mayhem; but I want a bath, and a garden room, and a cup of tea, and dinner, and bed, and you. . . ."

"I don't know about mayhem, but we've got a murder to solve, and a couple of ships to find, and . . . "

"Ask Father Takashi. He's holding out on you!"

"Yeah? You think?"

"Yeah! I know!"

"Father Takashi," said Alex to the assembled group, "do you have any idea who committed this murder?"

"I like these Americans, with their direct approach!" said the senior municipal police officer to his colleague.

"He's Russian, a Russian admiral," contradicted his junior.

"Then why was I told he's an adviser to the American president?" asked his boss, somewhat testily.

"Because he is," replied his junior.

"I don't understand these Americans," complained the senior municipal police officer.

"No," responded Father Takashi, "I don't know who committed the act. And I most certainly cannot explain to you how it was done in a locked room. But I have a pretty good idea of why the act was committed, unfortunately; and I feel I am largely to blame.

"Brother Tomoyo came to us a good dozen years ago seeking refuge from the yakuza. I asked Em to ask his advice and counsel about any possible yakuza connection in regard to the murder of Cardinal Matsumoto in Rome, given the way in which it was accomplished. I gather that Brother Tomoyo decided on his own to make some inquiries among his old contacts and was murdered as a consequence. I feel guilty about setting things in motion, and not being here to counsel a more conservative approach on his part. But one thing is clear to me.

"When he first entered the monastery, we bonded as friends and called each other by nicknames. I have a birthmark on my left hand in the shape of a butterfly, and he called me *cho-cho*. That message he left was for me. He gave his life to tell me I was right in thinking this whole story is directly connected in some way to the yakuza."

"See?" said Connie quietly to Alex.

"Connie and I will ponder all of this in our hearts—from the Okura," announced Alex. "We'll see you all in the morning."

CHRONICLE XLVII.

This morning Connie felt like a new woman. Wrapped in a demure pastel yukata and wearing geta, she was walking the elegant garden, looking at the flowers, fishponds, tea houses, and little Shinto shrines beneath the magnificent trees of the Okura's old Japanese garden in the heart of Tokyo. She was enchanted. Not the least by the geta, the outdoor wooden clogs she wore. They looked appropriate, but strange. In fact, they were the most comfortable and stable outdoor shoe she could imagine for a woman, and automatically she took smaller steps than usual.

Last night she and Alex had been met by one of the assistant managers, who ushered them quickly to their ground-floor room, several stories below the hillside lobby and reception areas. The large and airy Japanese-style room was highlighted by a *tokonoma* alcove set into one wall, where subtle recessed lighting bathed a perfectly understated and sparse flower arrangement of pussy willow with a single stem of cinnamon and ginger cymbidium in a tall, thin terra-cotta vase. A young woman in a stunning kimono glided into the room behind the assistant manager, motioned Connie and Alex to be seated facing the lighted garden, and served them tea while offering them a light dinner menu. She took their cocktail, wine, and dinner orders, and then suggested they might like to bathe while dinner was being prepared. They were shown into two large, separate bathrooms, where their two bathing assistants—young girls in short yukatas—awaited them and asked each to undress. Their clothes were whisked away to be cleaned and pressed after their hostess served the cocktails they had ordered.

Just in case they needed telling, they were informed that in Japan one washes one's body *before* bathing, not during a bath. And their bathing assistants each set about scrubbing them in their separate bathrooms. With soap and brushes. From head to toe. Then rinsed them thoroughly. Without embarrassment or favor. (When they compared notes later, they agreed they had never felt so clean.)

Only then were they shown into their shared bath, a deep pool heated to a temperature which both found initially almost intolerable, but soon luxuriant.

When they were asked to step up and out of the heated pool, they were told to hold each other steady. They both found this sensual and even arousing until the two assistants, who up to this point had proved a delight, repeatedly dumped wooden buckets of ice water over their heads, and then popped both of them into warmed bath robes, vigorously toweled their hair, slippered their feet, and led them to the lovely dinner that had been delivered and laid out for them in the main room of their Japanese suite. They were left alone with the dinner and wine, and asked to call when finished, at which time all evidence of the meal service was quickly removed.

As was traditional in Japanese rooms, their floor was covered in woven rice straw tatami mats, but the mats in this room were still new enough to retain a light green color, and that unique fragrance of new tatami. It is that fragrance of green tatami that brings the best sleep to Japanese people. Once dinner was cleared, two maids quickly presented Connie and Alex with their sleeping kimonos, and pulled futons, Japanese-style duvets, and barley-filled pillows from the two antique tansu chests with butterfly escutcheons that adorned the austere room. They made up the couples' bed on the floor, bowed, and departed.

"After that bath and dinner and wine," Connie had said, "I'm a pushover."

"I'm more of a rollover," her husband had replied sleepily. And once again, Connie had happily proven her husband wrong.

She smiled at the memory. This morning, however, he was going to be left on his own. Absolutely nothing, and certainly not murder, would pry her loose from this tranquil garden. In fact, she might even have another bath. And get her hair done. But before Alex returned to the monastery and the police, she wanted to suggest that he take a second look at that cell and see if Brother Tomoyo could possibly have managed suicide. If he was conflicted between the oath he swore to the yakuza and the oath he later swore to the monastery, this may have been his Japanese way of reconciling them. Alex needed to double check to see if anywhere in his cell Tomoyo could have jammed the hilt of the sword long enough to throw himself back upon it in a disciplined and calculated suicide, then falling forward, with the sword protruding from his chest, digging into the stone floor.

CHRONICLE XLVIII.

Alex slept late, politely skipped the proffered Japanese breakfast of soup, fish, and rice, drank his usual four cups of coffee instead, and walked to the Christopherian Priory from the hotel. He and Connie had stopped briefly at the embassy last night, across the street from the Okura, to allow Alex to send a situation report to the president, Senator Laughlin, and Tom. He had promised the municipal police he would return to the monastery this morning to review matters once Brother Liu was back from Beijing, and everyone else had had a night to think about what had transpired. Alex felt no wiser, but he was armed with Connie's idea.

Brother Liu had returned, been welcomed, introduced to the two municipal police officers, and brought up to date by the time Alex arrived. "Was there any sign of breaking and entering elsewhere in the monastery?" asked Brother Liu.

"No," replied the younger officer. "We checked every door and window, and even every iron grate."

Alex promptly spoke up: "Is there any chance Brother Tomoyo could have committed suicide? Could he have thrust himself backwards onto the sword, and then fallen forward onto the floor?"

"That possibility had occurred to us, as well," responded the senior officer. "We spent several hours, while we awaited your return from Beijing, attempting to find some way to jam the hilt of the sword into or between anything in the cell. But it's just not possible. Frankly, I would have much preferred that solution to the crime—despite the monastery's religious taboos against suicide—because we could have quickly closed the case. But no matter what we tried, we could find no way to hold the sword at the appropriate angle firmly enough to do the job. The sword cut through Brother Tomoyo's spine from behind and exited his chest. We simply cannot see how he could have managed that alone in his small cell, and there is no evidence that he was killed elsewhere and moved.

"So we are at an impasse; and I don't mind telling you that I am under a great deal of pressure to solve this murder quickly. The press will inevitably sensationalize the crime if we do not present a solution promptly. I would welcome any help you can give me. What more can you tell us about Brother Tomoyo?"

"When he first arrived, a dozen years ago," said Father Takashi, "he was just seeking refuge. He didn't even know our monastery was Christian. The monastery looks Buddhist, which it was from its inception in the eighteenth century until the early 1930s, when it was purchased by Admiral Stephen Yamamoto, who accompanied the emperor to Rome to meet the pope. Shortly thereafter he bought several Buddhist monasteries here and in Kyoto from an obscure and failing sect and gave them to the Christopherian Order. Brother Tomoyo at first thought he was seeking refuge in a Buddhist monastery!"

Brother Liu interrupted: "What was the Buddhist sect that Admiral Yamamoto purchased this monastery from back in the 1930s?"

"I don't recall the name, and my records are in Kyoto," responded Father Takashi. "I distinctly remember he called it small and obscure, and there's something in the back of my mind about it being somewhat disreputable. But I recall the early Christopherian monks remarking on how disappointed the neighbors were that the Buddhists had left."

"The back wall of Brother Tomoyo's cell—what is on the other side of it?" asked Brother Liu.

"Why, the garden," replied Father Takashi. "There's a cloistered garth on three sides of the inner garden, and the fourth side opens onto a little orchard and vegetable patch."

"Is that inner garden original to the monastery?" continued Brother Liu.

"Yes. There are plantings and pathways, a few stone benches, and two old stone lanterns. It's quite small."

"Are they all original to the garden?"

"No, we added the stone benches when they were given to us after the war."

"And the lanterns?"

"I believe they're original to the monastery. At least I can't ever remember them not being there. They are not at all unusual; typical late Edo period matching stone lanterns, each about a meter and a half high, quite lovely."

Brother Liu was looking increasingly agitated with every answer Father Takashi gave him. "We'd better go to the garden," he said.

"Will you tell us why?" asked Alex in consternation.

"Of course. But first let's see if I'm right. If I am, we can all thank God that my father was a Chinese Buddhist!"

Father Takashi led the group back through the monastery and out a side door opening onto the garth, a stone pathway around three sides of the garden with an overhanging roof buttressed on the garden side by columns and open archways.

"Admiral Stephen Yamamoto added these cloisters to the original building, thinking they made it look more in keeping with a European monastery," he explained.

Brother Liu wasn't listening. He walked out into the garden and followed the path to the left, in the direction of the back wall of Brother Tomoyo's cell. When he reached the stone lantern closest to Brother Tomoyo's cell, he put his hands on it and began to push. Nothing happened. Everyone except Brother Liu looked disappointed.

He then stepped to the next side of the lantern, and pushed at a ninety-degree angle from where he had started. The lantern slid easily around, pivoting on one corner, revealing a black hole beneath it about a meter wide. A crude, old, handmade ladder led down into the darkness.

The senior municipal police officer handed Brother Liu his junior's flashlight, and led the way for the three of them to descend into the ancient tunnel. "This is how the murderer got into Tomoyo's cell," Brother Liu called up to the others.

"How could he?" called down Father Takashi. "There's no way in!"

A few minutes past, and Brother Liu returned to the bottom of the ladder, about eight meters down. "There is a way in," he called up. "You need a machine to open it. An eighteenth century machine! If you will all go back to Brother Tomoyo's cell and wait, we'll show you. But please wait outside the cell. Don't go into it, as we don't know exactly where we're going to end up."

The others agreed, but Alex started down the ladder before Brother Liu could depart back up the tunnel toward the priory with the flashlight. Alex wanted to see an eighteenth-century machine and wasn't going to miss this opportunity.

As Alex reached the bottom of the rickety ladder and his feet touched earthen floor a good eight meters down the well-like hole, his first thought was, *I'm glad Connie's not down here, she wouldn't like it*, quickly followed by an honest *I'm getting too old to be doing this*. He turned to find that Brother Liu had already started down a low tunnel about a meter and a half high, leading off in the direction of the priory. Alex called out, "Oh Brother, where art thou?" but his voice was too muffled by all the dirt to reach Brother Liu, and his subterranean attempt at claustrophobic humor was lost on the surrounding worms. Alex pushed on, following the glow ahead.

After about thirty meters doubled over, Alex entered an underground room, and found he could stand up next to Brother Liu and the two municipal police officers. The room was roughly square, the walls slanting inward like a pyramid, apparently constructed by masons at the time the original monastery was built, using the same stone.

In the center of the room was an old wooden machine of some sort. It looked like it had come out of the Middle Ages, some sort of demonic Inquisition torture device, but Brother Liu had said it was eighteenth century. There was a vertical, deeply grooved pole, a giant screw in the center of the apparatus, inside a robust rectangular wooden frame that extended from floor to ceiling. On one side was a spoked wheel, like the wheel of an old sailing ship, but cruder, and a complicated catchment, gear train, and escapement that permitted the center pole to be raised or lowered in small increments by turning the spoked wheel.

Brother Liu shone his flashlight along the giant grooved pole screw, and Alex saw a large stone on top of it, shaped like an upside-down pyramid with the tip cut off. Instead of the tip, there was a hole and the grooved pole fitted neatly into that hole, so when the pole was raised or lowered, the large stone was raised or lowered with it.

It's counterintuitive, thought Alex. As a Westerner, I would have designed it to plug the hole in the floor. Instead, the stone—which must weigh three hundred pounds—simply settles into the hole, and having sides that slant inward, forms a perfect seal—a seal so tight that, once in place, water can't get through the cracks.

Using this mechanism, the stone can be raised by one person. *And I'll bet,* he thought, *they could grease these old wooden gears and raise it silently.* Once raised, the monk could use a ladder to crawl up to and in and out of the cell at will, then lower the stone from below afterward, and no one would ever be the wiser. *But why?* he wondered. *Why go to all this trouble?*

"Hold the flashlight," Brother Liu said to Alex, "while I turn this thing, and we'll see where it comes out. I believe we'll find it comes out in Brother Tomoyo's cell."

Alex held the light, Brother Liu applied pressure to turn the spoked wheel, the mechanical device multiplied that force, the vertical screw began to turn, and the stone ever so slowly began to rise.

Progress was tantalizingly slow. It took over seven minutes of Brother Liu's methodical work before the men saw a glimmer of light, as the bottom of the stone cleared the top of the floor above. And another good five or six minutes until Brother Liu was satisfied that the stone was raised sufficiently high to allow him to use the ladder nearby to climb up there, squeeze underneath it, and come out in what he presumed would be Brother Tomoyo's cell. He started up the crude ladder, followed closely by the two intrigued municipal police officers.

And Brother Liu proved to be prescient. They popped up just inside the north wall of the cell in which the murder had been committed. A small cheer rose from the monks and candidates gathered outside the broken door above. When the junior officer looked back down beneath the stone and could not see Alex following him, he called out "Admiral Rostov!"

"Don't shout," said Alex, walking in through the broken door, "I came around the long way. Brother Liu proved his point by climbing up, and I didn't need to prove my paunch by getting stuck." The short laugh that ensued was the first shared humor the group had enjoyed since the murder was discovered. It served to relieve some of the tension they had all felt.

Brother Liu turned to the gathered members of the monastery's little community, and apologized for asking them to remain outside the room: "I didn't know which of the stones would be raised, and didn't want to levitate one or two of you in the bargain!"

The senior municipal police officer said "Now, Brother Liu, you must tell us how you figured this out."

"We all deserve to hear this story, the whole monastery, as we all live here," said Father Takashi. "Let's make tea and gather in the garden in ten minutes and allow Brother Liu to take his time and tell us from the beginning how he solved the mystery of the locked cell."

Afterwards, Father Takashi regretted his words and open invitation. But how was he to know? He hadn't heard the story!

"When I was ten or eleven," Brother Liu began, once the candidates had served the tea in the garden, "as boys will do at that age, I asked my father about sex. And he explained it to me, both the physical and the emotional sides of love. My mother overheard us, and added that not everyone participated, pointing out that there used to be a Christian monastery nearby before the revolution, where monks practiced celibacy. She had attended a Catholic girls' school as a child and explained to me that some men choose to dedicate their lives to God, and that these monks sacrifice their own love between a man and a woman as evidence of this commitment to God. They remain chaste, celibate.

"My father, being a Buddhist, pointed out that not all monks are celibate. There was one small, unorthodox, and controversial Buddhist sect that despite its somewhat unrespectable reputation had no trouble recruiting novices.

"My father recounted to my mother and me how young, married women who had not conceived but wanted a child were advised to visit

Buddhist monasteries of this particular sect. There they would fast and pray. Then they were given some sort of potion to drink, and told to lock themselves into the cell closest to the garden for the night, a cell with only one entrance, no windows, a stout door, and a lock with a single key given to the woman who was told to carefully lock herself in.

"Apparently the potion was a soporific, combined with some sort of powerful Chinese aphrodisiac. The women would do as instructed, lock themselves in a cell that had but one entrance. During the night the monks would use the contraptions like the one we found in the tunnel to raise the keystones in the floors of the cells and sneak in one at a time. The drugged women would be highly receptive though half asleep, and it is said they remembered nothing in the morning.

"Over time," my father said, "about half the women who tried to conceive in this fashion, did so. Which makes sense if you figure that infertility is a fifty-fifty risk between men and women. But according to my father, over half the women kept coming back.

"My mother said she found it hard to believe that the women remembered nothing. My father concurred. He said that those who returned most often gave up drinking the potion, and some even gave up locking the door."

Father Takashi interrupted at this point with a stern reminder that everyone was due in chapel in five minutes, and that if any of the candidates, novices, or—God forbid—brothers, were entertaining thoughts that they might have chosen the wrong Order, he would hear special confessions immediately after midday prayers, traditionally called Sext, though today he chose to say simply after midday prayers.

CHRONICLE L.

Alex and Em were talking quietly in the monastery garden when the senior municipal police officer approached and said, "While the Christians are in chapel praying, I would like to take the opportunity to talk with the two of you discreetly about a new development that concerns you both."

Em felt that little niggle of warning about the dangers of cultural assumptions: because they were not in chapel with the monks, and because Japan was overwhelmingly Buddhist and Shinto, the officer had just assumed that they were not Christians. The error was inconsequential, but it reminded her to be careful of making similar mistakes.

Alex clearly was curious about the officer's opening line. What could possibly link him with Em here? She worked with Tom, and he had just met Tom in Washington through the president.

"Early this morning, before I left our headquarters, a senior police officer in plain clothes identified himself to me and requested printouts of our data on each of you."

"Municipal police or military police?" asked Alex.

"Neither," replied the officer. "And that's the point. He was with the Special Security Police attached to the Diet, our parliament."

"What did you do?" asked Alex.

"I gave him the background information we have on you when you served as admiral of the Russian Navy, our summary on the Krapotkin affair, your retirement and subsequent appointment as adviser to the president of the United States, your marriage to the former wife of the late banker Zimmerman, and your unofficial visit here. As to you, Ms. Peale, I gave him what information we have regarding your employment in Rome with the Foundation for the Propagation of Aid to Parish Priests, and your work with Father Takashi here. But I am troubled by this request. It is most unusual. In fact, it is the first time in my thirty-year career that this has happened."

"What do you make of it?" asked Alex.

"It could only have happened if some senior member of the Diet asked that it be done. And that would happen only if he in turn had been asked to do so by a very powerful constituent."

"I can understand a query about me," said Alex. "What I cannot understand is a query about Em, much less linking the two of us, unless it has something to do with this monastery."

"Or with the death of Cardinal Matsumoto," added the officer. "That subject came up in the talks between Ms. Paine and Brother Tomoyo and may have had something to do with Brother Tomoyo's subsequent inquiries, and his death."

"I keep getting the impression that you're trying to tell me something without actually coming out and telling me," said Alex, feeling somewhat frustrated with the officer.

"You must be learning our language," said the officer with a smile. "I'm used on the municipal force for the most sensitive of missions. Usually that's homicides involving important non-Japanese, senior politicians, and noted yakuza. But once in a while I get pulled off homicide for something especially sensitive. That happened last month, when I spent a week protecting twenty-one historians from the United States, Canada, China, and South Korea. They were in Tokyo to meet with senior officials to protest what they called the 'revisionist history' that some of our elected leaders are applying in an attempt to whitewash our role in World War II, the occupation of China, Manchuria, and Korea, the use of their women as sex slaves, and now, rehabilitating the reputations and roles of Japan's war criminals.

"We Japanese are today a profoundly pacifist people. China is taking advantage of this and pushing us around in the Pacific just like Putin pushed around Georgia and the Ukraine, and for the same reason—access to energy and natural resources—in this case in the disputed Pacific Islands. Those of us who want to see Japan stand up against this land grab, and counter China's claims, believe that we are handicapped by not having a military that can project influence—only a self-defense force. They look around and see our neighbors with nuclear capability and believe we should counter it by at least being seen to have the de facto potential to acquire that capability in short order.

"I could never say all this to you in front of my countrymen," the officer continued. "We are not explicit on these subjects with each other. But what you and I have witnessed here in the past few days is not just a crime with clear links to the yakuza. It is also linked to the nationalist, revisionist movement of the far right, which to my profound regret has overwhelmed the position I personally advocate—a sane and incremental strengthening of my country."

"I appreciate your sharing these views with us, and how difficult it is for you to do it!" said Alex.

"Well, after thirty years I've been offered retirement in a few months, and I think I'll accept—not because I'm ready to quit, but because I'm becoming too uncomfortable with what I see happening around me to remain an official part of it."

"My friend," said Alex, "you have come to the exact same conclusion that General Krapotkin and I reached in 2001, when the two of us decided we needed to step outside ourselves and our careers to make a difference."

"I think I will have to reread your file at home tonight," said the officer with a shy smile.

After the officer had left Alex and Em in the garden, Alex turned to Em and said, "Whatever we end up doing, my bet is that we can count on him for help, if we need it."

CHRONICLE LI.

When Tom stepped off the direct flight from Washington to Tokyo, he was astonished to find Sure waiting for him with a big smile and a hug. "I couldn't be more pleased to see you," he said, "but who's minding the store?"

"Have faith, dear cardinal!" replied Sure. "I've trained our Rome team well. They're fully capable. And His Holiness has Kurt keeping a close eye on everything. Far closer than you would imagine! In fact, it was His Holiness who insisted on my coming to meet you."

"I don't understand," said Tom.

"Look, Tom, the pope has been two steps ahead of us all the way. After you and Kurt bonded over that crazy assassination attempt, and Kurt gently pushed His Holiness up the learning curve about the Vatican's real-world involvement in nudging history, he saw you as the means to resolve a major problem that Cardinal Matsumoto delivered up to him before his death. The catch was he couldn't reveal exactly what the problem entailed without abrogating the confessional. Now he wants us here. I'm sure he has a good reason.

"And so do I," Sure continued. "The Italian police reviewed the Vatican hospital's security film and found a sort of a logo on the collar of that fantastic outfit the cardinal's murderer was wearing, just as she rose out of the soiled linen basket, the instant before she disappeared. According to Washington, it tracks to a major Japanese conglomerate. I've brought you the information they discovered, and the background that Langley has developed on it. Somebody clearly stole the prototype of a new technology developed by this corporation, and if we can figure out who, we may have our killer.

"One final point," Sure concluded. "His Holiness said to tell you: 'When in doubt, look to Father Takashi—that's where all of this started, and that's who we are all committed to helping.' I said I would repeat his message to you word for word."

"I guess we had better get to the monastery, then," said Tom. "But first, I have to pick up the bags from customs. I had just planned to stay here one night to recoup and then fly on to Rome. I'm acting as an official US courier for a diplomatic pouch addressed to Admiral Rostov in care of the US Embassy. At first they wanted me to carry a forty-five automatic! Can you imagine? I declined, of course, and explained that I had better protection from a much higher power.

"I must drop off two diplomatic pouch suitcases intended for Alex at the embassy, get them receipted, and then we'll be free to go to the monastery. I was told he would be at either of those two places, or at the Okura, where I'll be staying as well."

"As will I. I guess that's where the action is," said the young CIA agent, who just eighteen months earlier had herself been the center of the action on the north shore of Oahu.

CHRONICLE LII.

Father Takashi's little Tokyo Priory had received more attention in the last few days than it had received in the last hundred years. He had fended off the Tokyo press, the Italian paparazzi, the Associated Press, and Agence France-Presse, all keen on the murder; but for reasons he could not fathom, Bloomberg kept dogging his every step. He could not leave the monastery without a Bloomberg correspondent asking for an interview. It wasn't like the pushy, intrusive British; it was just that the Bloomies kept implying they knew something he wasn't telling. He knew a whole lot he wasn't telling, and was not about to try to outguess the investigative reporters, so he just smiled and blessed them. He had always liked Bloomberg, anyway. After midday prayers and a—let's admit it—rather meager lunch, he awaited the imminent and eminent arrival of Cardinal Gallagher, expected on the midmorning flight direct from Washington.

Father Takashi knew that it was stories like Brother Liu just told about the lascivious Buddhist sect that made celibacy that much more difficult for the younger brothers, and certainly for the novices and candidates. Thankfully, Father Takashi had coped, controlled, governed, and finally mastered those desires. Where he still succumbed was to serious temptations centered about the subject of cuisine. He did not believe in raw fish. He believed in boeuf bourguignon. He could subsist on inconsequential lunches. And dinners with o-sake were acceptable. But a week without a good burgundy, and a fine Kobe pot-au-feu, was just intolerable. When Father Takashi confessed, which frankly was not all that often, and until recently was only to his cardinal, his most grievous sin was that he had *une fine gueule.* The fact that he remained as thin as a rail, and looked so convincingly ascetic, was clearly a gift of a benevolent and forgiving God, whom Father Takashi suspected must be: (a) female, and (b) either French, or at the very least Italian.

In any case, despite the Shinto respect for nature and worship of ancestors, and the World War II nationalist nostalgia and revisionist history, and the latent sacredness and belief in the Emperor, of one thing Father Takashi was certain: God was not Japanese.

Admiral Rostov, Connie, and Em were in the garden when Father Takashi was notified that Cardinal Gallagher and Surely Devine had arrived at the monastery. Father Takashi was delighted and joined them all under the cloisters. Connie embraced Sure, Sure hugged Em, and after introductions and greetings all around, Alex said, "I believe we are here for a purpose. We have much work to do. And His Holiness must think so, too. The *Akatsuki Maru* and *Shiki-shima* are due off Nagasaki in a little less than two weeks' time, and we still have no idea who the enemy is, what the real risks are, where they're coming from, or when. All we know is that we have been assured that the danger is imminent."

Father Takashi spoke up on the subject for the first time: "I have new information. The two ships will be off Nagasaki in four days."

CHRONICLE LIII.

"Forgive me, Father, but that can't be right," observed Alex. "Those two little ships would be cruising at about seventeen knots, maximum, to conserve fuel, and on either route—around Africa, or around South America—there is no way they could cover the seventeen thousand nautical miles from France to Japan in that short a time. We were told that they would remain at least two hundred miles off the coast of any nation that protested their passage, and Greenpeace got just about everyone to protest, in one way or another. So unless you've found them somehow, and the US Navy certainly has tried but without success, my best guess is that twelve to sixteen days from now, depending upon the weather they encountered, they'll pop up off Nagasaki."

"Admiral," said Father Takashi, "I admit to withholding critical information from you until today, information that both Cardinal Matsumoto and His Holiness were made aware of early on, but I did so only because I—and they—had sworn silence to protect the plutonium shipment from what we perceived to be the greatest risk, terrorist attack on the high seas. If the route and location were known, the risk would be greatest. Seized by terrorists, the plutonium would be a valuable commodity for sale to states seeking entry into the nuclear club, or those like North Korea having trouble taking the longer, more complicated uranium route to that goal. And it could become a powerful instrument for political blackmail as well: once the critical ingredient, the plutonium, is acquired, any threat becomes credible, even if you lack a delivery system. All you need to do is blow the stuff up with standard explosives to make a city center uninhabitable for thousands of years.

"Seizure by terrorists wouldn't be that difficult if all that protected the four thousand-pound shipment was the couple of modern, high-powered Gatling guns on the Akatsuki Maru freighter, and the two unarmed helicopters and four small anti-aircraft batteries on the Coast Guard's *Shiki-shima* escort vessel. We thought the American Navy would make up the difference, and then the US Congress and the Japanese Diet got in that pissing match about who would pay for it, and who would be seen as mercenaries, and we Japanese ended up hung out to dry.

"That's when I asked my cardinal for permission to take matters into my own hands. It was a sin of pride on my part, which I promptly confessed, but when my cardinal heard me out, he encouraged me to act. In fact, he colluded with me, and went so far as to inform His Holiness of what we were up to, so that the Vatican—God forgive me for saying this—could prepare credible deniability if we were found out.

"As the working priest to Greenpeace-Japan for over twenty years, I was more than familiar with the risks involved. And the key to our success was, I believe, heaven-sent, when the Japanese hierarchy chose as captain of the *Shiki-shima* not a Coast Guard officer, but a fast-rising and level-headed Naval lieutenant, Lt. Mamoru Ito, a good Catholic, and a congregant of mine, essentially a crypto-Christian who visits our monastery in Kyoto at least once a month for confession, fellowship, and prayer.

"He accepted at my insistence to meet with a representative of Greenpeace-Japan on neutral territory, our monastery, and we arranged a modus vivendi. Greenpeace would call off its dogs of peace, its propaganda campaign in the press and TV, once the little two-ship convoy left port in France. Greenpeace would follow astern at least ten miles behind in their leased seagoing tug, all three ships running electronically silent. No emissions whatsoever.

"Importantly, Lieutenant Ito, after I reviewed Admiral Stephen Yamamoto's history with him, agreed to reconfigure the protection of the plutonium itself, following Yamamoto's example when he accompanied the emperor to visit the pope.

"And the *Akatsuki Maru* would use paint, plywood, and mylar to change its deck configuration, hide the two guns, rename the vessel, and use forged papers to make it appear to be a small Lebanese freighter. The *Shiki-shima* would alter its appearance to take on the aspect of a South Korean coastal minesweeper, with all the appropriate identification symbols, out on sea trials.

"And most importantly, they would radically change their route to Japan. Instead of staying two hundred miles seaward, they would mix in with the clutter of near-shore local vessels. Instead of taking the long way around, they would use the Suez Canal.

"So, Admiral, you asked if I had found them. Truth be told, I never lost them. While the two ships had ample fuel for a seventeen thousand or even twenty thousand-mile journey at seventeen knots, they could afford to push twenty-three knots on the much shorter route. And while I could not track them any better than the US Navy, my friends on the Greenpeace-Japan tug that trailed behind had no such luxury and kept stopping along the way to refuel. While they had sworn to no electronic transmissions, I had provided them with a prepaid phone to give me a ring and simply report on the weather wherever they found themselves. They called me 'mother,' and phoned every third day.

"I have just committed another sin of pride, by recounting all of this to you, but I can report that both ships are safe and close enough to Japan to be out of reach of the international terrorists we had feared. The problem we now face is that they are coming within range of what I never imagined—homegrown Japanese terrorists—for that is the only explanation I can imagine for the deaths of Cardinal Matsumoto and Brother Tomoyo."

CHRONICLE LIV.

The senior municipal police officer was shown into the garden, where he asked politely for a word with Alex, alone.

"Last night I read our extensive files on you," he began, "starting with your career in the Soviet Navy, continuing with the published account of the Krapotkin affair and your preemptory theft of the nuclear warheads from the depot in Ukraine, to your retirement, your move to America, your marriage, and your subsequent association with the White House.

"I realize now that my murder investigation must be peripheral to something much larger, more dangerous, and more important, if it involves all of you here today. As I explained to you yesterday, I'm about to accept retirement after thirty years on the force, in large part out of frustration with what I see going on around me. I would love to go out with a bang! How may I be of help?"

Alex took the man by the elbow and led him back to the rest of his assembled cohorts. "I would like to introduce and reintroduce all of you to Asahi Onishi, a full colonel in the municipal police, who has just volunteered to join our little band of brothers and sisters, at clear professional risk and personal cost to his thirty-year career on the force. He could not have joined us at a better time. Father Takashi, I would ask you to brief him over lunch on the background of our concerns, including all that we discussed this morning. But with so little time now left to us, we need to move with alacrity. Sure tells me she has evidence of a Japanese corporation's involvement in the murder of Cardinal Matsumoto in Rome. Sure, would you show that photo to Colonel Onishi?"

Colonel Onishi took the photo from Sure, saying "Please just call me Asahi, like the newspaper—it's a popular first name here; and if I'm joining you, I'd prefer not to be addressed as Colonel!" He looked at the photo of the raised white logo on the collar of the white bodysuit used by the murderer. It was taken from the surveillance camera tape, and was white on white, barely perceptible; but Langley had enhanced it, pixel by pixel, and gotten as much out of it as possible.

"I recognize it," said Asahi. "It's the logo of the developmental arm of a mid-size advanced electronics firm on the outskirts of Tokyo. It has an enviable reputation, and a well-known chairman. Armed with this photo, I could pursue an inquiry in my official capacity if that would help."

"It would, but only after lunch and Takashi's briefing. We need you to get up to speed to be aware of all the forces in play here, so you will know what to look out for. In the meantime, I would appreciate your giving all of us a short course on who could possibly be acting as Japanese terrorists today—for political reasons or for financial gain."

"Only two groups, to my knowledge and in my thirty-years' experience, would have the motivation, skills, and resources to be realistic threats. The first would be the far right, the neo-nationalists. And the second would be the yakuza, Japan's mafia.

"If you are referring to the possible theft of the plutonium currently in transit," said Asahi—and at this point everyone other than Asahi looked shocked at being told that their cat was out of the bag—"as I assume from your expressions, we are," he continued, "then I would not pick the neo-cons as the most obvious threat. Right now, they are already achieving almost everything they want. Japan is becoming a de facto nuclear power. Its leadership is revising history, rehabilitating World War II leadership, and looking to justify reorienting its military from purely self-defense to modest force projection. My guess is the last thing the neo-cons would want to do is anything overly adventurous that might rock that boat. And I should add that my guess about the plutonium results from the fact that the municipal police have known of Father Takashi's work with Greenpeace for a number of years now."

CHRONICLE LV.

"That leaves the yakuza," prompted Alex.

"And that's a misnomer," said Asahi, "literally. Traditionally, you have three—and these days, four—separate groups. The original three are referred to as 'ninkyo dantai,' the 'chivalrous organizations' that formed toward the end of the Edo Period in the mid-nineteenth century, when the old social structures of Japan began to break down, and various factions formed self-protection societies. These were the lower classes, the social groups who owned no property, homes, or livestock. They saw themselves as society's outcasts, those who had everything to lose and little to gain—the itinerant peddlers, hucksters, traders, entertainers, and gamblers associated with the outdoor fairs that traveled the land. Over the past 150 years they evolved what they perceive to be an honorable if illegal tradition, based on the samurai code of self-preservation and acknowledging only one master. Today they see themselves as fervently patriotic and almost part of the establishment.

"Then there is the fourth group, the newer syndicates that deal in drugs and human trafficking. They have even been known to funnel financial support to North Korea. They are essentially thugs for hire, as in old Indian Thugees. While there may be honor among the old-line yakuza, and a close connection to the *nyoku*, the right-wing political groups, these newer thugs have no loyalties. They will do anything to anyone for money and power, including acting as professional assassins."

"Given what we're up against," said Tom, "I would recommend we approach the problem head on. We don't have the luxury of time or finesse. I propose we send someone to interview the chairman of the Japanese company that Asahi identified by that logo, and another delegation to interview the most senior traditional yakuza we can find—and ask directly for their help."

"Why in God's name would they choose to help us?" asked Connie.

"Because," said Tom, "if what Asahi says is true, we can ask the yakuza to help on the grounds that they patriotically would be saving Japan, and protecting themselves from blame; and we can ask the corporation chairman for help on the grounds that he patriotically would be saving Japan from the yakuza, and protecting himself from complicity!"

"Strange as it may sound, that actually makes sense," said Asahi.

"Who should do what?" asked Connie.

"Well," said Asahi, "I should be the one to beard the corporate chairman in his den. Corporate chairmen are considered gods here and are overly protected. The only chance we have of seeing him is if I pull my rank and position in the municipal police, and let his office know that we have specific evidence incriminating his firm and therefore his good self."

"And what about the yakuza?" asked Father Takashi.

"That's more difficult," replied Asahi. "If we go to any single traditional faction, it will try to use us against the others. But there is one possible approach, if Admiral Rostov is willing."

"And that would be?" prompted Alex.

"There is an old *oyabun* who is above it all, a former head of the largest yakuza clan, the Yamaguchi-gumi of Kobe, the strongest yakuza family since World War II. He is the only yakuza ever to be given the official right to carry the long sword, the sign of a samurai, by the government during the war. He is respected by all the clans. He's eighty-two years old, in poor health, long since retired, and has become a recluse—in an eighteenth-century farmhouse that he had moved to the heart of an old district of Tokyo. But if we were to tell his wife that the president of the United States has sent a personal emissary to see him, he might relent and accept to talk with you. And he is unquestionably the most knowledgeable and revered yakuza in Japan today."

"Alex," said Connie, "there is no way you are going to meet him without me."

Alex quickly replied, "Connie, I really don't think that . . ."

And then he got "That Look," and knew his argument was lost before he even started.

"If you think for one minute, Alex Rostov," said Connie, "that you are going to get to meet the godfather of all Japan—and not take me with you—then, as my sainted mother would say, you've got another think coming!"

"I cede the point," said Alex, glancing at Asahi and raising his eyebrows.

"It's a bad idea, Mrs. Rostov," said Asahi on cue. "Very un-Japanese. Simply not done. No women."

"Actually," interrupted Father Takashi, "I think it might be just the thing to throw the old guy off stride. He's so reclusive that if he does accept to see Alex, he can hardly refuse to see the wife of the president's personal emissary. Connie, I think it's a genial idea."

"Well," said Connie, "I'm happy that's all settled, then."

"How should we address him? As a representative of the president, I can't very well use his yakuza title," said Alex.

"Address him as 'Sensei'—it means 'honored teacher' in Japanese, and is both appropriate and polite, given his age," said Father Takashi.

"I agree," added Asahi. "That's the perfect solution."

"Well, that just leaves the tough part: how do we get Alex an appointment with him?" asked Tom. "I strongly doubt that the embassy would be the appropriate route. And I'm sure the municipal police would not be the way to go."

"Oh, that's easy," replied Asahi. "Just ask the manager at the Okura to call and make the appointment for you. Believe me, he's handled much more delicate matters than this!"

CHRONICLE LVI.

The Okura arranged a tea-time appointment with the old yakuza without blinking an eye. Back in their Japanese garden suite, Connie and Alex were getting ready to be picked up by the embassy car Alex requested to take them to the appointment when Connie had a thought. At her age, new thoughts no longer occurred all that often, so she paid attention to it. She remembered that *miyage*—little gifts—in Japan were an important part of the culture. And she had received a parting gift from her closest bosom buddy when she flew out of Washington with Alex—a Michael Kors "Signature Hamilton Tote," a handsome leather bag any woman would love, but as a "signature" bag, it bore that famous "MK" logo printed all over its silvered exterior.

"What was the name again of this notorious crook we're about to meet?" she asked.

"I wouldn't call him a crook, Connie, at least while we're in Japan. We're about to experience a formal Japanese tea ceremony with Masa Kondo, age eighty-two, and his equally famous wife, age sixty-two, a renowned geisha, musician, and poet—until she married Kondo. Quite apart from him, and his notoriety, it's a great honor in Japan to meet her, and should be for you too. She is considered a 'living national treasure.'"

When Connie had opened her friend's gift on the plane, she had carefully rewrapped it in the original paper and ribbon. She really didn't know why—women just do these things, instinctively. And now she was so glad she had. This was the appropriate American gift for the geisha.

Connie was well-enough read to know that geishas have nothing to do with sex; they are the highest paid entertainers in all Japan, having trained a lifetime in the traditional folk instruments: the flute, the lute, and the ancient harp. They have to be skilled in the accompanying accomplishments of poetry and dance, and often published in the former. And they have spent years perfecting their appearance and comportment, so they are elegance personified. They personally embody the essence of the eighteenth-century Edo Period, all of the beauty of old Japan.

Nothing said "American" like Michael Kors. By good fortune, Connie had the perfect gift for a Japanese woman whose husband's initials were MK! She took off her friend's card, thanked her lucky stars, and brought the gift with her.

As they were getting into the embassy limousine, the driver asked, "Admiral, flags or no flags?"

"Flags today, please," replied the admiral. "This one is official."

After the driver-body guard returned to the front seat from placing the US flag and the Japanese flag on the little chrome stanchions on either side of the front hood of the limousine, he said "Admiral, are you sure about this address?"

"No," replied Alex. "All I'm sure about is that it is the address I was given by the Okura manager. Why?"

"Well, it's not the address of a private home. It's the address of an old Shinto shrine," replied the driver.

"Let's just go there and see what happens," said Alex.

When the limo, flags flying, pulled up in front of the small and clearly ancient Shinto shrine, an old, senior priest stepped up and bowed deeply, waiting for the driver to open the door. As Alex stepped out, the priest said in perfect English, "Admiral Rostov, you are welcome here," and then turning to Connie, who followed Alex, added "We are doubly fortunate that you chose to accompany your husband today, Mrs. Rostov. Please follow me through the shrine."

The priest led them through the shrine, amongst a scattering of pigeons, pilgrims, priests, and monks, around the central temple, the huge bells and swinging logs to ring them, the storage sheds filled with offerings of sacks of rice, the prayer papers tied to trees and fences, the drawings and paintings of horses, especially white horses, speeding express prayers to the gods, and finally to a back fence and a modest gong, which he hit resoundingly.

After a moment's wait, the gate was opened, the priest bowed farewell as they passed through, and they were led on by a comely woman of perhaps sixty years in a simple peasant blue shift and head scarf.

When they looked up, they were greeted by a vision so ethereal, so perfect in its beauty that they simply stopped dead in their tracks, and Connie instinctively reached out for Alex's hand. They had never encountered anything like it before in their lives; yet they both realized they were in the presence of something extraordinary. It was a big, two-story, early eighteenth-century Edo Period farmhouse. All wood. Not a nail in it, as they would later learn. Mortise and tenon construction throughout, held together with wooden keys and pegs. A great, high, thick thatch roof. Large, shuttered windows to let in the light and air, keep out the rain and snow, and allow the indoors to be part of the outdoors as much as possible. There was a covered well, a two-wheel horse cart, minus the horse, and a goat and a few brightly colored chickens nearby. When Connie had partly recovered her composure, she turned to Alex and said, "We've found the heart of old Tokyo."

CHRONICLE LVII.

"Ah, but you haven't!" said a voice from off to their left.

A beautiful Japanese woman in a stunning *nishiki-de* kimono stepped out from behind the bougainvillea hedge, smiled, and continued in perfect English: "In fact, this old farmhouse was brought piece by piece and board by board from the southern tip of Kyushu, where it surely would have deteriorated in the milder, more humid climate. I fell in love with it the first time I saw it, and immediately told my husband. After months of negotiations, he managed to buy it for the two of us to retire to. And a few years later it turned up here. You have no idea how much it means to us!"

"I think I can imagine," said Connie.

"After we are both gone," continued the wife of the old *oyabun*, "it will officially become a museum dedicated to Japanese craftsmen."

"It is quite simply the most beautiful home I have ever seen," said Alex.

"Then you must both come in, and meet my husband," said the ageless, lovely woman. "I tend to judge our infrequent visitors by their first reactions to this old homestead, and you two have certainly passed the test."

Once inside, introductions were made, everyone was seated in front of a huge fireplace beneath a beamed ceiling, awaiting the elaborate tea ceremony to be served formally to the four of them: an old man, the godfather of Japanese yakuza; his ethereal beauty of a wife, considered a national treasure of Japan; a Russian admiral now representing an American president; and the American wife of a late Swiss banker, now married to the admiral—all politely awaiting the age-old ritual of preparing and drinking Japanese green tea.

Alex reached his right hand up to his forehead, wiped his open palm down across his eyes, then his nose and mouth, and said, "Kondo-sensei, I am here representing my president with a message and a request, but I cannot express myself until I begin to recover from seeing the beauty of your home, and the honor of meeting your wife."

Connie had played bridge and poker with and against her former husband for years, and as she invariably won, she was inordinately proud of her ability to spot "tells." She picked up three from her host, right off the bat, on the words "sensei," "home," and "wife." He turned to his wife, asking for a translation of Alex's opening gambit, but Connie knew from the "tells" that he understood English even if he chose not to speak it. While his wife translated Alex's words into Japanese, Connie caught Alex's eye and deftly nodded her approval.

The old man leaned over and spoke at some length with his wife. She translated for the benefit of their two guests:

"My husband suggests that if we are ever to speak *dusha-dushe*, or soul to soul as you Russians say, perhaps we should forgo the politeness of the Japanese green tea ceremony and go straight to the vodka. As it happens, my husband has a few bottles of *starka*, a gift from an old friend. Mrs. Rostov, this is a very old, smooth vodka that my husband has gotten out on only one other occasion, to my memory. While you and I need not keep up with the men, we do need to at least join in the first toast, as it will be important."

Connie nodded and smiled concurrence, having no idea what was coming next.

Almost magically, iced vodka bottles and glasses appeared, together with bits of pickled Japanese herring, onions, little pickles, tiny potatoes the size of marbles, and a delicious looking coarse black bread. The old man had chosen to honor Alex's Russian heritage, used the appropriate

Russian expression, and—as his guest—Alex was moved by this exceptional gesture.

Glasses were poured, and the old man paused, as if making up his mind about something. Then, once decided, he forged ahead. He raised his glass, signaling he wished to make a toast. And then in perfect, unaccented English, he said: "To the man who provided this vodka, our mutual friend and mentor, and I trust now our spiritual guide, General Georgiy Krapotkin!"

Alex was so stunned he almost forgot to toss back the wonderful, dark, cold *starka* to Georgiy's memory. Almost.

CHRONICLE LVIII.

If the old man was looking to catch his visitors off guard, he had clearly succeeded. First the house, then the wife, and now this revelation. "You knew Georgiy?" asked Alex.

"I knew him as Gosha, his affectionate family nickname, as I first met him with his father when he was twelve. And the last time I saw him, he brought me a few bottles of this vodka and sat in that chair you are sitting in now. He explained to me that you and he were about to preempt the theft of strategic nuclear warheads from the Soviet depot in Ukraine, and asked if I thought he could park them in the Kurile Islands, with my help.

"I replied that I would gladly help him, but that those islands were a poor choice. While Russia deemed them to be Russian, in fact they're inhabited by Japanese fishermen and their families and have been for over a hundred years. The arrival of any Soviet craft, much less your submarine, Admiral, would create quite a stir—and every one of those fishing boats has a radio!

"That was our final time together. The next news I received was of his death on Vieques. That was the only other time we opened his vodka. But here, I'm being a poor host. We must drink again to his memory!"

said the old man, pouring the glasses to the rim all around. And once that was accomplished, Kondo-sensei continued: "So, Admiral, who's stealing what from whom this time?"

Alex summarized their case to date, and—without attribution—provided the analysis of why they thought it was probably not the work of the far-right, despite the clues of a disappearing ninja in Rome and an antique samurai sword in Tokyo clearly pointing in that direction. He added that they were following up separately on the Japanese developer of the hi-tech chameleon outfit used by the ninja. And then Alex played his hole card by concluding that the US president requested Kondo-sensei's advice and counsel regarding who among the Japanese yakuza might attempt the theft of the plutonium upon its arrival at Nagasaki.

There was a long pause while Kondo-sensei pondered the question, using the time to pour yet another round of vodka. When he had gathered his thoughts, he raised his glass and said, "To the president, for the honor he does me in asking my help, for the balls he has in taking such a direct approach to resolving such a delicate matter, and for the man he picked to carry out his mission! I would not have expected this in a thousand years. But I will give you all the help I can.

"First, give me a day to confirm your theory that the *nyoku* right-wing political groups are innocent of complicity or collusion. I hope you are right.

"Second, I will of course use my own sources to endeavor to find any yakuza connection. The fact that I do not already know of one means that the chances of finding one are slim, as I pride myself on being well-informed, even though I am long since out of 'the game.' Again, I shall need no more than one day.

"Thirdly, while I understand your thinking as you've explained it to me, I get the feeling we're both missing something. I agree the greater threat was terrorist attack en route, and that Lieutenant Ito cleverly obviated that by changing route, and indeed the rules of the game.

"But attacking the two ships in Japanese waters strikes me as sheer folly, unless there's something here we're not seeing. Moreover, if this is a yakuza operation, murder in Rome is a long and uncharacteristic reach for the yakuza. I find it surprisingly bold. In any case, however, you have my help, and I will be in touch tomorrow at the latest."

As Connie and Alex rose to leave, the beautiful wife of Kondo-sensei said, "I still owe you tea, Connie, if I may call you that. Please call me Aoi. I understand you have two girlfriends staying with you at the Okura. Why not bring them and come back tomorrow at three o'clock, and I will introduce you to something of old Japan."

"Nothing would please me more!" said Connie.

As Kondo-sensei extended his hand, Alex realized it contained something. "This is a dedicated, encrypted phone that will allow you to reach me, and I you, without our official friends—on your side or mine—able to hear us. It's quite advanced, so please don't lose it. I'd like to maintain the advantage as long as I can!"

"Thank you, Sensei," said Alex, and accepted a piece of technology he did not even know existed.

I wonder how she knew about Sure and Em, thought Connie.

CHRONICLE LIX.

The next day Connie felt guilty and said so. Here she was, dragging Em and Sure away from the strategy and logistics planning at the monastery, to go back and visit Aoi, when they should all be involved in preparing for their early departure the next day. Perhaps she should just phone Aoi and beg off.

"Absolutely not," said Alex. "Consider your mission an intelligence-gathering exercise, and a bonding experience with a woman whom any Japanese would give his or her right arm to spend some time with! We've got our preparations under control. There's a limit to what we can do but wait. Go. Look. Listen. Report back. I love you. Goodbye!"

It turned out to be a felicitous decision. Sure and Em were in love with what they saw and learned from the moment they arrived at the ancient Shinto shrine. Connie had not realized how much she had been affected by the old farmhouse until she saw it a second time, through the younger eyes of her two enthusiastic and less-reserved friends. And Aoi pulled out all the stops to teach them about what they were seeing, its origins and history. It was an afternoon that the three Americans would never forget.

It was also a most un-Japanese experience for Aoi. She was not at all accustomed to American directness, openness, frankness, and certainly not to the youthful and totally refreshing enthusiasm these women shared with her—as if all four of them were conspiring together. She astonished herself when she offered to reveal some of the secrets of the Japanese tea ceremony. She would only do this for a daughter—if she had a daughter. And here she was sharing age-old secrets with foreigners. How could she? How could she!

Well, she was lonely, and missed seeing other women. The joy and appreciation of what she had to teach and show these three new acquaintances was so infectious. They loved learning so much. That was it! The indefatigable curiosity, the probing intellect of the American female. What a different breed from their repressed and diminished Japanese counterparts!

So she told them secrets. How the tea ceremony had evolved over more than a thousand years, and on the surface was simply an expression of respect and etiquette through grace and discipline. But underneath that surface was a strong Zen aesthetic of "*wabi*" and "*sabi.*" Wabi was inner strength in the form of humility, simplicity, quiet, and sober refinement, while sabi was characterized by the exterior or material side of life that was open, worn, weathered, asymetric, imperfect. The implements of the tea ceremony, the studied movements, even its history all reflected the interplay of these two transformative forces.

It was then that Connie bowled her over by saying, "Just like your home! You've just described why I love your home so much! It's the combination of sabis and wabis!"

And here I'm supposed to be teaching you, thought Aoi.

Aoi went on to explain that often non-Japanese got the tea ceremony all wrong. First, they thought it was a ritual about drinking tea; and second, they thought it was an elaborate ceremony to honor guests. Neither conclusion was correct—but both reflected the egocentric philosophies of Western thought.

She told them that the tea ceremony can take half a dozen forms, from the relatively informal and brief, to the most formal and elaborate, lasting four hours or more. But in each of them, there is an interplay of the traditional movements and gestures, implements and, importantly, the setting—from the tea bowls, the caddy and scoop, whisk, iron teapot, and water ladle, to the hanging scroll and its calligraphy—often written by Zen Buddhist priests emphasizing harmony, respect, purity, and tranquility—to the "*chabana*" or tea flower arrangement, and the highly embroidered kimono worn by the host. The interplay of all these elements says it's not about you, it's about one thousand years of doing this, fifty generations of tradition, each seeking to honor those who have gone before and related to the same transformative forces of wabi and sabi.

"Give me a concrete example," said Sure, in typical American style.

Aoi replied, "You've noticed how sparse and studied and elegant our flower arrangements are. But you may not have noticed that when petals drop, they are never removed. They are an essential part of the arrangement; they complete the picture."

After tea, Aoi had invited one of her former protégées, a beautiful young geisha, published poet, and recorded harpist, to perform for the four of them. (Had it not been done simply as a favor for Aoi, her Sensei, the cost to a Japanese host would have approached the price of a small car.) Her guests were enchanted with the performance, especially when afterward she submitted to their questions, and astonished them further by revealing that it took three hours and four assistants for her to prepare her hair and makeup for Aoi's little party.

Later in the afternoon, when Sure asked so very directly, "What has your husband not done yet that he still wishes to do?"

Aoi had no hesitation in replying, "I know he's been reading about a new heart procedure developed at Cedars Lebanon that his doctors say is appropriate. And, of course, I know he has longed to take me to Las Vegas for years. But other than that, I think he's quite at peace with himself and his life."

"What prevents him for fulfilling those two wishes?" asked Connie in all innocence.

"Why, the FBI," said Aoi. "He's on their NO ENTRY list."

"Nice tea," said Connie.

CHRONICLE LX.

Connie, Em, and Sure returned directly to the Tokyo Priory of the Christopherians to find everyone awaiting them. Alex recounted what had transpired in their planning so far, saying that they should all be prepared for an early departure for Nagasaki the following morning. They had chosen the Unzen Miyazaki Ryokan as their base of operations, a comfortable inn and spa about forty-five minutes by car from the port of Nagasaki, far enough for them not to be noticed but close enough to gain port access quickly. More importantly, the inn was just two kilometers up the mountain from the Unzen Police Station, which was on the water in Tachibana Bay, just around the peninsula from Nagasaki Harbour and the port. The station served the Marine Police, the Coast Guard, and the municipal police, and had several large docks. Their helicopters would land them there, and two rental cars would be available for them from there on.

As an old municipal police hand, Colonel Asahi Onishi had to repress the urge to stand at attention to give his report to the little group of coconspirators, when his turn came to fill everyone in on what he had learned. "This turned out to be one of the most difficult interviews of my career," he began. "At first, I was refused an appointment. Even when I showed up in person, I was told the chairman was indisposed. After formally presenting my credentials and insisting officially, I was shown to his outer office, where all of his personal staff seemed to be treating the situation as if he was ill. When he finally relented and agreed to see me, I must admit he looked terrible.

"At first, he would not let me question him, just insisting he had nothing to say to me. I asked all of his hovering staff to leave us, closed the door to his office, looked around until I found a liquor cabinet, poured him a whiskey, and just sat down and waited. He looked at me for a long time without saying a word. I said, 'Whatever it is, I'm here to help.'

"His hand began to tremble. He picked up the whiskey, drank it, and began to weep convulsively. 'They've kidnapped my youngest son! They said if I talk with the police they will kill him.' Then he opened his briefcase and showed me a photo of a boy of about sixteen holding up a newspaper. He said he got one of them every three days as proof of life. And then he started sobbing again and handed me a rolled-up handkerchief. 'And my wife was handed this when she was in the grocery store, as proof they mean business! Can you imagine that cruelty, and how she felt?' I could guess what was in the little bundle but had to make sure. It was a severed little finger."

"So," concluded Asahi, "we are in a new ballgame. We must add extortion and kidnapping to murder and whatever else they have planned. They demanded that the chairman give them the prototype chameleon suit, and he did so personally. But they have not returned his son. That was almost a month ago. And now he is so distraught he does not know what to do. Moreover, he could not enlighten me on who 'they' are, except to say he suspects they are yakuza. The only break we caught in the case is that in one of the proof-of-life photos with a newspaper showing the date, there appears to be a second captive. I'm having my people run a photo recognition scan against teenage students, as it was of a young girl about fourteen or fifteeen. It's the only lead to come out of the interview."

Alex said, "We're still all questions and no answers. Time is short, and day after tomorrow we need to be in Nagasaki, ready for whatever happens. Tom has brought me some advanced gear that may prove helpful and has been trained up on its use. I'll have to learn on the fly, literally. Tom, I need you to give me a short course later today.

"Asahi, I need you to request a patrol craft in Nagasaki from the Coast Guard, a small, fast craft that can carry all of us. I know it won't have any serious armament, but it must have a major, seaworthy spotlight, 220-240 volts. That shouldn't be difficult, as almost every Coast Guard vessel has at least one of them."

It was at this point that Alex was taken off guard by the ringing of the little phone he had been given the previous day. He answered, and heard: "Alex, this is Masa. Please forgive the familiarity, but I hate using last names, even if we are encrypted. I've done my homework. You were right. There is a yakuza connection, but it's not the old guard; it's with the new thugs. They have no allegiances or loyalties. They give an honorable and ancient tradition a bad name. If we could get rid of them or control them we would; but so far we've not been able to.

"And there's a foreign connection as well. That's where the money is coming from. But I have no further information on that, or who it is, at this point.

"What I did learn is that they have kidnapped the fourteen-year-old daughter of the CEO of Nagasaki's fishing fleet. He owns a huge refrigerator and packing vessel and a fleet of fishing boats, all based in Nagasaki. I'm told they are in port as we speak."

And then the old man again surprised the admiral by asking, "Where do you think the choke point will be?"

"My guess is the Megami Ohashi Bridge," said Alex. "It's the narrowest point in Nagasaki Bay—before you reach the port. We plan to travel to Nagasaki tomorrow, and be prepared for anything the following morning, and every morning thereafter, until the plutonium arrives."

"You'll need a spotter," said Masa. "The bridge is the highest point in the area. I'll be up there with a good scope and will call you."

Alex was about to thank the old man, when he realized the line was already dead. He reported the gist of his conversation with Kondo-sensei to the group, and then continued.

"Father Takashi, I need to sit down with you and some naval charts and study Nagasaki's surrounding waters. We want to position ourselves, and the patrol craft Asahi is requesting, somewhere outside of Nagasaki Bay, far enough from the harbor to allow whatever these guys are planning to transpire without our getting caught up in it, but close enough so that we can intervene if we can do any good. Clearly we're not strong enough to prevent an attack, but we might be able to outflank it. Speaking of which, I've asked an old friend for help, and if I hear back, I'll fill you in. Where can we quickly get our hands on naval charts of Nagasaki?"

Tom leaned toward Connie and quietly said, "I guess we know now why Alex got to be an admiral!"

Father Takashi spoke up: "Charts are in the priory library. They're seventeenth- and eighteenth-century Edo Period charts, but the waters haven't changed, and I'll read the Japanese for you."

"One last point," added Alex, "Connie, Em, Sure—it would help if the three of you could tell us anything you may have learned this afternoon that might give us some leverage or insight into Kondo-sensei. Yesterday, when he told us he had long been 'out of the game,' Connie picked up a contradictory 'tell,' which may mean he's lying, or just wishful thinking."

As Sure had asked the key question of Aoi, Connie signaled her to take the lead in responding to Alex.

CHRONICLE LXI.

At six the next morning, after Alex and Connie had showered and were having a quick Continental breakfast, while packing up their last items and closing up their suitcases, Alex said, "I've got good news and bad news: Which first?"

"The bad, of course," replied Connie.

"I won't be with you during the action tomorrow, or the day after, whenever it occurs," confessed Alex.

"And why?' asked Connie, with some asperity.

"Because you're the best photographer we've got. I need you up on the Nagasaki bridge directly overlooking the port, recording what goes on, so we can track and prove who's doing what to whom."

"No way, José! I'm sticking with you."

"Of course," added Alex, "you won't be alone. The *oyabun*, Kondo-sensei, will be up there with you—undoubtedly well-guarded—with a good scope, acting as a spotter for us. It's the highest point around, and he's volunteered to serve as lookout."

"Well, why didn't you start with that! I get to be with the Godfather up with the angels while you and the boys and girls float around down below with the fishes. I like it. So what's the better news?"

"I've just bought you a new camera, another Lumix like the one you brought, but this one's the new FZ270, with a sixty-power stabilized optical zoom. It's tiny compared to a big camcorder, so you shouldn't be noticed; but it will give us all we need, in stills or video. The only problem is that you may be spending two full days on the sidewalk of that bridge, with the *oyabun*."

"Before we leave, I'll just have a little chat with that nice Okura assistant manager of ours," said Connie.

A short while later, after they had checked out and thanked everyone, Alex and Connie were pleased by the convenience of having the municipal police on their side. All they had to do was take the elevator to the roof of the Okura, where Colonel Asahi Onishi awaited with the second helicopter, on the Okura's rooftop helipad. The first 'copter, with Cardinal Gallagher, Father Takashi, Emery Peele, and Surely Devine aboard, according to the manifest, had departed five minutes earlier, bound for Nagasaki Prefecture's Unzen Police Station.

En route, Asahi gave the pilot detailed instructions, and an hour later, upon arrival over Nagasaki peninsula, he began briefing Alex and Connie and the other helicopter by radio link:

"Below us is a long north-south oriented cape that ends on its southern tip in a long bay and harbor, Nagasaki, which means long cape. Kyushu is Japan's most southwestern island, and Nagasaki is its best natural harbor, closest to the Asian mainland. That means if you are coming to Japan from China, Korea, Southeast Asia, north in the China Sea, then Nagasaki is your first, best Japanese port. During the war, Japan's Imperial Fleet was based here, which made Nagasaki a prime target for the Allies.

"As we fly south, we'll pass over the city of Nagasaki, about a half million people including suburbs; but the city center itself, the valley floor between the two mountain ranges and the two rivers, is only about four square miles. The long bay extends right up into the city, but the shipping port is halfway down the bay on the east side, your left, just before that lovely new bridge. It's the Megami Ohashi Bridge, which reminds everyone of San Francisco's Golden Gate, even though it's only one-third the size. Connie and Kondo-sensei will be stationed there tomorrow, and if necessary, the following day.

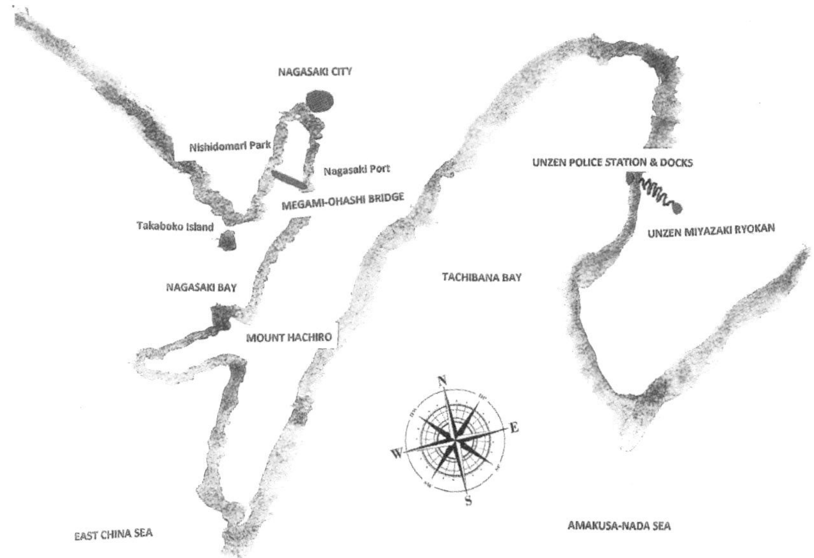

"If you will look down and to the left, as we fly over the port, you will see the large refrigerator and packing ship that Kondo-sensei referred to, the one with the yellow and blue house flag; and each of those fishing vessels in the port with the same flag—there must be forty of them—belong to the same company. Its CEO's daughter has been abducted, according to Kondo-sensei.

"Before we fly over the bridge, look across the bay to your right. That is Nishidomari Park, the huge city park that extends to the other side of the bridge and forms the tip of the cape. It is here that Alex thinks there is a natural 'choke point,' the ideal spot to attack—if you're planning to attack—because it's the narrowest point in the bay, and it gets quite shallow on the Nishidomari Park side.

"Now, as we fly over the bridge, Connie, you'll see that traffic isn't too bad, and that you have wide sidewalks on both sides. I've brought two little folding stools we use for stakeouts for you and Kondo-sensei, as that is essentially what you will be doing most of the time.

"After the bridge, we exit the bay, and go out to sea, passing a small island on our right. That's Takaboko Island, and Alex plans to stage our two small craft there early tomorrow to be ready for whatever may happen. The island's not very big but should give us ample cover.

"But now we're going to bank left, or east, fly over the remains of this little peninsula, and here we are at another bay, Tachibana Bay. You can see directly ahead of us across the bay, down at the shoreline, the Unzen Police Station and its series of docks, where we'll be landing in a few moments. And if you'll look a couple of kilometers directly up the mountain from the police station, following that little road, you will see the Unzen Miyazaki Ryokan. I've asked the pilot to overfly it, without getting too close so as not to disturb the guests, so you can enjoy from the air where you will be staying."

As they flew discreetly near the ryokan, and Connie looked down on the traditional inn and spa, her impression was of the Okura's beautiful garden, but much larger, with open-air hot spring baths scattered about. "Another hardship assignment!" she said to Alex.

CHRONICLE LXII.

They landed on the pier of the Unzen Police Station and were greeted by Major Watanabe of the Maritime Police, who showed them the Coast Guard cutter that had been placed at their disposal, introduced them to Captain Nishihara and his crew, and added that his Maritime Police team and accompanying escort vessel would be arriving later that morning. Meanwhile, the two civilian rental cars were parked out front, and the Miyazaki Ryokan awaited their arrival just up the road.

Alex was pleased to learn that the cutter, with a crew of six, had not one but two 240-volt spotlights, and that it could do almost thirty knots if it had to. *And it might have to*, he thought.

Father Takashi asked if he could drive one of the cars, and of course all agreed. Asahi took the wheel of the other and led the way. When Father Takashi hadn't arrived after ten minutes, on a journey of two kilometers to the ryokan, Asahi became concerned—until Father Takashi appeared around the last bend in the road, and pulled up at the ryokan, grinning from ear to ear.

As it turned out, the good father had never driven a car before, had no license, and had just broken a good half dozen laws, to the acute embarrassment of Asahi, and the delight of everyone else.

They all entered the ryokan in great good humor and were promptly shown to their Japanese-style rooms on the garden, each by a hostess in traditional kimono, who served their guests a welcoming tea. Their hostesses informed each of them that lunch would be served in the garden momentarily for them as a group, but that dinner would be served individually in their rooms, as it was understood they would be going to bed early in order to rise at 4:00 a.m.

They were offered a pleasant lunch of sushi, sashimi, and tempura *à volonté*, seated at a round table for seven in the garden, accompanied by several choices of tea, a half dozen possible sakes, or a house white wine. Connie, Tom, Father Takashi, and Alex opted for the house white. "Ah," said Father Takashi, after seeing the color and tasting the wine. "It's a Tomi! We are drinking a Japanese wine, one that is much prized. How delightful."

"I didn't know the Japanese made wine," said Tom.

"It took us a long time to learn," responded Father Takashi. "The vines arrived here from the Middle East in trade over a thousand years ago, and we began growing grapes in modest quantities. But we didn't start to press them for wine until after the Meiji Revolution of 1868, and the reopening of Japan to the West after two hundred years of living as a closed society. How cut off from the rest of the world were we? Well, we didn't know wine was made from grapes. And we thought silver was three times more valuable than gold. It was only after Commodore Perry arrived that we learned.

"This Tomi wine comes from Kai, near Mount Fuji. It's from an old grape called Koshu, with a thick skin to withstand all our rain; and it produces a fruity wine that's drunk young and served with exactly what we have here—raw and cooked fish, flavored with sauces like soy or miso. I'm pleased you have a chance to try it."

Alex asked everyone to join him after lunch for an orientation cruise aboard the Coast Guard cutter. He planned to cross Tachibana Bay, round Nagasaki Cape, and go as far toward the harbor as south of Takaboko Island. He did not want to approach the island, Nagasaki Bay, or the port any closer than that, as he was certain the opposition would be watching, but that would at least give everyone a geographical orientation as to what's where, so that in the following days, directions and compass points would not be confusing.

Essentially, he added, they would be seeing in reverse what Asahi had pointed out to them from the air. And as they had been in two different helicopters at the time, this would provide an opportunity for them to ask questions.

Finally, he concluded, he wanted to be back early, so that they could all relax, bathe, walk in the garden, and enjoy some peace and tranquility before an early bedtime, and the following few days. "What you are about to face are the most debilitating parts of any battle. Do not underestimate them for a moment. They are subversive. They can be crippling.

"It's the waiting and the uncertainty. If we let them get to us, we are lost from the start. And the odds are bad enough already. Take care of yourself in this regard. And then take care of each other."

"Alex," said Connie, "I have a tough question. I know you told us, me in particular, to be discreet and not stand out. Especially up on that bridge. But if it's a choice between being invisible and being comfortable, what should we do?"

"Choose comfort, by all means," concluded Alex. "We're too long in the tooth to be uncomfortable while we save the world out of the goodness of our hearts."

"I'm going to hold you to that," said Connie.

CHRONICLE LXIII.

"If you want to be popular," Alex said quietly to Connie the next morning, "don't make people get up at 4:00 a.m." The dry run yesterday afternoon had been uneventful, even pleasant. And the early night clearly suited everyone, after a long and busy day. But it was now 4:30 a.m., and the little group was gathered rather grumpily in the lobby of the ryokan, where exceptionally their host had permitted coffee, juice, toast, and marmalade to be made available at this un-spa-like hour.

The gracious lady had, however, agreed the night before to have the kitchen prepare six boxed Japanese "picnic lunches" for them to take on their "outing." Connie had declined, but everyone else was happy to see that the boxes were ready for them, next to the desperately needed coffee.

Before leaving, Sure and Em called for a collective decision of the group, which they later agreed was probably the smartest group decision made all day. They decided that as the Unzen Police Station and their awaiting cutter were on the bay at the foot of a two-kilometer steep downhill drive, Father Takashi would not get to drive this time.

Em and Sure were given the driving duty, as they appeared the most alert of the bunch at this hour, and they safely wended their way down the mountain again. There, a Maritime Police officer took the wheel of one of the cars to deliver Connie to the middle of the Megami Ohashi Bridge. He estimated that she would be in position a good half hour before Major Watanabe and Captain Nishihara had the Maritime Police cutter in place behind Takaboko Island with the rest of the group.

Before leaving the dock, Alex asked Father Takashi to check his personal cell phone reception, which turned out to be good. Alex then asked the father to try calling his coconspirator and secret weapon, his friend and parishioner Lt. Mamoru Ito, serving as captain of the *Shiki-shima*. While Lt. Ito was sworn not to break radio silence, Father Onishi had assured Alex that if the lieutenant saw he had an incoming call from Father Takashi, he would answer. The problem was these phones were not advanced satellite phones but simple cell phones. They would need to be in range. Alex had said that in his experience that would be no more than thirty nautical miles out to sea. If they could reach Lt. Ito, they could warn him to expect some sort of attack in or near Nagasaki Bay. Father Takashi tried his phone, but no luck.

They were still a good ten miles from Takaboko Island when Alex's special little phone rang, and he knew it was Kondo-sensei calling. "Alex, Masa. I'm set up on the seaward side in the center of the bridge, with a good scope. Where are you?"

"We're about ten miles south east of Takaboko Island, and will be coming up behind it shortly, staying to the southwest, out of sight. I didn't get a chance to tell you last time we talked, but Connie will be joining you on the bridge with a camera to record things," said Alex.

"Good idea—oh, and here she is now. I'll call you back."

Just then Alex's second phone rang. It was Connie: "I'm on the bridge, right at the center on the south side, and have found you-know-who. Call you back."

Hope they get along, thought Alex to himself, *they're both hard-headed individuals, and it's a long way down.*

Connie's driver opened the trunk of the car and took out the two folding stools that Asahi had promised. "That's thoughtful," said Masa.

"You ain't seen nothin' yet!" exclaimed Connie with a big grin.

I wonder what that means? wondered Masa. *Must be some American colloquialism.*

But at his age, with a long day ahead of him, and perhaps another after that, he clearly relished the thought of occasionally being able to rest his old bones on the canvas stool. He motioned to his companion, who stood discreetly twenty feet to his left, and introduced her to Connie.

"Connie, I would like you to meet the only other woman in my life. Don't worry, Aoi knows and approves. This woman would be our family's second living national treasure, if she existed. She does not exist. The diminutive woman I introduce to you is a true Sensei. But she is a creature of folklore, myth, legend—and regrettably now, Hollywood. Mrs. Rostov, may I present Kunoichi Shinobi, as she is properly addressed. Shinobi-sensei—may I introduce Connie Rostov, wife of Admiral Alex Rostov, and the former Connie Zimmerman." The Sensei bowed formally, and without saying a word returned to her post twenty feet away.

"Were you trying to tell me she is a ninja?" asked Connie, somewhat confused.

"I was trying to tell you there are no ninja. They are a figment of legend and folklore, now garnished by greedy filmmakers. But this diminutive woman of a certain age is more powerful, highly trained, disciplined, and sensitive than anyone else I have ever met. Aoi and I are in awe of her. She is not a ninja but a *shinobi-no-mono*, the antithesis of a *samurai.* While the old samurai obeyed strict rules of honor, dress, weapons, and combat, the shinobi breaks all rules—including rules of nature. She can become invisible by being unnoticed. She can walk on water or fly with a kite. A perfect spy, she can infiltrate anywhere in almost any disguise. And her physical abilities are astounding. She appears to us mere mortals as supernatural or even superhuman. But she is simply highly trained, diligent in her practice, and devoted to her eighth century, over 1,400-year-old traditions. You and I are in safe hands."

Periodically, Masa checked the spotting scope on its tripod, pointed south down the Nagasaki Bay and out to sea. He showed it to Connie and taught her how to focus it for her eyes.

Then they both became aware of a large white truck very slowly approaching them in the inside lane. The truck had a crane on the back and carried a row of new construction-site portable metal bathrooms. When they reached Connie, two white suited and white gloved attendants hopped off the truck, the crane popped one of the portable johns onto the sidewalk, the two attendants skidded it over to the railing, and one of them came over to Connie, showed her his clipboard with a fax with her photograph on it, and said something in Japanese.

"He says he's sorry they are fifteen minutes late, but they had the wrong side of the bridge at first. No signature necessary, as the Okura prepaid, and ordered that if the photo matched, just drop off the unit," translated Masa, totally flummoxed by what was happening.

"Arigato!" said Connie, and then turned to Masa as the truck pulled away. "I thought as long as we were going to be here together for so long a time, we might as well be comfortable. So I ordered this at the Okura before we left Tokyo."

"No wonder we lost the war," thought Kono-sensei to himself, surreptitiously taking an empty soup can from his pocket and tossing it over the railing to the waters below.

Just then Masa's "Alex phone" rang. "Haven't heard back from you. How's it going?" asked Alex.

"Fine," replied Masa. "Connie is a delight, and we've been talking. Nothing in sight on the scope to report."

"I hope Connie doesn't attract too much attention as an American photographer on that bridge," said Alex.

Masa caught Connie's eye, and said, "Fear not, your wife is the soul of discretion, Alex." And then he winked. Later he reflected he did this before he knew what would happen next.

CHRONICLE LXIV.

By noon, the group on board the cutter was running out of things to do in preparation for—they didn't know what. Alex had received a call on his third phone, his satellite phone, and was able to tell his companions that the friend he had mentioned earlier had indeed just checked in. If all else failed, and they lost control of the plutonium to foreign terrorists, they still had one ace in the hole. He would like to tell them more but could not. What he could say is that their tenuous position had just gotten a little stronger.

Tom had tested and retested the little heli-drone, taking it out to 1,500 yards, up to 1,500 feet, and was quite comfortable now "threading the needle" as they called it, which meant bringing it in close to windows and portholes to use its versatile camera to peer inside—in this case, their own cutter's cabins, and those of the accompanying escort vessel, for practice. He was now recharging the back-up batteries.

This little suitcase-sized drone was one of the two special pieces of equipment that he had carried as a courier to Tokyo for Alex, and was his personal favorite, the one he had chosen to be trained on at the agency before he left Washington this last time. This weapon was non-lethal. It carried the advanced, weaponized propofol that could knock out anyone for thirty to sixty minutes, depending on the amount inhaled, in a radius of two hundred feet from the tiny, four-propeller-driven miniature helicopter. He flew it from a book-sized computer, joystick, and laptop screen that gave him a zoom lens on the 'copter's camera.

For their part, Em and Sure had asked the crew to teach them the fine art of throwing a grappling hook and boarding line, a knotted line that might enable them to swing aboard another vessel, even while moving. Their youth and agility proved an advantage; they were quick learners.

They also asked to be shown the basics of the inflated Zodiac rubber boat carried on the stern, with its small, mounted outboard engine. Again, they learned with a minimum of time and fuss.

Alex spent his time wiring up the other suitcase-size weapon system Tom had brought, the sonic emitter, or "bang stick" as Alex called it: a hemispherical, directional pulse gun with an antenna the size of a basketball hoop. It sent a wave of energy at the precise amplitude and frequency that rattled someone's brain against his skull hard enough to knock him unconscious. It had a range of 1,100 yards.

However, it also had two handicaps. If used too long or too often, it could cause a concussion. And if used without protective, over-ear noise-cancelling headphones, the backwash from the antenna would knock out whoever was using it, and whoever was around them.

First invented by the Italians during World War II, and then tried out by the French during the riots of 1968, the weapon's backwash problem was why both nations gave up trying to develop or use the technology further. (The French had seriously hurt twenty-three of their own gendarmes in the Sixth Arrondissement in July of 1968.)

It was only after the agency had found a company in Connecticut that knew how to solve the problem that the nonlethal weapon could be developed without risk to the home team. While it could be used on battery, Alex wanted the full range available, and therefore wired it up to the 240-volt circuit used normally for one of the spotlights.

Meanwhile, Asahi had used the downtime to transfer to the accompanying escort vessel to brief his Maritime Police colleagues on the background, purpose, and risks of their assignment. To a man, they said they understood the importance of success.

And Father Takashi continued to try to reach Lt. Mamoru Ito aboard the *Shiki-shima*, a frustrating task until, just as everyone else was about to have lunch, he heard the voice he knew so well saying, "Moshi Moshi!"

CHRONICLE LXV.

Connie's phone rang. It was Alex. "Father Takashi just reached Lt. Mamoru Ito aboard the *Shiki-shima*. Please pass the word to Kondo-sensei. Father Takashi briefed Lt. Ito in detail about what we have learned so far and passed the phone to me. Ito confirmed that before leaving France, they had reconfigured the storage of the plutonium, and told me to ask Father Takashi about the details. He said he would prepare for a surprise attack, but that there was little he could do that he had not already done. We expect their arrival in about two and a half hours."

"Oh good," said Connie. "That gives us time for lunch."

She filled Masa in on Alex's news, just as a caterer's delivery van pulled up. The crew of three plus driver set up a table, four folding chairs, and table settings for four in short order, asked Connie, Masa, and his companion to be seated, and promptly served them red miso soup, barely seared tuna, with a celadon green sauce on the side made from heavy cream, wasabi, and fresh ginger. There was a sliced cucumber salad with rice wine vinegar, with a sprinkling of edible flowers on top. And the whole accompanied by green tea. Simple, quick, elegant. They bowed politely, promising to return to pick up everything in an hour. Connie had checked her watch. The whole production took less than five minutes. Again, Kondo-sensei just shook his head.

"It's a treat! But why four?" he asked.

"I ordered it in Tokyo at the Okura, and simply guessed that you would have two bodyguards," replied Connie.

Connie caught his incredulity, and said, "We aren't going to do anyone any good unless we keep up our strength. Alex told me if I had to choose between being incognito and being comfortable, to choose the latter. If we are being watched, just think of this as a diversionary tactic. Now eat your soup before it gets cold."

"You like red miso rather than white miso soup?" asked Masa.

"Oh yes," replied Connie. "Red miso has strength of character; white miso soup had always seemed effete to me." At this, Masa laughed so hard Connie was afraid he might choke. He translated for his companion, who made a comment. Masa translated: "She thinks you have the reincarnated soul of a samurai! It's quite a compliment."

Everyone was hungry, having spent a long morning in the open air, and the luncheon was sublime. Kondo-sensei surprised Connie by saying, "Shinobi-no-mono, our companion, tells me she believes she knows who the murderer of Cardinal Matsumoto and Brother Tomoyo is. I described to her in detail the two deaths, as recounted to me, and she said she recognized the work. She is certain that the woman is not a Japanese shinobi, and from the combination of tactics . . . " and here he was interrupted by a harsh exclamation from his companion, " . . . and the obvious lack of certain skills," he translated, "she is convinced that she recognizes the work of a Korean assassin employed by the yakuza."

Shinobi-sensei spat out a harsh exclamation that Connie was sure included the English phrase "chameleon," though pronounced with a strong Japanese accent, a phrase which Masa was about to translate when Connie said: "You don't have to translate that one. I bet she said, 'This woman *needs* a chameleon suit; that's how incompetent she is!'"

Masa laughed until tears formed in the corners of his eyes. Then he translated for Shinobi-sensei, who looked at Connie in a new light, and smiled warmly.

It was then that the police showed up, a Nagasaki Municipal Police car with two white-gloved officers.

Connie looked at Masa and said, "I've got this." She later learned that the senior officer had politely asked how in the world she thought she could camp out on the famous Megami Ohashi Bridge, set up a tin potty, and serve lunch. Connie simply handed them the note she had asked Colonel Asahi Onishi of the Tokyo Metropolitan Police to prepare on his official stationery for just such an eventuality. The senior officer read the note and passed it to his junior. Whatever it said, the reaction was unequivocal. First the junior officer jumped from the driver's seat to join his boss. Then they both saluted crisply, bowed deeply, and left.

All Masa could say was a quiet, "Wow."

Connie picked up her phone and called Alex to relay the news about the possible murderer, suggest he promptly inform Asahi, and at the same time thank him for his note.

Alex promised to do so and asked if everything was all right. Connie replied that if he had paid the Okura bill before leaving, then everything was perfect. Alex said that of course he had and would call back if things changed on his end. When he hung up, once again he pondered the imponderable Connie: Asahi's note? The Okura bill? Would he ever fully understand this woman? He thought not.

CHRONICLE LXVI.

"Lt. Ito suggested that I ask you about the reconfigured plutonium storage," Alex said to Father Takashi. "What's the story?"

"Well, you'll recall that I told you of the meeting on neutral ground—at our monastery—between a representative of Greenpeace and Lt. Ito, to find out if their mutual interests would permit a way to cooperate."

Alex nodded.

"To inspire and perhaps even suggest a way of protecting the plutonium, I recounted how Admiral Stephan Yamamoto had protected the emperor and his priceless cargo in the 1930s, when they sailed from Nagasaki to Rome to meet the pope. Not everyone favored the initiative. In fact, right-wing elements strongly opposed allowing Western religion back into Japan. They argued that it was the enemy of science, and a Trojan horse for colonialism.

"Moreover, the emperor was carrying with him one of the three most valuable, ancient Japanese pottery pieces of the Imperial collection—as a gift to the pope. Those same right-wingers felt it was sacrilege for it to leave Japanese soil. The newspapers had published the timing and route of the trip, and Admiral Yamamoto feared the right wing might try to abort the trip, or even that pirates might attack his vessel to hold the artifact, and the emperor, for ransom."

"So what did he do?" prompted Alex.

"First, he altered the route, without informing anyone—not even the emperor—as he didn't know who in the palace he could trust. And second, he slipped the famous pottery into the straw basket with all of his mundane tea implements, disguising it as of no more value than a common part of his daily tea service."

"Well," said Alex, "it seems Ito-san has followed your advice. But I trust he's not broken international law and safety standards, or risked his crew with radiation poisoning, by taking the plutonium out of the special hundred-kilo casks required by the International Atomic Energy Agency. Those casks are damage resistant in a collision or grounding, fire-resistant up to eight hundred degrees Celsius, and leak-tested down to ten thousand meters of ocean depth. Not perfect, but pretty damn good!"

"I'm sure anything he might have done would not increase risk. Just the contrary," said Father Takashi.

Now that Asahi was back on board, and Alex was into the technical specifications he knew so well, he continued on for everyone's benefit.

"You should all know what we will be seeing today. The *Shiki-shima* is armed with hand-operated 20mm Vulcan machine guns port and starboard, and a couple of dual 35mm anti-aircraft gun turrets fore and aft. If my risk assessment is correct, we have nothing to fear from the air—unless Tom gets careless or the hiccups. So that makes Lt. Ito's main defense guns useless, because as anti-aircraft batteries they can't train downward and fire below the horizon line at something on the sea.

"That leaves his Vulcans, which can be devastating at a thousand rounds per minute. And that's exactly why I believe he won't use them on his fellow countrymen. If he did, Japan's modest Self Defense Force would never recover politically in his lifetime.

"The *Akatsuki Maru*," he continued, "the reconditioned little plutonium-carrying freighter, is essentially unarmed; but even if they added a couple of Vulcans before she left port in France—which is what I would have done—the same analysis applies. They wouldn't risk firing on their own countrymen.

"As to the opposition, I simply have no idea what they will do, much less what they will use. But my best guess is that they will not use overwhelming force in order not to justify overwhelming retaliation. Remember: If they do manage to seize the plutonium, they still have to get it someplace where they can retain it. Our job is of course to stop them if we can, and to free their captives, if they are still alive."

Alex's "Masa phone" rang. "Here they come," announced the *oyabun*. "They're about six miles to the southeast."

CHRONICLE LXVII.

As everyone watched through binoculars from the cutter and its escort vessel tucked to the west of Takaboko Island, Alex couldn't believe what he was seeing. Now he deeply regretted briefing Lt. Ito by phone and doubted Father Takashi's assessment of his brilliance . . . for the lieutenant had reversed the order of the little two-ship convoy! The *Shiki-shima* was leading the *Akatsuke Maru* into port. The armed protector was leading the vulnerable little freighter into the possible trap.

What could Lt. Ito be thinking? Perhaps he thought to take the attackers head-on, and let Alex protect the freighter from the rear. The problem with that plan was that if the opposition did succeed in gaining control of the freighter, the armed *Shiki-shima* would be on the wrong side to prevent a commandeered *Akatsuki Maru* from making a run for open waters and the sea. And Alex and company had no armament that could forstall it. *Who am I to say*, thought Alex, *but it's not what I would have done.*

Masa and Connie watched from above, Masa glued to the scope and Connie clicking away with her new camera. Neither noticed Shinobi-sensei undoing a long, black canvas roll that had been at her feet the whole time where she stood on the bridge.

The two small ships passed Takaboko Island, entered Nagasaki Bay, and continued toward the bridge, without incident. There were pleasure boats about, a seagoing tug over by Nishidomari Park, but the fishing fleet and the big refrigerator and packing ship remained in port, with no sign of activity. *Perhaps there's nothing to fear*, thought Connie. *Wouldn't it be wonderful if we've just over-imagined all this, after two murders?* Nothing continued to happen, and Connie crossed her fingers.

The *Shiki-shima* was almost at the bridge when all hell broke loose. Everything happened at once, and Connie was hard-pressed to photograph it all, though she had to admit she had the perfect vantage point with the camera shooting three frames a second.

The big refrigerator and packing ship came steaming out of the port at flank speed, turned left full rudder, backed down two thirds on its port engine, and continued at flank on its starboard engine. This put it into a skidding maneuver that sent it sideways into the *Shiki-shima*, which being much smaller and lighter, found itself being forced into the shallows near Nishidomari Park. At this point, the sea-going tug that had been idling nearby simply nudged the bow of the *Shiki-shima*, sending it aground.

At the same time, a "cigarette boat," a pleasure craft that could exceed forty knots skimming on top of the water, screamed toward the *Akatsuki Maru*'s port side, a diminutive figure all in white clinging to the bow. The boat slowed abruptly as it reached the freighter, the white figure threw a grappling hook and knotted line and swung aboard. Half-way aboard, the figure just disappeared, turned grey, and blended in with the grey of the freighter's side.

Connie glanced toward Shinobi-sensei, only to find she was gone. She called to Masa, asking where his companion was. Masa pointed to a parasail just above the deck of the *Akatsuki Maru*. Connie started clicking away again. The parasail crashed onto the deck, but through the viewfinder Connie saw Shinobi-sensei had first dropped off and was running toward the bridge, armed with what appeared to be a can of spray paint. Up on the bridge deck, Shinobi-sensei did a pirouette, spraying a fluorescent mist in a cloud around her. A fluorescent head became visible for a moment, and then simply dropped to the deck. Shinobi-sensei disappeared down a steel ladder, picked up her parasail, and leaped off the ship in the direction of Nishidomari Park.

Connie hadn't seen the blows. Later, when she checked the camera, she learned that Shinobi-sensei was not only faster than the naked eye, she was faster than Lumix. The camera had nothing but one woman standing perfectly still looking at a fluorescent head, and then the same woman looking at an empty space. (The coroner would subsequently report that there were two blows that killed the yakuza assassin. The first was a powerful thrust of the hand, fingers straight out and rigid, crushing the larynx and trachea, causing suffocation. The second was an upward thrust of an open hand, with a force of perhaps two hundred pounds, the base of the palm hitting the bridge of the nose, causing an instant lobotomy as it drove the nasal bones into the brain, and brain death before the assassin hit the deck. In effect she was killed twice, once to incapacitate instantly, and the second time to be absolutely certain, both within less than a second.)

Meanwhile, some twenty fishing boats had steamed out of port and swarmed the *Akatsuki Maru*. It collided with three of them, almost capsized one, and had to stop. Forty men swept aboard, guns pointed, but not a shot was fired. The unarmed Japanese sailors simply raised their arms.

By now, the seagoing tug was back from helping with the intentional grounding. While the *Shiki-shima* was double-hulled, and it was not a hard grounding, for the time being at least she had effectively been taken out of the picture.

With the *Akatsuki Maru* dead in the water, the tug assisted as the leader of the boarding party took over the bridge at gunpoint and quickly turned the little freighter around, now heading it back down the bay, toward the open sea, followed closely by the much larger refrigerator and packing vessel.

CHRONICLE LXVIII.

Alex had counted on the superior speed of his Coast Guard cutter and accompanying Maritime Police escort vessel to give him an advantage, but so far the action had played out over a surprisingly small part of the long bay: south of the bridge, and south of the port on the east side just north of the bridge. *Connie must have a perfect view,* he thought; but Alex was following developments closely too, from the screen of Tom's drone, which Tom was flying with admirable dexterity.

While the refrigerator and packing ship used its size, bulk, and kinetic energy to sideswipe the *Shiki-shima* and, with the help of the tug, send her aground, Tom used the time and the distraction of that action to take his drone from window to window and porthole to porthole on the port side of the refrigerator-packer, which Alex thought was the most likely place the opposition would be holding their two teenage hostages. It didn't take long for the drone's camera to spot them through the wardroom window, bound to chairs in the wardroom. Sure and Em were shown where they were, and asked to prepare to swing on board from the cutter on cue, see quickly to their release, and carry them fireman-fashion to the waiting Maritime Police boarding ladders and a jury-rigged sling that—if all went well—would by then be positioned at the stern of the refrigerator-packer.

Alex used the speed of the cutter to race up the east side of the bay while first the tug and then the much larger refrigerator-packer broke off from the grounding maneuver to continue down the bay chasing the *Akatsuki Maru.* Alex allowed the tug to pass by without incident. But with the refrigerator-packer barely underway, it was the ideal point for Alex to give Tom the go-ahead to try the drone's weaponized propofol that the agency was so proud of.

And well it should be, thought Alex, as everyone on the cutter and escort watched the crew of the refrigerator-packer keel over in their tracks on deck. The weaponized gas should dissipate harmlessly within the next four or five minutes, according to Tom.

The drone simply made two passes, fore to aft and back again, and then hovered over the air intake for the bridge. When Alex was reasonably sure that everyone aboard the target vessel, with the possible exception of the engine room crew in the bowels of the ship, had succumbed to a peaceful, pleasant, and dreamless sleep, he moved the cutter in, and matched the slow forward speed of the ship, so that Em and Sure could throw their grappling hooks and boarding lines and climb swiftly aboard. Alex watched the attractive shapes disappear above, remembering a time when he used to be that strong, well-trained, and agile—but quickly got his mind back to business.

Em and Sure were followed up the ropes by two Maritime Police commandos and two Coast Guard officers. The first two would use plastic restraints to cuff and shackle all on board, while the second two would take control of the vessel, turn it about and bring it into port, arrest everyone on board, and impound the vessel.

As soon as the two Coast Guard officers had cut the engines, the Maritime Police escort vessel moved to the stern of the ship, mounted boarding ladders and a canvas sling for the hostages, who would still be anesthetized, and went to the aid of their colleagues, beginning with the engine room and lower spaces that might have to be taken at gunpoint.

Meanwhile, Alex set off after the tug and the *Akatsuki Maru.* As he ordered the Coast Guard cutter to pull abreast of the tug, one of the tug's occupants in its wheelhouse had the temerity to raise an automatic weapon and point it in the direction of the cutter—at which point

Alex, who had gotten everyone to put on his suitcase-full of the special over-ear headphones, pulled the trigger on his "bang stick" and sent a pulse of energy across the two-hundred feet that separated the two boats, knocking out everyone on board the tug and sending the automatic weapon flying.

Quite prepared to do it again, Alex was pleased to see he didn't have to. The cutter quickly pulled up beside the moving tug, and two Coast Guardsmen plus two Maritime Police crossed easily, to repeat the earlier procedure used by their colleagues on the refrigerator-packer ship.

Alex left them to it and continued after the *Akatsuki Maru*. "Here's where it gets really interesting—and risky," said Alex to his remaining team. "If we press on at flank speed, we can catch up with the *Akatsuki Maru* in a few minutes, as we have that high an advantage. If she continues going as fast as she is now, we can't use the propofol with the drone because the speed would dissipate the gas before it did any good. We could use the sonic weapon. It would knock out everyone on board, including the crew as well as the yakuza; and frankly the crew didn't seem to put up much of a fight. Our first priority—after saving the hostages—is to save the plutonium, even if it gives sore heads to the crew. But if we do that now, we'll never know how these crooks thought they could get away with a blatant hijacking in broad daylight, and still manage to escape with 1,700 kilos of plutonium in hundred-kilo IAEA casks, much less who's paying them and where they're taking it.

"Asahi just heard from the Maritime Police escort vessel. Em and Sure have the two hostages safely on board. They're already awake, healthy, and joyful to be alive and freed. Em and Sure are with them. And the escort is on its way back to rejoin us, at flank speed. I suggest we take a brief pause, let them catch up, give the commandeered *Akatsuki Maru* a chance to move toward the mouth of the bay, and follow at a distance of no more than three thousand yards astern." Asahi, Father Takashi, and Tom concurred; and Tom used the break in the action to bring the little drone home to change its batteries, and insert two new propofol cartridges.

Connie saw from the bridge that the Coast Guard cutter was slowing. She turned to ask Masa why that could be and saw Shinobi-sensei standing twenty feet to his left.

CHRONICLE LXIX.

With Em and Sure back on board, Tom felt much better about life, Alex felt happy to have his full crew aboard, and Sure and Em were delighted to have seen some real action and take part in rescuing a fourteen-year-old girl and a sixteen-year-old boy. The rigorous training Em and Sure had received at Job's behest had stood them in good stead, as they had been promised.

Alex gave the order to follow the *Akatsuki Maru*, remaining three thousand yards astern, with the Maritime Police escort vessel close behind him. Everyone was becoming increasingly edgy, including Alex. First Connie called, then Masa reinforced Connie's initial query. Both wanted to know what the hell was going on. All Alex could say was, "Not much, for the moment. Have patience. Keep a sharp lookout."

In fact, it was Shinobi-sensei who saw it first, and called to Masa, who immediately pointed it out to Connie, and then phoned Alex. Alex and his crew were at water level, with their view blocked by the *Akatsuki Maru*, which had stopped dead in the water. When Alex answered Masa's call, he was informed that the conning tower of a submarine had just broken the surface a quarter mile in front of the *Akatsuki Maru*. Alex took the wheel of the cutter, turned slightly to port to get a better angle, and looked through the best pair of binoculars on board. "She's North Korean!" he declared.

He explained quickly to Tom what he had seen: on the surface, the sub was dead in the water, opening the conning tower to allow her captain to talk with the yakuza aboard the *Akatsuki Maru*. She would be gulping in fresh air, forcing it throughout the submarine under pressure, preparing to dive as soon as their business was transacted and the plutonium transferred. And the air intake would be just above the captain's head, on the conning tower. This was an ideal situation to use the drone and its propofol.

As soon as Tom's drone was in position above the submarine, Alex could fire the sonic emitter, taking out everyone on the *Akatsuki Maru*, friend and foe alike. It would not be pleasant for the crew, but it would allow the Maritime Police to board, with enough time to cuff and shackle the yakuza.

Colonel Asahi, as the senior Japanese officer present, said he had to report immediately to Tokyo the presence of a hostile submarine belonging to North Korea in waters off Nagasaki. Asahi said, "They will ask for my recommendation of official action. What should I tell them?"

As Tom prepared and launched his drone, and the Coast Guard helmsman increased the speed of the cutter, Alex paused and then said, "My father and I surprised a bear behind our dacha in Russia early one evening when I was eight. It was much larger than my father but turned and ran up a tree. I asked him why. He said it wasn't afraid and told me not to point to it or even look at it—just to ignore it. He said it went up a tree out of pure embarrassment—being caught out where it wasn't supposed to be. If we just ignored it, and pretended it wasn't there, by the next morning it would be gone, without any confrontation. If the propofol works," he concluded, "that would be my recommendation to the Japanese government."

Asahi got on the phone, a call that lasted for the next half hour. Meanwhile, Alex and Tom proceeded with the plan. Tom took the drone up to five hundred feet and brought it down slowly above the conning tower, using the camera as a guide. Alex pointed out the air intake on the little screen of Tom's computer.

Alex moved the cutter to within 1,100 yards of the *Akatsuki Maru*, turned the wheel over to a Coast Guardsman, picked up the sonic emitter, and said "FIRE!"

Both the *Akatsuki Maru* and the North Korean submarine were stopped, a hundred yards from each other, preparing to launch boats. The crews on each simply collapsed, those on the submarine peacefully, the captain slumped over the waist-high edge of the conning tower, the crew on the long, narrow deck holding an inflatable raft, and those on the *Akatsuki Maru* clearly less comfortably, their arms thrown up defensively as if to shield their heads from the blows of an unseen adversary. But collapse they all did.

The Maritime Police escort moved swiftly to the side of the *Akatsuki Maru*, police climbing with handsful of plastic restraints to cuff and shackle the yakuza. There was little they could do for the crew. They had been told to check for bleeding ears, a possible indicator of concussion, but in the absence of that, just to try to make the crew as comfortable as possible, and wait until they came around naturally, then hand out aspirin.

As the police moved toward the *Akatsuki Maru*, Sure and Em pushed the Zodiac up and over the side of the cutter and took off for the North Korean submarine—without a word to Tom or Alex or Asahi, who looked on in total surprise. They tied up to the submarine, now only one hundred yards away, climbed to the conning tower, and darted down inside. A full ten minutes passed before they reappeared, popped back up, their knapsacks full, and climbed down to the deck.

It was at this point that Sure saw the captain's hat, which had fallen to the deck when he passed out and slumped over the edge of the conning tower. She spoke with Em briefly, who laughed. Then the two of them climbed back up into the conning tower and rejoined the unconscious captain. Sure took out her phone and clearly called someone. There was no one on board the cutter, as no one's phone rang, and only later did they learn she was calling Connie.

Then the most extraordinary thing happened. Sure put on the captain's hat. She and Em took off their knapsacks. Then they both took off their shirts, revealing themselves in all their glorious youth and freshness. They each ducked under one of the captain's arms, held him up in a drunken, happy pose, and waved at Connie up the bay on the bridge.

On the bridge, as Connie clicked away, Masa had his eye glued to his scope, and said, "Connie, I want a copy of that one!"

Tom was horrified. Alex thought it hilarious and used his own little camera to record the unexpected event. Father Takashi smiled, realizing exactly what was going on. And Asahi, to his lasting regret, missed the whole episode, still talking to Tokyo, while the Coast Guard and the Maritime Police crews remaining on the cutter and the escort, patriots to a man, cheered for America.

Asahi covered the mouthpiece on his phone and said to Alex, "Tokyo wonders if some sort of official arrest and punishment of the submarine captain is not appropriate?" Alex replied, "There's no greater punishment for a North Korean than sending him home to North Korea—unless it's sending him home empty handed!"

Asahi translated what Alex had said, and there was a long pause. Then Asahi looked up, smiled, and said "Arigato!" He pressed the disconnect button and told Alex, "They concur with your very Japanese solution to the problem!"

CHRONICLE LXX.

When Sure and Em were back on board, they asked to speak to Tom, Alex, Father Takashi, and especially to Asahi. "First," began Em, "we want to promise Asahi that all we have purloined will be shared with JCIA. The two of us guarantee it and will follow up to make sure it happens. Frankly, we have a treasure trove. The captain apparently had 'Open only upon arrival at rendezvous' orders, and as a consequence the sub's safe was still open. We have all of his orders, all of the sub's codes, and much more—two knapsacks full.'"

"Second," continued Sure, "we both want to apologize for pulling this foray off without asking permission, but we didn't think we would get it, so we went ahead on our own."

"But why the nude photo op?" asked Tom in some frustration.

"Just think about it, Tom," said Sure. "Apart from the fact that it was the first pure fun we've had the whole trip, it solved the one problem we couldn't manage: the captain will go home empty handed and face the enmity of his superiors; but how can we—and, importantly, Japan—get back at the superiors who sent him? That whole totalitarian regime is built around the unquestioning worship of 'Great Leader' Kim Jong Un.

Embarrass him and he will strike out in retaliation. Embarrass him on his sacred birthday, and he'll take down anyone who caused it.

"So, on his birthday, we are going to send him a birthday card. On YouTube. From two unidentified females (it's a long lens shot). But what is easily identifiable, with those huge letters and numbers on the conning tower, is his submarine. And we're going to thank Kim Jong Un, and his captain, for a wonderful time."

"Think of it as giving your boobs for your country," added Em.

"And for Japan!" said Father Takashi, grinning broadly.

Driving that car for the first time, and now the boobs, thought Sure to herself, *the only two times I've seen that big grin. Perhaps he's a crypto-American.*

Tom look mollified, and said "You're right, I hadn't thought of that."

Alex said, "It's damn brilliant."

Asahi admitted, "I wasn't even going to press you for the intelligence you gleaned, after all you've done for us—but I want you to know how much I appreciate your offer!"

Alex added that he still had one hole card that had not been played, and that now was the time to play it. He picked up his satellite phone and spoke at length in Russian, finally laughed heartily, said "Dosvidan'ya!" and turned to his colleagues. "I told you I asked an old friend for help as a last resort. He is captain of a Russian attack submarine and used to serve under my command before I retired. I prevailed upon him to lurk submerged at the twenty-mile limit off the coast, just in case the plutonium got away from us. I just called to thank him for acting as lifeguard. I gave him a short version of what has happened. He said he would stick around another day, and have fun harassing the North Korean sub on its way back home. When I again expressed our appreciation, he said he had done nothing, and that I knew who to call any time I wanted nothing done again!"

Tom made one more pass over the sub's air intake, expending the last of the propofol and giving the cutter and escort vessel an extra forty-five minutes to an hour to return to the Port of Nagasaki, leaving the submariners to awake to find that the *Akatsuki Maru* had magically vanished, together with their orders, codes, and all sensitive information on board, and that they were floating unmolested and unremarked, totally ignored in one of the world's busiest shipping lanes. Not to mention that the captain was missing his hat.

Father Takashi's phone rang, and while he answered and spoke in Japanese, Alex heard him warmly say "Mamoru," and knew he must be talking to Lt. Ito, who would undoubtedly be feeling a little chagrined to have been taken out of the action. As Father Takashi finished his call, and Tom retrieved his drone, Alex said, "Let's make for the Port of Nagasaki and join up with all the others. Asahi, could you send the car back to pick up Connie and Masa? It's time we got this plutonium safely to where it belongs."

Father Takashi grinned broadly and said, "Alex, it's already there! That was Lt. Ito on the phone. Shortly after we took off from disabling the refrigerator-packer and its crew, he managed to extricate the *Shiki-shima* from its soft grounding, and sail into port, where she is moored at a special, well-guarded dock awaiting our arrival. It turns out that Ito reconfigured the storage of the plutonium by putting the International Atomic Energy Agency casks in steel oil drums that he had previously welded to the deck and rear cabin bulkhead of the *Shiki-shima*. It appeared to be a stack of eighteen drums of extra fuel piled up between two stanchions in a pyramid, 6-5-4-3, about eight feet high, seventeen with a hundred-kilo IAEA cask in each and one filled with seawater. Welded to the deck and bulkhead, they were immovable, an integral part of the ship, but appeared to be a temporary fuel stack."

"So the plutonium never was on board the *Akatsuki Maru*?" asked Alex.

"No."

"It was all a diversion, then. And that's why the crew didn't put up a fight . . . . And that's also why the *Shiki-shima* came into the bay ahead of the *Akatsuki Maru*! Brilliant! Absolutely brilliant! And I'll bet Ito isn't a lieutenant, either, is he?" asked Alex.

"No," said Father Takashi, "he's the second-youngest admiral in the history of the Japanese Navy."

"And I bet I know the youngest!" exclaimed Alex.

They both said the name simultaneously: "Stephen Yamamoto"

CHRONICLE LXXI.

It took over an hour for all five remaining vessels to be moored securely at the guarded Coast Guard dock inside the Port of Nagasaki. Next to the *Shiki-shima*, already berthed, was the seagoing tug, the refrigerator-packer, the *Akatsuki Maru*, the Coast Guard clipper with Alex and company aboard, and the Maritime Police escort vessel.

Alex was first met by a big hug and kiss from Connie, who had been brought down by car. She explained that Masa had declined to accompany her, saying it would not be appropriate given the inevitable government officialdom, but promised that he and Aoi would join them later at the Miyazaki Ryokan. Connie reported that she had phoned their rather formal and staid hostess-owner, requesting that a dinner party in the garden be arranged for the group that evening, plus two additional guests, Masa and Aoi Kondo. The owner had pressed her to repeat the names and asked if these were *the* Aoi and Masa Kondo. With a great intake of breath, she said she would handle everything; she would arrange a wonderful evening, not to worry about a thing. Clearly, in Japan a US presidential envoy on an unofficial visit ranked far below an officially recognized living national treasure and her infamous, if retired, *oyabun* consort! Connie also reported she had met Lt. Ito while waiting for Alex, had found him handsome and charming, and insisted he join them all this evening for dinner at the ryokan. He had said he would be delighted. He added that he was just on the phone with the prime minister, recounting what had transpired, and that the PM was about to call the US president to express his thanks on behalf of the Japanese people for all that you had done!

Alex's second encounter was at the hands of Asahi, who introduced him to the chairman of the advanced electronics firm that had developed the chameleon suit prototype, and to the CEO of the fishing fleet whose refrigerator-packer and fishing vessels had caused such havoc today. It was their son and daughter, respectively, that Alex and his friends had rescued.

While the chairman and CEO had been placed under arrest for their roles in the attempted theft of the plutonium, Asahi said that he felt no jury in Japan would convict them for acting under the duress of complying with orders from the yakuza to save the lives of their children. They wished to meet Alex to thank him on behalf of everyone who had played a role in freeing their teenagers. At this point the two senior executives bowed so deeply and often that Alex became embarrassed. Then they both spoke to Asahi, and Asahi translated. "Is there anything—anything at all—that they could do to show their profound gratitude?" Alex was about to shake his head, when he paused.

"Yes," he said, "something quite wonderful. It will cost you considerable time, and a great deal of money, but I can think of no more rewarding endeavor that you and your families could accomplish together." Then he took these two wealthy and powerful men aside, and with Asahi's help, described what he had in mind. After five minutes of detailed discussion, all four of them were looking very happy indeed.

Alex proceeded to make the rounds, thanking each of the Coast Guard and Maritime Police who had participated that day, getting each of their full names, ranks, and addresses, and telling each in turn—with Asahi translating—how much his or her personal participation was valued. They were all proud of what had been accomplished; but when Alex had finished his rounds, they were bursting their buttons.

As the sun set over Nishidomari Park across bay, Alex, Connie, Tom, Father Takashi, Em, Sure, and Asahi got into their cars brought by the Maritime Police for the drive back to the ryokan. Just before they left,

Asahi said to Connie: “I hope you’ll forgive me, but I too phoned the ryokan, after you called, and spoke with the owner. I asked her to pull out all the stops for your party this evening; and I added that I would be charging it to the emperor.”

— EPILOGUE —

Father Takashi wanted to sit in the sun in the garden, warm his bones, and reflect. He realized that since World War II, nuclear power in fact had brought energy to places and people needing it and saved the atmosphere in some small part from being used as a sewer to dump carbon waste from coal, oil, and gas. That's why he had spent his senior years supporting nuclear energy—and fighting through Greenpeace against its diversion and misuse.

And he knew the argument that, if the Americans had not dropped bombs on Hiroshima and Nagasaki, Japan would have proceeded with its own nuclear weapons program. Japan had in fact tested a nuclear device of its own just two days after the Nagasaki bombing back in 1945, a device that had been developed and then sabotaged by a Japanese nuclear physicist working in a secret Japanese Naval facility in North Korea at that time. That was how North Korea first developed nuclear technology. Takashi had even been shown the piece of paper on which that physicist had intentionally altered a single decimal point, changing the yield of the device to be tested, thereby undermining at the most crucial moment Japanese military confidence in their own bomb to retaliate against the Americans. That courageous act by that Japanese had itself shortened the war. And he had had the opportunity to tell the man, who later became a tenured professor in the American southeast, just that, in person.

And the priest was well aware of the plausible argument that, had the Americans not killed 250,000 Japanese at Hiroshima and Nagasaki, including his fellow orphans and teachers, nuns and priests at his school and orphanage, at least 2.5 million more would have died when the war continued another year—as it most surely would have—but with no change in the final outcome.

The old priest had never gotten an answer to the question he had asked Father Junichi on the morning of August 9, 1945, however. Had God visited the Cathedral that day?

Father Takashi looked down at his left sandal and saw a cricket, a little brown one this time. It spat out a stream of dark liquid. *That's supposed to be tobacco juice,* thought Father Takashi to himself, smiling. Father Junichi had told him that.

Later in life Father Takashi had looked into it further, as he looked into everything Father Junichi had taught him during their brief acquaintance. That brown liquid was toxic, a poison used by crickets to annihilate their enemies. Or each other. But it was also a powerful aphrodisiac. In the right amount, at the right time, it had a certain allure, a seductive power that was hard to resist. And when used carefully, it could assure the survival of the next generation. *Perhaps we have more to learn from these little guys after all,* he thought.

He yawned and considered a nap after a good lunch of boeuf bourguignon and a glass of Juliénas. It had been more than a month since he had treated himself.

The pope would shortly leave the Vatican and Rome for Washington, he reflected, to address a joint session of Congress on what was being billed as the first State of the World address. Tom was hastening back to Rome to relieve Kurt Uri as acting head of what had become a successful and busy foundation, so that the commander of the Swiss Guard could accompany His Holiness to Washington.

Awaiting Tom was a handwritten note from the pope, congratulating him and Sure and Em on a job well done, adding the names of three priests who he thought needed to be sent special telephones urgently, and concluding with a plea that he had sixty-six older cardinals now relieved of duties, no longer participating in the College, maybe somewhat resentful, in any case missing the Collegial intrigue of old. Perhaps they could form part of a plan c. In any case, His Holiness offered Tom a list of twenty of the sixty-six whom he nominated to be recruited by Tom to the foundation's growing international fold.

Also awaiting Tom was a nicely framed photograph, hung conspicuously in his office, taken surreptitiously by Sure: A photo of Tom in the village of Gandolfo, wearing Sister Lucia's habit. Tom would realize that while he and Em were in the field, he may have imposed too much office time on Sure, a lesson he would remember.

Em and Sure, assisted by two reassigned Swiss Guards, would find that they were going to get to continue to work with Tom, but with more field responsibility and less Vatican office time, which made Sure particularly happy. Points to the photo!

After the US president had heard personally from the Japanese prime minister, he nominated Alex and Connie to be the US ambassadorial team to Tokyo. When the announcement was made, the Rostovs had promptly received a bottle of old *starka* vodka addressed to them in care of the Okura. There was no card accompanying the gift, but they said they knew who it was from. They planned to return to Tokyo following congressional approval of the nomination and, they hoped, in time for the cherry blossoms.

A few days later, a short article had appeared in the Japanese press reporting that an old, retired *oyabun* had undergone a new heart surgery procedure at Cedars of Lebanon hospital in Los Angeles, and was recovering nicely at Caesars Palace in Las Vegas, accompanied by his Japanese wife. They said they would be returning to Tokyo in time for the cherry blossoms.

Father Takashi looked around his garden at the cherry trees and thought, *It won't be long now. And it will be an interesting spring this year.* God, it seems, was back in her heaven, and all was right with her world.

Brother Liu interrupted his peaceful musings to say, "There are people here to see you. The two kidnapped teenagers that were saved in Nagasaki, and their four parents. They say they are here to finance and help you rebuild the school and orphanage you lost in 1945."

"Brother," said Father Takashi, "let us embrace our future."

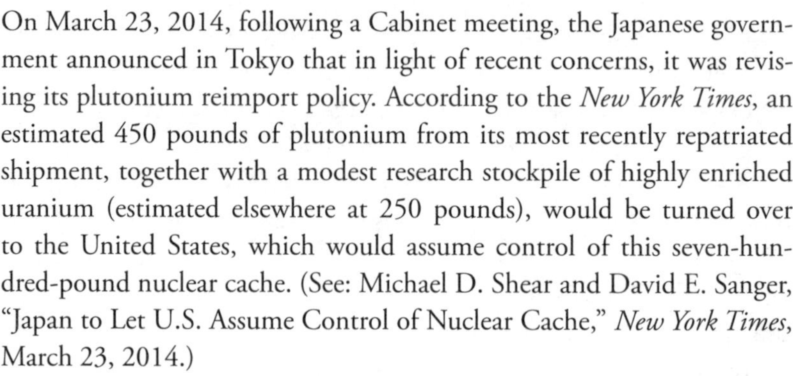

On March 23, 2014, following a Cabinet meeting, the Japanese government announced in Tokyo that in light of recent concerns, it was revising its plutonium reimport policy. According to the *New York Times*, an estimated 450 pounds of plutonium from its most recently repatriated shipment, together with a modest research stockpile of highly enriched uranium (estimated elsewhere at 250 pounds), would be turned over to the United States, which would assume control of this seven-hundred-pound nuclear cache. (See: Michael D. Shear and David E. Sanger, "Japan to Let U.S. Assume Control of Nuclear Cache," *New York Times*, March 23, 2014.)

The following day, March 24, 2014, President Obama confirmed this one-time arrangement—the lynchpin in his five-year-long push to help secure the world's deadliest weapons. And on that day Japan's prime minister and America's president each received personal messages of congratulations from His Holiness Pope Francis.